BLOOI
Enslavem

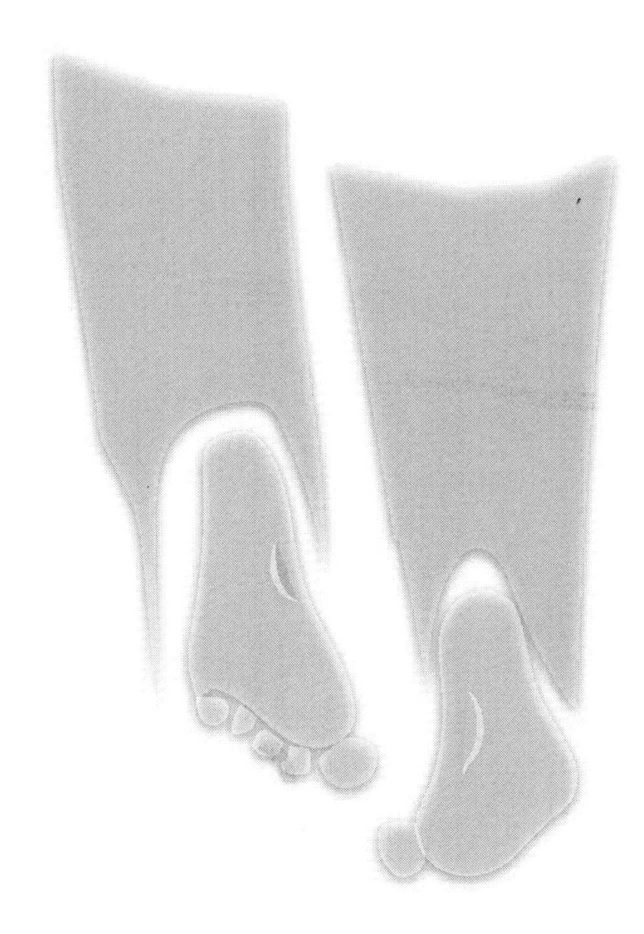

Historical Novel

by

JUDITH C. OWENS-LALUDE

BLOODY TRAILS: Enslavement & Freedom
AnikePress, © Copyright 2021, Henderson, Nevada

AnikePress
Worldwide Publisher
Henderson, Nevada, USA
Orders:
jcamille@AnikePress.com
http://AnikePress.com

ISBN 978-0-9972613-5-6
LCCN 2020922294

BLOODY TRAIL: Enslavement & Freedom
includes:
Discussion Questions
Glossary
Historical photographs

Book illustrations, layouts, and cover photo and design
by Judith C. Owens-Lalude

To contact the author and publisher or receive information regarding programs and presentations related to *BLOODY TRAILS: Enslavement & Freedom*:
jcamille@AnikePress.com
http://jcamilleculturalacademy.com

Dedication

This book was written in honor of my ancestors, who were noble Africans not seeking to be enslaved. My loving husband, A. O'tayo Lalude, MD; my two wonderful sons, A. Adesina Lalude and Akinwande A. Lalude whose endorsements were invaluable. My dream of telling this story would not have been realized if it were not for their tenacious love and the support of my other family members and friends.

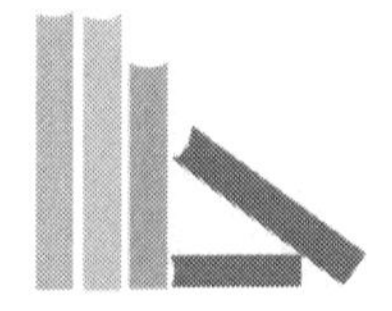

Books by Judith C. Owens-Lalude

Write for Children & Teens PROMPTER

The Long Walk: Slavery to Freedom
(Paperback and Audio)

Miss Lucy: Slave and Civil War Nurse
(Paperback, Audio, and Braille)

DUNKER

Boots and Blisters

Wedding Drums and the Tall-Tall Tree

The Midnight Boy from South Sudan

BOO! That's My Pumpkin

Peas and the Popover

Kaleidoscope Kids

Kaleidoscope Kids Coloring Book

AnikePress
Worldwide Publisher
Henderson, NevadForeword

Foreword

FREEDOM! FREEDOM! FREEDOM! That is the overarching theme, the underpinnings, the motivation, the inspiration, and the beating heart of *Bloody Trails: Enslavement & Freedom* and its predecessor, *The Long Walk: Slavery to Freedom.*

The driving force of *Bloody Trails: Enslavement & Freedom* is the struggle and fight to obliterate forever the shackles of physical and psychological enslavement, no matter its dangers, pain, sacrifices, and sorrows. It is the blazing torch within the soul of Toby to be free and to unite his family. It is his all-encompassing, relentless passion and reason for life, just as it was for his mother, Clarissa, in *The Long Walk: Slavey to Freedom.*

Clarissa's saga depicted brutality, violent, and a *plantation apartheid system* that controlled the thoughts, waking moments, nightmares, dreams, and very existence of the enslaved. Cruelty was the expectation. Subservience and working beyond exhaustion and pain were normalized realities. Being regarded and treated as *tools* and *beasts of burden* to produce wealth and prosperity for slavers was the rule.

Bloody Trails gives us the cruelty of slavery, but with two disparate views:

- Psychological enslavement: The seemingly *benign bondage* that appeared to reflect caring, nurturance, and even affection and friendship by enslavers. This was a *deceiving veil* of caregiving, concern, and affection that Toby and his twin sisters experienced.

- Physically brutal enslavement: Brutality and violence were acknowledge in the *typical* slaver-enslaved relationship. Slavers believed in their *ultimate and absolute power over the enslaved.* They believed their property a thing to produce wealth and prosperity; a thing to demand and expect unquestioned submission; a thing to sexually exploit, if so desired, and the power to control life and death of their *bonded property*—no matter how that was masked in a *perceived, benign, slaver-enslaved relationship.*

Owens-Lalude brilliantly situated her characters in settings that revealed slavery was not *one size fits all.* The realities of bondage evoked cruelty and terror throughout this saga. However, the element of *betrayed loyalty* was the most insidious in deceiving the enslaved to believe their conditions of bondage were not as awful as their chained and downtrodden brethren. Yet, they were caught in a web of deception created to generate loyalty to and trust for their enslavers.

Finally, the many followers of Judith C. Owens-Lalude's books can enjoy the excitement of reading what happened to Toby and his sisters. We have patiently awaited the spirits of Clarissa's children to reveal themselves to Owens-Lalude so she could chronicle their harrowing journeys to FREEDOM!

Dr. Toni-*Mokjaetji* Humber
Professor Emeritus
Ethnic and Women's Studies Department
California State Polytechnic University, Pomona
Pomona, California

Introduction

Family elders of Judith C. Owens-Lalude spoke excitedly about their history, each topping one vignette with another. "We're from Fairfield, Kentucky," they all agreed. However, there was never mention of the early ancestors who were among those captured from a Nigerian village and sold into bondage.

The acclaimed *1619 Project* spoke extensively about the arrival of West Africans at the Colony of Virginia. Centuries later, an 1860 census report revealed Owens-Lalude's family, in Kentucky, was brought from Virginia to northern Kentucky where they were auctioned and sold to Ben Miller's father, a prosperous dairy farmer. She often wondered if they were held in Matthew Garrison's slave pen in Louisville.

Owens-Lalude's search expanded with trips to Nelson County, Kentucky, where her family elders lived or spent time during their younger lives. After casual visits and additional research, she presented readings and interpretive programs highlighting enslavement in North Central Kentucky. Owens-Lalude learned that her family members were not held in bondage there. Instead, they were enslaved about a mile north of the Nelson and Spencer County lines in Goodwin Spring. This was an unknown fact that was not revealed to her family elders until an ancestral search, initiated in 2007.

Over the years, Owens-Lalude's research and collected data led to the writing of *The Long Walk: Slavery to Freedom*, a historical fiction that traces the journey of a mother and her son from abusive enslavement to the cradle of freedom. Readers roused and intrigued by the story's events demanded to know more about what became of the family, five members separated on the auction block, the same as Owens-Lalude's real family.

The interest expressed for a sequel led to the writing of *Bloody Trails: Enslavement & Freedom*, also a historical novel that is constructed from various aspects of enslavement–throughout Kentucky, Tennessee, Louisiana, Missouri, and Canada–including family separation, bondage, freedom seeking, the life of freed Negroes, and the Underground Railroad. *Bloody Trails: Enslavement & Freedom* exposes a seemingly privileged lifestyle for some. At the same time, the horrific psychological trepidation of bondage without the typical physical abuse cannot be minimized. It equally distorted life for the enslaved.

Figure 1: Map of 1850 South Central US and Southwestern Ontario, Canada by Majorie Lorene Laine White, Cartographer

Table of Contents

While painting a graphic picture of some of the many horrors of the American institution of slavery, Judith C. Owens-Lalude also humanizes her characters, thereby creating a must-read. *Bloody Trails: Enslavement & Freedom* dramatizes the Auction Block and other horrific aspects of slavery that led the enslaved to risk escaping and to experience the unforgettable perils of the Underground Railroad. As I read *Bloody Trails: Enslavement & Freedom,* I found myself connecting to the protagonist, his twin sisters, and his extended family—cheering them onward to better lives.

Lonnetta M. Gaines, Ph.D.
Retired Educator, Lecturer, Performer, and
author of *Fia and the Butterfly: 7 Stories for Character Education*

1

Auction Block

Shaken and sickened by the sight of spluttering, worn-out, fettered Negroes shuffling one behind the other–jostled up and down the auction block steps. Toby watched and waited his turn to be sold. A tall, menacing auctioneer, wearing a dark brown top hat, polished boots, leather pants, and a waistcoat beneath a frock coat, braced himself against a podium not much broader than his shoulders. The auctioneer guffawed at the darkies whose inner selves fought to not be bartered for. With a raised mallet, he thwacked a wooden block and then aimed the grip of it at Toby. The young buck's body quickened, the same as those sold before him.

Toby's feet stumbled up the four wooden steps till he stood merged in the flesh and blood of the souls who mounted them ahead of him. The lad parted his feet among the still warm, smeared footprints. Cold, terrified, and shivering, he gripped hard on his lower, tasting his own blood. Not wanting his mother to fret, he held his body erect. With his shoulders back, he snatched what were surely the last glimpses of her; his sisters, Mary and Molly; his younger brother, George Henry; and Jake, not his real pa, but felt like he was to Toby.

Boisterous bidders leaned in for a better view of the lad, pulled from the cluster of newest stock. Jeering and pointing, the onlookers passed a jug of moonshine mouth to mouth. Some who roared with laughter now slouched where they once stood steady. Moe, less intoxicated, leaped onto the block, took hold of Toby's shoulders, shook him, and rotated him for a better head-to-heel inspection.

"Open ya mouth." Toby did. "Boy's got a good amount of teeth in his head," Moe announced to the crowd.

Moe cupped a hand, shoved it between Toby's legs, and rough-fondled his scrotum. The pain put the boy on his toes. "Seems things be all right down der. Dis here boy gonna make a bunch of good lookin' pickaninnies fa somebody." He flicked Toby's genitals. The lad grunted and gritted his teeth. Clench-fisted, Moe clubbed the buck's shoulders, each blow heavier than the prior.

"Des here be a strong one." The mallet slammed. The auctioneer raised his voice, "Hey! Hey! Watch yourself. Take ya hands off dat darkie or you gonna be buyin' goods ya damaged and don't be wantin'. Best ya step down. Dat boy don't belong ta ya yet."

As Moe was about to leave the block, his feet slipped from beneath him. He fell into the hands of rowdy bidders who shoved his drunken body aside to crowd against the block. They waved fisted notes as one shouted an offer and another shouted one better.

"Last call fa dis here buck. He's a good one. Near 'bout twelve. Be tall. Well built. Special breed. What do I hear?"

"Se-se-seven, hu-hu-hundred da-da-dollars."

"Do I hear another bid?"

After a long pause, the auctioneer pounded the gavel the same as he did after each bid. The sound vibrated up the spine of every captive who heard it.

"Sold! Come git ya stock, Humphrey."

Toby shut out the cries of the other Negroes, pulled from their loved ones, same as he was. He gawked at his family still bunched at the same spot, sure it would be the last time he'd see them.

"Give me back my boy!" Toby's ma shrieked loud as she could.

Toby thrashed his arms about, walloping darkies who passed him on the steps, as he was hustled off the block to a far corner. His heels, gouged by the splintered wood, caused him to bobble on one foot while the other flailed above his head, about to knock over a passing soul to be auctioned. An assistant snatched Toby's arm and pulled him off the steps to avoid chaos.

"Gonna have ta tighten dem shackles on ya, boy. Dem legs ya got, be like dem of a wild deer. Ain't got time ta or wantin' ta chase no buck."

Toby was tugged by the shackles, past gawkers, to the far corner of the barn.

"Stay here till ya come fa."

As Toby stood alongside other sorrowers waiting to be claimed as property, conflicted, he struggled to manage fearful thoughts that taunted him. He shivered in his patched, snow-wet britches and tattered coat as his toes gripped icy mud. Cold and lonely, the boy grieved for his family. His front teeth shaved his fingernails beyond the quick when his hands weren't smacking his restive thighs.

Toby eyed new owners lined up at a dilapidated table, braced on unsteady legs to pay for their stock. They deliberated about the auction events as they waited their turn to pay their due. They cackled and thumbed at the stock they were about to acquire. Some establish ownership by groping and patting down their new property to be listed with their land, livestock, and other slaves–an indication of their power and wealth.

"Bruce Humphrey, gitcha money ready." The auctioneer pointed the butt of his gavel toward the table. "Git in dat payin' line ova der."

Through slitted eyelids, Toby quick-peeped at Humphrey. He was a short, stout man whose frayed, blue paisley neckerchief choked his beefy-red neck. A greasy wide-brimmed, over-worn hat hid his eyes; but, didn't block the view of his lower face that sported a mass of unkempt beard blanketing his cheeks and chin.

Toby took care not to stare at Humphrey. He didn't want to get hanged by the prickly rope that replaced the shackles tied to his waist, rubbing it raw, or the one knotted at his ankles, scouring off the flesh. Instead, he scanned the fasteners on the fat fella's unkept cowhide jacket. The missing ones wouldn't have made him appear better kempt, even if they had been tacked in place. The coat sleeves engulfed his brown, clawed fingers and warmed them when his arms dangled at his sides. The man's tattered trousers bunched across dusty, roughed-up boots, not a proper fit, and curled up at the toes.

"Next!" shouted the clerk who gave Humphrey an annoyed look.

"Git over here."

"I-I'm a–comin'."

The recorder squinted at Humphrey. "Stop dat damn stammering. We talks straight here in Kentuck'." He slapped his hand on the rickety table. "Be quick. Putcha money down here. Gitcha stock. Keep movin'."

With an unsteady hand, Humphrey laid a wad of crumpled notes down on the table and turned toward Toby, who knew he was coming for him, but wished it wasn't so.

"Hey! Hey, you! Come back here. Dis here money ain't enough fa dat buck. He's prime stock. The last call for him was seven hundred dollars."

"I–I got the rest. W–w–won't take long ta–ta git it. M–my horse, tied up . . . " Humphrey indicated with a crooked index finger, puffy lips, and pockmarked nose toward the barn door. "Ju-ju-just ou–outside der."

After his new master faded from sight, Toby scrambled to decipher what had happened to him from the fireside in Virginia to here in Kentucky, from his ma's side to the auction block, and now, to a corner crammed with grieving souls who waited to be transported to what was certain to be a continuum of hellacious bondage.

Wretched loneliness cramped Toby's body as he pondered survival without his family from whom he'd never been separated before. He discreetly raised his head when a gang of grotty men entered the barn in search of new stock. Sure that his new master had a quick clobbering hand, he contemplated the sort of master each of them might be.

Cries from Toby's mother compelled him to take note of his folks who reeled and wailed as Jake, more depleted and bent with age, was pulled from them, dragged, and boot-kicked up the auction block steps. Their cries fought against the sounds of the gavel slammed and slammed again. After the third one, Jake was hauled away by a tight grip on his left arm already painfully swollen and tender. Toby squinted to see more through his tear-filled eyes. After blinking to clear them, he peered into a heap of auctioned souls. Jake wasn't among them. He was gone.

Clarissa's voice was afflicted with anguish. His mother clamored above the commotion. "Mary! Molly!" she howled.

Clutched together on the auction block, the girls appeared more delicate than Toby remembered them just minutes before. He set his jaw to call out to them as he strained to decipher one from the other. Mingled with fear and anxiety, he couldn't project even a murmur.

Perplexed, Toby struggled to stave off the outside world when a gruff voice seized his attention. A horse's length from him was a strange mix of musty men, various shades of filthy flesh. Three of them, obviously farmers, all tall and bony, not the same height, but near to it, had damp matted hair the color of scuzzy straw plastered to their narrow heads. Their bird-wing ears supported grubby farm hats that cast shadows across their thin, cracked lips, stretched nearly ear-to-ear, and pointy noses. Toby felt they must be, without a doubt, relations.

Another Joe in the mix leaned against a post with his hands pocketed. He wore a dusty gambler's hat; a time-worn, black-patched frock coat; and a grayish-brown shirt–once stark white. His nervous eyes shifted beneath a mess of bushy brows. Standing next to him was a younger fellow not much out of boyhood. He wore faded green-plaid pants with hems well above his boot spurs and a once frippery jacket with sleeves hiked a quarter way up his arm.

The pack stood, with their boot-heels dug deep into the same mud Toby was plastered in. They haggled about what they'd pay for their stock and how they intended to profit from it.

A farmer in a Panama hat, waving and gesturing, spit-shouted over the heads of others to make a point that didn't seem to have one, finally asked, "Who got dem pretty little twin gals?" Another farmer, a smidge from the cluster, rubbed his hands together in a crude way and grinned. His tobacco-stained teeth gripped a corncob pipe that he bounced from corner to corner of his mouth. "Wish I could'a got my hands on one of dem little gals. Dey sho be pretty."

The tallest of the might-be-brothers backed away from the group to tug the farmer's arm. "Who got dem gals?" he asked.

Toby's ears were hot and attentive to the voice of the man who grinned, proud that he had the answer to the question. The farmer who gripped a long-stemmed corncob pipe, drew his shoulders back, and raised his chest. "Nobody around des here parts. Dem gals be sold for more den twelve hundred dollars. Maybe some more, maybe some less. Don't rightly 'member jes' how much. But I knows dey's bought by a high-brow business man dat come in from St. Louis. He be totin' one of dem 'spensive leather cash bags wid plenty buying money in it."

2

The Twins

Pleased he had the mind to bring along a couple of heavy linsey-woolsey blankets, Lawrence Piper lifted one twin to bundle her and planned to swaddle her sister in the second covering. They kicked up such a fuss, he put down the child he held. The two small bodies snapped together same as loose magnets dropped into a wooden bucket.

To ward off the cold, Lawrence draped the girls in one of the coverlets, adjusted them on the carriage seat in front of him, and tented the two from head to toe with the second blanket. The little ones shivered and sniffled so that locks of their grimy hair plastered to the sides of their faces escaped from beneath the coverings. Lawrence knew the hawkish winter air seeping through door casings could cause death-laden sicknesses and, for gals so fragile, death. With a tender pat on the heads, weighted with a degree of confliction, he strived to let them know they were safe. Satisfied, he leaned back with a deeper than usual sigh.

"Let's go, Num. The dark's pursuing us. I want to get some distance before we have to stop."

"Yes sa, Massa."

Num snapped the reins, slapping the horses' rumps. Following the bits' indications, the animals neighed as they swerved leftward, heading west to St. Louis, Missouri. Lawrence savored what he hoped was a lucky buy. Pleased he came upon the twins and outbid others to get them, he felt confident Virginia, his wife of five years, would praise him with a generous hug.

Days later, the coach thundered to a stop in front of the house. Hearing the racket, Tipper, the Pipers' feisty house hand, hurried down the front steps to greet her massa as he clambered down from the carriage.

"Welcome home, Massa."

"Thank you. How's your missus?"

"She be well, sir. But she be takin' huh meals in huh room since ya done left. She be missin' ya a terrible lot."

Low-pitch nasal whining from the coach compelled Tipper to glance around Lawrence's shoulder.

"Got somethin' in der, Massa?"

"See for yourself."

Tipper stepped around him, stuck her head inside the carriage for a better look, and quickly withdrew it. The pungent odor assured her animals occupied the coach bench.

"What kinda critters ya got in der, sir?"

"Couple little pickaninnies to cheer up your missus."

Lawrence pulled back the top cover; two small, bushy heads with inquisitive eyes emerged. Doubtful about what she was seeing, Tipper stretched her neck for a better assessment. She knew Massa Lawrence wanted to purchase a hand able to clean and do heavy lifting, but what was there wasn't so.

"Sir, dem little bucks or little gals, ya got der?"

"Gals, Mary and Molly. They need baths and clean clothes. They reek with piss and fear. Burn those rags they have on. I'm sure they're full of lice, nits, and who knows what else."

Tipper tilted her head, speculated about the girls, and said, "Not sure, but dey looks lak dey might be pretty little things. Missus gonna lak dem no matter what."

"Hope so."

"I takes care of dem. I rides wid dem to da rear of da house."

Tipper clambered into the coach, sat where Lawrence had, and closed the door. The twins drew themselves down into the coverlets with only the white of their eyes exposed.

"Take us to the back door," she hollered to Num.

The buggy wobbled its way down Perry Street and around the corner to the rear of the house. Tipper took careful note of her new charges before she said, "I's goin' ta take dem coverin's off ya and fold dem. When I's done, we gonna hurry inta dat house. Der be a fire fa ya. Ya can warm dem little feet."

Disoriented by Tipper's meek voice, the girls didn't resist when she took their coverings and rolled each one into a tight bundle that she tucked under their arms to carry.

"Follow me."

She lifted each twin down to the ground. They doddered behind their new protector who led them hurriedly up the backdoor steps and into a warm kitchen that smelled of sweet bread, bacon, and beans. The twins were guided to the pantry, a good-sized room off from the kitchen. Tall hutches with see-through glass doors lined three walls. In the center was a large work table that would seat eight to ten people.

"Go head. Sit ya selves down der. Ain't no harm gonna be comin' to ya."

The twins waddled toward a low table in the corner, with the two footstools underneath it. They dropped their loads on the floor, scooted the stools side by side, and sat on them. Tipper placed a tin cup of warm vegetable broth in front of each gal. However, they picked up one tin with both sets of hands and took turns sipping from it. When empty, they did the same with the second tin.

After Lawrence left the carriage, he went straight to his office, removed his coat, and teased a package from his carpet bag before he anxiously climbed the stairs to Virginia's *boudoir*. He had been gone for better than two months and wanted to be sure she was well. Tipper smiled when she heard his feet shuffle above her head as he made his way to her *boudoir*.

Virginia, who rested on the chaise lounge absorbing slathering sunbeams from the window, answered her husband's timid knock on the door.

"Please come in," she said.

At her invitation, he entered the room with one hand extended and the other behind his back. She smiled and raised a graceful hand to him. He took it with all the care he had, soft-pressed his lips against it, and then anointed her lips with a fresh kiss.

"I'm home, my dear," he said, but was concerned seeing her pale, near-translucent skin, and dark circles under her eyes that had advanced her age too far beyond her twenty-five years.

Virginia adjusted herself to allow Lawrence to sit next to her. "I've missed you, dear. How was your trip?"

"Better than I thought it might be. The fur generated a good price, and the request for additional hides was surprisingly higher than expected. This year will be profitable for us. And while I was in Kentucky, not far from Louisville, I decided to check on the new stock brought there for auctioning, and ended up buying a couple of pets for you. Care has to be taken before you see them. But close your eyes and hold out your hands. I have a little something else for you."

Lawrence presented the package from behind his back. His excitable hands placed hers around it. When Virginia opened her eyes, she cradled the gift to her bosom as if it were a young kitten. She rocked it before drawing the fuchsia ribbon toward her thumping heart to loosen the knot. She just as slowly peeled away crisp, floral wrapping from a gold-embossed, cherubs embellished wooden box.

"How splendid!" Virginia said and lifted the lid. "Lawrence, they're absolutely beautiful. I've never seen such a lovely vanity set with such an array of colorful stones. And they're on both sides of the comb. This must have cost a shameful sum of money."

Virginia's fingers researched every stone, large and small: amber, azure-blue, leafy green, rose pink, royal purple, and ruby red. "And look here, Lawrence, the artistry of these silver ringlets and leaves is exquisite. The ones snugged around the stones add such a depth of grace. This dresser set is indeed a treasure."

Purchased from a jeweler, Lawrence thought it was a bit pricey. "But this vanity set is imported. And, one of a kind," he was told. Now, he laughs as he visualizes Virginia filing her nails, fastening her shoes with the buttonhook, smiling at herself in the handheld mirror, and Tipper combing and brushing his wife's golden curls around her fingers.

"I'm going down to check on Tipper and the task I left her with." Lawrence began to leave the room but hesitated before he pulled the door open to exit. "I'll come back to have supper with you later," he said.

From the top of the stairs, whimpers and chatter not decipherable added to the stockpile of thoughts that clogged his mind about how Virginia might respond when she saw the pickaninnies for the first time.

Both tiny heads, as if they belonged to one person, rotated when Lawrence entered the kitchen. The gals, meek and cold, glanced at him and quickly turned their stares back to Tipper, who dumped the last kettle of hot water into a copper tub, before she added drops of rose oil. With a firm hand, she gave the bathwater a good swishing. By the time the temperature satisfied her, Lawrence had gone back up the stairs.

Tipper deposited the filthy threadbare pieces of clothing stripped from the twins into a bucket. When she attempted to lift the gal into the tub, patches of blue fabric that stuck to their hips surprised her. She peeled them off and hid the remnants in a drawer before putting the twins into the washtub or the bucket of rags on the outside step for Num.

With a heavily soaped sponge, Tipper scrubbed the two from head to toe. Dirt and scum clung to the tub, creating a massive ring around the inside while a thick film of filth floated on the water's surface. The girls peered at Tipper with the biggest, brightest, almond-shaped brown eyes she had ever seen. What was beneath the days of encrusted grit awed her. She never dreamed they'd have such blemish-free flesh the color of walnut meat and smooth as churned butter. Their shiny, cocoa-brown hair, with gentle waves, fell limp over their shoulder blades. One look at them, and she knew they hadn't been abused like most Negro children who bore scars from their master's hand or a vindictive whip.

Tipper bundled the girls in a large huckaback towel to keep them warm. She didn't bother to separate the two who had finally stopped crying, but their faces were sorrowful and eyes puffy-red.

Once again Lawrence came to assess the progress of the baths and was told, "Massa, der be nothin' ta dress des here gals in."

"Num's gone to fetch nightgowns and simple clothing for them. He should be back soon. Tomorrow proper garments will be sent from Durry's Dry Goods," Lawrence said as he noted the sound of footsteps outside of the rear door on his way back upstairs.

Num entered the kitchen toting three cord-tied parcels. "Put dem down der," Tipper said pointing to a heap of clean, folded laundry near the pantry. "Den take dat bucket I done sit at da door and burn dem rags I done put in it."

Tipper removed the cord from the first package and unwrapped it one corner at a time. Two gray, long-sleeved Negro cloth dresses with white cotton collars and cuffs were neatly folded inside. With a snap of the wrist, she shook them out and hung the garments on wooden pegs beneath a row of bells mounted high on the wall behind the kitchen. She helped the girls into the woolen bloomers and muslin nightshifts from the second package. The button-up shoes, folded chemises, and cotton stockings in the last package were set on the floor beneath the hanging garments.

The twins fed each other from the bowls of soft-cooked apples and buttered toast soaked in warm milk placed in front of them.

"Hey! Hey! Jes' eat bits at a time. Der be plenty food fa ya. Can have much as ya be wantin'." The girls peered over their spoons at Tipper. "Don't want ya gittin' sick 'fore ya git full."

Once they seemed content, Tipper checked on her missus. When she returned to the kitchen, she bedded the gals down on a quilt near the cooking stove, padded two small logs to pillow their heads, and covered them with warmed woolen blankets. They were asleep before Tipper finished snuggling covers around them.

Not to delay supper for the Pipers, Tipper let the girls be to prepare a tray of smoked pork and sweet potatoes. She was pleased she had already taken up the tea service without incident. It seemed the missus was obsessed with her new gift and didn't take note of her hand entering and leaving the *boudoir*.

Lawrence didn't knock on the opened door when he returned, astonished that Virginia was on her feet and waiting for him.

"You seem to be feeling better."

"I cleaned up some and put on a fresh gown. After Tipper groomed my hair with the new comb and brush, it spiked my spirit," Virginia said with a song in her voice.

"She seems to have the gift of being upstairs and downstairs at the same time. I don't know how she does it," Lawerence said.

Virginia yanked the embroidered pull cord on the wall next to the fireplace that rang one of the bells in the pantry. Tipper knew the call was for their dinner and stepped back to assess her work. Feeling it was her best, she lifted the food tray and carried it up to the waiting diners.

The door was ajar, Massa Lawrence and the missus sat close as he recalled the particulars of his travels.

"Come in," said Virginia.

Tipper positioned her load on a mahogany drop-leaf table placed in the room for such occasions. The Pipers pulled their chairs to the table. Unhurried, they enjoyed the meal and conversations about Lawrence's new auction purchase and how it might change the flow of the household events.

Although achy and fatigued from his trip, Lawrence rose early the next morning eager to check on his new purchases. Barefoot, he rushed down to the kitchen where the gals snuggled together in a deep sleep. He didn't tarry, just peeped and hurried back up the stairs to Virginia. Tipper stirred oats and cooked eggs for the household and never knew he had come down. When done, she woke the girls curled beneath the blanket. Their inquisitive tear-encrusted eyes studied the kitchen, the pantry, and the copper tub.

Not knowing where they were, they cried, "Want Ma. Where my ma?"

"I cain't tell ya where she be. But I can tell ya dat no harm gonna come ta ya here. Ya gotta be brave. I got somethin' fa ya to eat. Ya hongry?" she asked the twins who nodded.

Tipper gestured for them to follow her. The little ones tiptoed behind her to a washroom where she blotted their faces and hands with a soft wet rag; dried them off; and dressed them in fresh, white, handkerchief-cotton chemises. Tipper seated them at the low table in the pantry and gave each a scoop of cooked oats with warm cream floated on top. They nudged one bowl aside and ate from the same dish. Tipper left them to continue her morning tasks. They eyed her over their spoons as she placed the rest of the breakfast food on an oval tray to take up to the Pipers.

"Ya two stay put. Don't ya move. I be back in a snap."

Tipper hurried the hot breakfast up the back stairs and waited at the opened door.

"Come in. Sit the tray here," said Virginia as she collected the papers to create space on the table for the tray.

"Missus, if der be nothin' mo fa me ta do, I goes on back down ta da kitchen ta take care of dem little gals Massa done brought ya from Kentuck'."

"Tell me, what's your opinion of them."

"Dey could be da two prettiest little things ever. Soon as dey fed and properly dressed, I be bring'um up fa ya ta get a glimpse of."

As Tipper was leaving the bedroom, Lawrence came in.

"Mornin', Massa."

"Tipper."

"Can I gitcha anythin'?"

"Send Num up with extra coal for the fire."

Soon as the message was delivered, Num collected nuggets from the coal bin and climbed the stairs to the bedroom. At the door, he heard his master telling the missus he was concerned about her health and how he hoped the gals he brought from Kentucky would bring her back to the woman he married five years ago. Num tapped on the door.

"Mornin', Massa. Mornin', Missus. Gotcha some coal. Should I be puttin' dis here on da fire?"

"Yes, and be quick," Lawrence said and took a serious stance. "Then go tell Tipper to hurry and bring those gals up to meet their new missus. She's eager to see them."

"Yes, sa."

Num tilted the coal kettle; lumps tumbled onto the fire he stoked with a poker, sending up a yellow-tipped blue flame flaring a bright light. The remainder was dumped into the scuttle next to the hearth.

"I be comin' back later wid da ash hopper. I cleans away dem ashes."

Num returned to the kitchen where Tipper sat with the girls while they ate.

"Massa say he wants ya ta hurry dem gals up ta see da missus."

"Did he say when?"

"Naw. Don't believe he did. He only say soon."

Tipper took measure of the girls before she said to them, "Ya new missus be wantin' ta meet ya. Hurry and finish eatin' dem vittles. I be gittin' ya prettied up some. Den we be goin' up ta say hello. Won't take long. I comb ya hair out and dress ya in dem new frocks hangin' on dem pegs."

Using the spoon tips, the girls scooped warm oat lobs to feed to one another. When Tipper determined they were done eating, she caught a breath and said, "I'm gonna comb dem heads out. It ain't gonna be easy cause ya slept wid dem wet heads and dey be a heap of mangled mass. Gonna hurt some, but I do my best ta cause ya as little pain as I can."

With a brush in one hand and a bowl of tepid water next to her, Tipper sat the twins on the stool wedged between her knees. To assess the situation, she brushed over the mess of matted hair. The tangles were serious and wouldn't ease their hold. When a bit more aggressive with the comb and brush, the girls squealed and kicked. Tipper was forced to sit them on the floor bundled in a blanket, braced between her legs with a tighter hold on to them.

"Num. Come."

"Miss Tipper, ya be callin' me?"

"Tell Missus and da massa I got a problem wid des here gals. Ain't gonna be able to git dem ready ta be seen no way soon. Might be up in tamorrow 'fore I be done wid dem. Go now. Hurry. Tell dem what I done told ya."

"Yes, um."

Tipper turned her attention back to Mary and Molly. Using her fingers, she continued to tease aside small portions of hair. Alternating a damp brush with a comb, she easy smoothed the hair flat on her palm. Each tamed section was twisted into a knot till both heads had a half dozen and needed that many more.

Tipper encircled the girls with her comforting arms. "I knows ya be tired, 'cause I am. Dis here's a big job. Gonna take some time. Let's rest some. I give ya a sip of warm milk."

Their sad faces were more than Tipper wanted to endure. She rolled back the blankets clammy from tears of agony and battle sweat. She wiped their bloated faces with a cool, moist rag, put them back on their stools at the small table, and gave each a half tin of milk.

"I see dem sorrowful cheeks and dem wet eyes. I knows dat gittin' dem locks taken care of be hurtin' ya, but ya missus be wantin' ta seein' ya. If her eyes take hold of ya lookin' lak dis, she be sendin' ya back to where ya come from. Drink ya milk, den put dem heads down on dat pallet and rest some."

Num stood in the kitchen with the warning from the missus and an expression that reflected her displeasure. Unable to make eye contact with Tipper, who inquisitively observed his behavior as he rung his hat.

"If ya gotta message, best ya be lettin' me know 'fore ya bust a gut standin' der lak a frighten' calf."

"Missus be mighty upset 'bout what ya done told me ta be tellin' dem. She say dat ya best be gittin' dem gals up der ta see huh and ya can stay down here in da kitchen."

"She say when?"

"Naw. Only dat it best be shortly. She say, too, if ya late, she gonna take da switch ta ya and dat might not be all."

Staring at Num, Tipper took in a troubling breath. She mumbled, "How I gonna git dem gals up dem steps ta knock on dat door? Dat woman be thinkin' crazy. Ya go on back to ya doin's. Don't want no trouble fa ya." Tipper shook her head."Did ya see Massa?"

"Naw. He be gone on."

With so little time, Tipper got the girls up, loosened their knots, pulled their hair back in sturdy twists, and hair-pinned them at the nape. She put a mop cap on each head and then attempted to pull stockings over their feet and up their legs. They bucked so she forwent them and didn't bother about the shoes. The twins were only cooperative enough for the dresses to be buttoned on them.

"Looka der. Ya be pretty as butterflies. Let's go see ya missus. Mind ya manners. Don't pout. Don't sob. If ya be good, I be havin' a treat fa ya when ya come back down."

Tipper, along with the wide-eyed twins, stood at the bottom of the steps staring up. "Wait here. Don't ya move. I goes up first and come back down."

Grasping a red and purple bandana in her right hand, Tipper went up each step minding her feet to not make a sound. She moved close to Virginia's bedroom door and discreetly looped the bandana around the doorknob before backing herself down the stairs.

In her most submissive voice, she said to the gals, "Ya gonna have ta go up dem stairs and partway down dat hall ta da missus room. Ya gonna tap on dat door wid da bandana. Missus let ya in. Ain't no way 'round dat. Ya hafta be brave. Den ya can come back ta da kitchen. Missus ain't gonna hurt ya none. Go on up der like I done showed ya. Git, now."

The girls wrapped together with a tight hold on one another. Tipper was challenged when she tried to part them without injury to one or the other. The three ended up rolling on the floor with mop caps flying, hairpins scattering, and hair twists undone. Tipper corralled the fussy gals, one under each arm, and made her way up to the hallway. She tapped the door with her foot.

When Virginia heard the ruckus, she opened the door a half-arm length. Tipper pushed the wailing twins into the *boudoir*. Before she could withdraw her left hand, Virginia flung the door against it with a powerful slam. Tipper fell back with a scream that radiated throughout the house. Lawrence ran up the front stairs. Num came up the rear to find Tipper on her knees with her hand clutched to her chest and reeling from pain.

"Come, come. Let me see what my husband brought me from Louisville."

Virginia wanted to greet the girls, but they refused to be touched and spun around, butted their foreheads against the door, and cried for Tipper. When the missus reached again, they dropped to the floor on their butts, pulled their knees up, and covered their faces. Unable to enter through the preferred door, Lawrence was forced to use an alternate entrance farther from the sitting area.

"What the devil is going on in here?"

"Tipper brought these uncontrollable gals up for me to see, shoved them into the room, and left them. I haven't a clue what to do with them. She needs to come back up here and get these little wenches."

Lawrence rang for Tipper. In a short time, she was at the door, about to turn the knob when Virginia said, "Come in the other door."

"Ya send fa me, Missus?" Tipper asked, holding onto her throbbing hand.

"I did. You get those little pickaninnies out of here. Don't ever shove them in my room again and then have the audacity to go off and leave them acting like this. I won't tolerate such behavior from you. Take those gals now. Don't bring them back till you can present them properly with some degree of manners. This is absolutely unacceptable!"

Back in the kitchen, Tipper seated the girls at the small pantry table and finished plucking the chickens she had left in order to answer the missus' call. In the meantime, the girls disrobed and sat on the bedding with their legs crossed. Tipper didn't know how they got out of their dresses in such a short time and without her help. Mary and Molly refused to let her remove their chemises to put nightshifts back on them.

"You two gonna have to open up dem eyes and let da missus see what she want to be seein' in dem. Ain't gonna do ya no harm. Ya gonna hav ta let me comb dat hair and dress ya proper."

Later that evening, unsure about what to do about the gals, Tipper fed them a light meal and recited fables her mama subdued her with when she was their age. They listened with captive ears and lazed into a light sleep. Smiling down on them, Tipper drew the quilt up and snuggled it around their small frames. Because some of Tipper's days were unbearable, she worried what life might be for the twins growing up under Lawrence Piper's roof.

3

Virginia's Gift

Three months later, with the twins clinging to her skirt, Tipper hurried up the stairs to answer the call bell and suddenly paused midway across the floor. The gals bumped her hips and were knocked to the floor. They shielded their eyes with Tipper's skirt.

"My! My! What have we here?" asked Virginia.

"Dey be Mary and Molly. Don't know which be which. But dey been eatin' well. Gained dem some weight. But not growin' much. I say dey be 'bout three harvests and some. Dey be needin' a smidge more growin' time 'fore I can say fa sho."

Virginia hastened toward the girls who ducked beneath Tipper's hand-gathered garment. Overcome with excitement, Virginia tumbled in her attempt to sit on the floor with the girls who refused to be seen by eyes outside of the kitchen area or speak to anyone other than Tipper.

Tipper lifted her skirt above their heads. "Come out. Come out, my little ducklings," she sang as she swayed her skirt.

Thrilled to see the girls, Virginia cupped one twin's chin with her right hand and the other one with her left.

"Mary?" the twin to her left blinked. "Molly?" The other blinked. When she released their chins, they lowered them to their collarbones.

"Tipper, if you have ribbons, I'll tie them on the girls."

The ribbons Tipper planned to use to prettify the girls' hair were handed over to the missus. But when Virginia attempted to attach the soft blue satin strip to Mary's hair, with the intent to do the same to Molly with the mint-green one, they refused to be touched by her. Flustered, Virginia moaned, "Take them and go. When you know the difference and have ribbons tied on them in some fashion, bring them back."

After Tipper and the girls left the room, Lawrence approached Virginia to help her off the floor.

"What do you think, dear?"

"They're beautiful, so dainty, and not much larger than dolls."

Back in the kitchen, Tipper held up the streamers. Mary took the blue and Molly the mint-green. They toyed with them and chuckled as one as they slipped into their private world.

Five months later, Lawrence sent for the buggy. Virginia, excited, was the first in. He handed Mary to her, with a blue ribbon braided in her hair. She was positioned next to the window and Molly, with a mint-green ribbon, was placed on the other bench facing her. When Lawrence got in and closed the carriage door behind him, the twins scurried down to the floorboard. It was heart-wrenching for him and Virginia to experience such behavior whenever they attempted to enjoy the girls' company.

Not knowing what else to do, Virginia stroked their heads, smiled, and begged, "Come up. You won't see much of the flowers or trees from down there."

Lawrence gingerly palmed his wife's hand. "Let them be. They need more time to adjust. It isn't easy for gals so young to be snatched from their mother. I wish I had bought her, too, but she wasn't on the block with them, and I wasn't thinking. At the time, I was rushed to get them and get back home to surprise you."

Lawrence and Virginia sat in solitude as they sorted their private thoughts of what might be ahead for them and the twins. Not once during the ride through the hinterlands did the girls glance up to take note of them. Instead, they picked at the flowers and creases in their skirts.

"Lawrence."

"Yes, my dear."

"Sitting here, I ponder how two young people, so small, could be such terrors. Remember how they ransacked the pantry the other day when they pulled flour bags off the shelf creating a dust storm? What a mess! Plus, they nearly destroyed my camellias and beautiful hawthorns as they raced through them on those tiny feet of theirs. The poor flowers struggled to reach full bloom. Tipper keeps an eye on them. Blink, and they're gone. We might need to hire guardian angels to keep them safe and out of trouble," Virginia said with a light-hearted laugh.

After the ride, Lawrence and Virginia stepped down from the carriage box and collected the girls. Once their feet touched down, Lawrence grasped their hands to climb the front doorsteps. He released them inside the house, where they raced to the kitchen. The twins lifted Tipper's skirt, clutched her legs, and hid beneath the petticoats. In meditated silence, the Pipers continued to Virginia's *boudoir* and waited for Tipper to bring up the supper tray.

As another month passed, Virginia grew more fond of the girls, especially since they were able to let go of Tipper's protective apron strings to explore the house, upending furnishings and pulling down bedding to create their make-believe worlds.

One day, at the top of the rear staircase, they belly crawled along the wall to Virginia's room. With pointed index fingers, they nudged the door, got up on their hands and knees, and poked their heads inside to see. When they thought Virginia wasn't looking, they scampered across the floor to hide beneath the bed. The twins hunkered down as they giggled and scooted back into the shadows.

Reclined on her golden brocade chaise lounge with a book on her lap, Virginia thumbed a button tufting as she swung a pink *boudoir* slipper hanging from the toes of her right foot. She kicked it off and drew her feet and legs up beneath her skirt. Twisting her body, she leaned over the back of the chaise lounge but pretended not to notice the girls. Amused, she chuckled, "I think angels are fluttering beneath my bed. Perhaps I can have sweet tea with them."

The twins giggled with delight, rolled from beneath the bed, and bustled across the floor.

"Go ahead. Tug the bell pull."

In a brief time, Tipper appeared at the door. The girls rushed to her with open arms. They clasped her waist and giggled more.

"Can I help ya, Missus? Des here gals been troublesome?"

"No, no. They're fine. We'd like a tea tray with a plate of crumpets. Bring along the sugarloaf. Today, we'll sweeten our tea."

Tipper stepped back with a curtsy to leave. "Will der be anything mo?"

"Not at this time.

With shy smiles, Mary and Molly faced Virginia, lifted the wings of their skirts, lowered themselves with proper curtsies, and waited to be invited to join her.

"Come, come," said Virginia playfully.

Butted next to each other, the girls peered past the missus as they moved closer to her, but not close enough to be touched.

"Be patient," Virginia whispered to herself and returned to her reading.

The twins remained standing where they were till Tipper re-entered the room. Virginia took in a deep relaxing breath at the sight of Tipper, who placed the tray of treats on the highly polished mahogany table and raised a leaf. She arranged the chairs designed to boost the girls high enough to fit properly at the table. The little ones toed the rims, hopped on the seats, and sat quietly studying their hands.

Tipper filled the cups with warm tea and shave sugar from the tip of the cone over the surface of the tea. She stirred and added cream as the missus had directed her many times before. The girls sipped the tea and played with the crumpets before nibbling the edges of them.

Days later, no longer able to hold her tongue, Virginia nudged Lawrence. "We've had the girls for some time now. We need to decide their age and consider formal lessons for them."

"Are you sure it's what you want?"

Virginia gave her husband, who was figuring in his ledger, a stern glance. Prompted by her gesture, he thumbed to the page with the girls' entry on it: Mary and Molly, twin gals, mulattresses born in Virginia to a woman named Clarissa; purchased in Louisville, Kentucky, for $1,250.00, January 6, 1846. Lawrence raised his head to Virginia's continued stare.

In a nervous voice she said, "Since the twins have put on weight and become more verbal, Tipper thinks the girls are older than she first estimated. She said they're possibly closer to four and maybe some. If so, it would mean they were born around the summer or fall of 1842."

"My dear, what month and day do you have a preference for?" said and Virginia shrugged her shoulders with indifference.

"If you can't decide, it'll be recorded as Sunday, September 18, 1842. That will afford you plenty time to plan their fifth birthday party and not be distracted by the school admission requirements." Lawrence chuckled as he penned the notation in the ledger.

"Please, be serious, Mr. Piper. I don't want them to fall behind their peers and be looked down upon. It's essential they acquire the best the mulatto community has to offer. We must ensure they attract upstanding suitors, marry well, be properly cared for, and have suitable homes."

"Virginia, I'm warning you, as I've done before, be careful. You mustn't forget those girls are little Negro wenches who have a specific place in society, and it's not among our kind. If you raise them with finery, they'll think they're no different from you and me and begin acting privileged. You got to be certain they know their places. If not, and you're knowledgeable of this, the least bit of arrogance they display–the bob of their heads or flick of a finger–can get them lashed to a point you wouldn't recognize them. I'm certain you don't want nooses around their necks either."

Shaken by Lawrence's words, Virginia's voice quivered when she said, "I'll take care."

"Be sure that you do."

4

Toby’s New Owner

It was early on the fifth night when Humphrey arrived in Bardstown, Kentucky, with Toby straddled behind him. The horse was pulled to a stop in front of a two-story structure. A swift jab from Humphrey’s elbow sent the buck backward off the animal’s rump nearly into the arms of a darkie who had filtered from a shadow into the glow of the sunset. He dutifully collected the horse's reins and took charge without a spoken word. B U R P S easy-to-read white-trimmed, red letters above the front entrance jumped out at Toby as he was yanked by the arm.

“Come on, boy,” a lad, whose face he couldn’t clearly see, said.

Toby trailed him through a musty saloon and down a dark, dank hallway not much broader than a pair of shoulders. At the rear door, he was ushered across a small, dirt-packed yard to a shed the size of a springhouse. Its bone-handled door was propped open with a slug hammer. A pungent odor that spewed out, caused Toby to back-step into a poke which sent him stumbling into the crude space with a slime-slick floor that pulled his feet from beneath him. Dumbfounded and sickened to the stomach, he lay flummoxed on his back. The darkie who led Toby to the shed dragged his body back against the wall to a sitting position.

"Dey call me Gus. What dey call ya, boy?"

"Toby."

"Good 'nough name," he said and looked up. "Ain't much daylight left. Da moon gonna be bright ta night."

Gus handed Toby an empty knee-high bucket, bags of onions, and a stubby knife. "Peel dem. Den put da skins in dat bucket. Take da vegetables ta Lena at da kitchen," he said, pointing to a structure about ten feet from the shed. "Den, put dem skins on da garden back of it."

To get his bloodied heels off the floor, Toby propped them on a stray log. A gesture that generated a gut-wrenching moan. He shifted his weight till he could sit comfortable enough to peel the onions he dumped next to his hip. The first batch of peelings was used to scoop floor slime into the bucket he later, as instructed, hauled to the heap he had seen near the vegetable patch back of the kitchen.

A slice of cold air, followed by a blinding sunray the next morning, snapped Toby from a deathlike sleep. The obnoxious fumes had irritated his eyes and throat and caused his nose to drip continuously. Scanning the space around him, he saw what he didn't see before: maggots twisted between the slight gaps in the wooden planks, mice squeezing in where the floor didn't meet the wall. Wet chicken feathers plastered most of the surfaces. Toby felt sickened even more.

The lad continued to peel and toss. When done, the bucket was lugged to the kitchen garden. He scurried back to the shed where a bowl of gruel was placed just inside the door. He took time to regard its presence. The last food he ate was a blurred recollection of his ma handing him a dry biscuit and a handful of cooked beans. A brazen rat shimmied up to the bowl and a smite sent it airborne, headfirst against the wall. It dropped to the floor, tongue out.

"Hey! Hey! Let dem rats be, boy."

Gus took the onions and put down two burlap bags crammed with potatoes and carrots. "Lena already got dem caldrons on da coals heatin' up da cookin' water. Don't ya foot drag. She be needin' des here. Guests be comin' through dem doors shortly."

Not checking to see if the rat was dead, Toby retrieved the bowl and consumed the gruel with a single gulp before he emptied the bags of carrots on the earthen floor next to his leg. Quick as his young hands allowed, he skinned them only to get more buckets and bags. The lad worked through to the evening.

Drunk and hungover, Bruce Humphrey ventured out to the rear yard. He surveyed the lad's progress and turned; Toby thought to walk away. Instead, he snatched his belt from its loops striking the boy so fast and furious he hardly knew what happened to him. Humphrey waddled away dragging the belt buckle at his side.

A rooster's crow roused Toby from a fretful sleep while cooking smells gave his stomach cause to grumble and hanker for his ma's fatback, biscuits, and grits. Exhausted and sore all over, he labored to sit up. When he did, his hand brushed a short stack of hoecakes and a tin of soured milk that was slid beneath the door, with a six-inch gap between it and the dirt floor. He cracked the door, scanned the yard for human life, but saw none. Before he devoured the food, he eased the indigo remnant from his ma's auction skirt out of his pocket. He held it with his hand and then in a devotional mode to his lips. He whispered into its gathers, "*Ma, I'm tired. I hurt bad. But, I pray you, Jake, the twins, and George*

Henry don't have nefarious owners. I asked the Lord to keep you protected from all the evils."

Called from the shed, Toby stuffed the remnants back into his pocket, scoffed down the food, and scurried through the hall he had followed Gus down two nights before. Humphrey, braced against the bar, held a broom that he shoved at him.

"Ta-ta-take this here. S-s-sweep dis here floor. Stand dem chairs and tables up. Pi-pi-pick up dat trash outside. Git dat pail out der on da stoop and sc-sc-scoop the hay out of the troughs. Then, co-co-collect da horse manure. T-t-take it on ta da-da garden."

Nearly a year had passed when the fall of 1847 tumbled into the cold winter months. Trees shifted their palette from vibrant greens to gold-reds and oranges. The leaves rained down till branches were bared and the ground carpeted. Soon, the smells of gingerbread, that filled the air, were savored by noses while sweetening tastebuds. Church bells rang out. Caroling pleased the ears and hearts. Tiny flames that blinked in most windows, announced the coming of Christmas.

BURPS saloon and the Eating House were filled daily by holiday cheers and drunken laughter. Interlaced scents of sweaty toilet waters, stale food, and whiskey wafted through the air. Each meal brought an increase of guests to the eating house. The demanded seating forced some to wait for tables or eat at the saloon.

One cold, drizzly morning, Gus pulled Toby from the shed to make way for scaled chickens. They were dumped on the spot where he slept. Using his thumbs, the boy scraped off the feathers and cut up the birds till his hands swelled and his back and neck throbbed.

Chatter and chuckles from the front of the saloon spoke excitedly about an upcoming weddin'. ". . . gonna be a big crowd comin' in town fa dat Christmas wedding," an unfamiliar voice said.

Another replied, "Mayor's daughter gonna marry herself dat tall, good lookin' lad dat's 'pose ta be a German lawyer from Nashville. Da one who be comin' 'round da saloon from time ta time."

Gus's forceful boot kicked to the shed door, followed by a stern order. "Git up, boy. Be needin' a fire to warm dat eatin' house. Gonna open up early fa coffee and quick breads. City be swellin' wid folks soon. Some be strangers, others be travelers."

Buckets with a mix of vegetables were lined against the shed. Bushels of corn lined the inside walls. As Toby worked, his sly hand teased carrots, cobs, and spuds into an empty burlap bag. He pushed it beneath an overturned bucket. He toiled past midnight. His hands and feet resembled toasty loaves of fresh-baked yeast bread.

After the last guests were out of sight, Humphrey closed the doors for the day. Toby cleaned up the messes left behind.

On the wedding day, Humphrey was at the church for final instructions from the wedding family regarding meal plans. The saloon was in a state of perfect silence. Gus and Lena sat on the kitchen steps, sharing stories and jokes about the white folks, while Toby took time to breathe without worry. Those moments never lasted long, at least not with sufficient time to create deep-down peacefulness.

When the ceremony ended, BURPS bulged with wedding guests whose constant demands kept Toby shuffling back and forth from the kitchen to the saloon and eating house with platters of roasted mutton, boiled beef, stewed rabbit, and the usual pork and wild turkey. Lena had decorated the table with poinsettia bouquets, cut-glass bowls, and serving plates. The wedding cake along with jam cookies and rice pudding added a sweet touch.

As the guests drifted out of town, after the celebration, they bought the leftover chickens from the wedding feast to take along with them. Later that night, local drunkards fired off gunshots and started fistfights inside and outside BURPS. Frustrated by the rowdiness, Humphrey booted the celebrants out and locked the doors. By then, drunk himself, he tottered down the hall to the rear door with Toby lagging behind him. Humphrey's clumsy feet slipped off the back steps. His head slammed against the last step and pillowed on it. The lad gawked, leapfrogged over him, and squatted to poke Humphrey's shoulder, making sure he was unconscious.

Feeling confident, Toby easy-stepped to the shack and snatched the burlap bag from beneath the overturned bucket. With his eyes pushed to the corners, the boy monitored the splay-legged body bellowing out a roaring snore as he crossed the yard to ease open the kitchen door. Lena, who was curled up in the far corner, where she slept on the floor near the hearth, watched Toby but didn't say a word. Instead, she turned her head not to see more.

Toby thrust cooked mutton, chicken, and a handful of cookies into the tote. Then, after listening tentatively for concerning sounds and hearing any, he ran to the turnpike, crossed it, and pushed through the winter foliage. He glanced back over his shoulder at the candlewick lights in the windows that blinked at him.

Running and talking he muttered: "*Ma, I'm a freedom seeker, not a fugitive. I never done nothing wrong. Got no reason to run except for the freedom due me. I be on my way. Watch over me. Got plenty food. Gonna find you and the others. They won't call us slaves no more.*"

The boy's feet raced his heart as he searched the sky for the Big Dipper. He followed the North Star till daylight dissolved the constellations. Depleted, he hid among bushes as numbing sleep devoured him. When something crossed his face, he sat straight up with no sense of place or time and scrambled to stand before he continued to zigzag through the thicket. Toby's legs, paralyzed by the bark of dogs, folded beneath him. His body bunched into a quivering mass with his arms layered over his head. Before he could think a thought, three pattyrollers, he had never seen before, stood over him. The lad held his breath and waited for the dog bites and thrashing whips.

"Git on your knees, boy 'fore I slice ya hide wid da whip and leave ya fa dem wild boars," one of the catchers said.

The lad's hands were pulled to the back and tied to his ankles. His tattered coat and sweat-soaked shirt were peeled down by the first catcher who gripped the whip. Hounds, held by a third catcher, growled, gnashed their teeth, and nipped at his hide. The thrash of the whip with three snapping blows' split the boy's flesh and drew blood. He shuddered from the pain as his warm urine bathed his legs.

When the catcher raised his cat-o-nine to execute the fourth blow, the third catcher, who seemed to be in charge, warned, "Stop! That boy won't be worth nothin' if you keep dat up. We got a ways to go fo we get ta Louisville where the best prices fa a buck can be gotten. We'll have to answer to Humphrey if his property is damaged and he doesn't get what he's askin' for. We don't want ta lose dem dollars due us," he said and then nudged Toby. "Put them clothes back on, boy."

After Toby dressed, he was rope-dragged down the trail headed back to the turnpike he had crossed to escape bondage. The catchers didn't backpedal, they traveled on northward, passing BURPS.

5

Back on the Block

Bewildered, Toby fretted about being back at the same auction site from which he had been sold a year earlier. The sound of rattling keys and the squeak of the pen gate's hinges, plus Matthew Garrison, who owned the cage and monitored the new arrivals, was all too familiar. Toby staggered toward the rear where he had clustered with his family waiting to be sold.

"Hey, you! Come back here."

Toby recognized the raspy voice that loomed over the aggregated howls of other captives. Considering if he was being spoken to, Toby turned toward the voice. Before he took a step, Garrison came toward him with the handle of a bloody whip pointed at him. "Weren't you here not so long ago?"

"Yes sa, Massa."

"Had look-a-lak gals in ya pack?"

Stifled by fear, barely responding, Toby said, "Yes, sa."

"I remember ya and dat butterfly mark dat be on the back of ya neck. Git now. Take care. Don't ya make no trouble," he said and walked away.

Challenged, Toby hurried to the spot he remembered his family occupying, squatted, and searched for evidence possibly left behind by Ma, Jake, the twins, or George Henry. He fingered blood smears next to his hip, and hoped they weren't from his kin. Desperately wanting to ask Garrison about them, his lips parted, but he knew he couldn't. Instead, he fiddled with the remnant in his pocket and recollected, fresh as yesterday, how he held onto his ma when wrenched from her grip. With his forearms braced across his knees, he rested his head on them and wonder how he might run, cross the river to Jordan, find his clan, and breathe freedom till interrupted by the clatter of keys and the creak of the gate. Garrison stepped forward and aimed the head knot of his whip at Toby, who flinched at its sight.

"Get dat stock. Get it up der. Now!" Garrison told two muscular bucks who kicked aside darkies to catch hold of the ropes tied around Toby's waist and wrists.

They yanked him out of the pen, lugged him across the courtyard to the auction block, and catapulted him up on it. One of the fetchers spun him in a dizzying circle. Terrified and tottery, Toby faced a cantankerous crowd with scoffing mouths and felt the hate that festered behind their faces.

The auctioneer slammed the gavel repeatedly on the knocker as he barked Toby's attributes over the ruckus. He demanded a bid higher than the first. None came. He called out a few more attributes.

"This one's twelve, thirteen, give or take a harvest. A slim one. Got a good set of steady feet. Experienced houseboy. Comes from prime stock. Can cook. Clean. Do laundry. Buck's a bit beat up and puny, but he's a hard worker. Been told he can be trusted. Might not be ready fa da fields. Take ya time wid him. Be easy on dis here boy. 'Fo ya know it, he be plantin', plowin', sowin', hoein', and makin' ya a nice batcha picaninnies. What do I hear fa dis here buck?"

"Seventy-five dollars."

"Eighty-five dollars."

A lad from the far corner of the barn yelled, "One ninety dollars."

No bids followed that one. The auctioneer directed his gavel at Joe Jammer, a sixteen-year-old. The young farmer shuffled through the crowd up to the block to view his newly acquired stock, about his size, if he weren't a mere skin and bones. Even though the buck appeared near death's door, Jammer was in no position to buy better but was confident he got decent stock for his money.

The clerk urged the young fellow, "Gitcha darkie and put ya pay down here."

With flighty hands, he laid his notes, about all the money he had, on the table.

"What's your name, boy?"

On Jammer's left cheek, near his earlobe, was a blueberry-sized mole with three spiking hairs. A tuft of dusty-blond hair dithered when he removed his grungy, ill-fitting hat. His head, full of teeth, generated an acceptable smile.

"Joe Jammer," he said.

The clerk penned a document, folded it, and handed it to Toby's new owner. "Dis here be ya ownership paper. Take care, boy, ya be mighty young ta be buyin' a buck."

Jammer proudly shoved the title document into his overall pocket and took hold of the hemp rope tied to Toby. It was the first time he had bought anything worth anything. With a whistling sigh, he said, "Come on. We goin' ta Madison, Tennessee."

Toby rode on Pub, a broad-back, dark-gray ox, till he plummeted from its barrel facedown on the road. Filth and slush bathed his face and filled his mouth and nostrils causing him to snort and spit. Alarmed his new stock might be ailing, Jammer dismounted and carefully put the buck back on the animal.

Toby gripped hold to Pub's ropes as best he could and shifted his weight to sit on what didn't hurt. His aching legs could barely hug the barrel of the ox as he struggled to keep pace with the stranger who rode on a sleek, dark-brown quarter horse he called Noble.

Led along, he reminisced about his ma and professed under his breath, *Sure as God lets me keep breathing, I'll find you, Ma. I'll find all of you. I won't rest 'til I do!*

The hills and trees up ahead wavered, eventually, fading into a blurry mess. Woozy, Toby tumbled off the ox's back, landing on the pathway with the wind knocked out of him. Pain ripped through his body, not missing a spot. Jammer stood foot-parted, coat fronts pushed back, and hands shoved into his overall pockets where his fingers manipulated the ownership papers.

"Git up, boy! Done paid too much fa ya to be layin' down dis soon." Jammer's boot toe to Toby's ribs didn't generate a grunt or flinch. "Good Lord! You be hurt. Bad, too. Best we stop a spell. Don't want ta lose ya hide before I gitcha ta da farm."

Horse crop in hand, Joe Jammer slapped his side with such disgust a mean cloud of dust surfaced from his pant leg. Toby remained in the middle of the road while Joe led the horse and ox into a clearing to rest and graze.

When the buck regained consciousness, he was stretched out beneath a warm blanket next to a crackling fire, fully clothed with socks on his feet and boots dangling over his heels.

"Hungry?"

Toby shifted his eyes, peered past his new master and focused on the firelight. He grappled to reclaim what bit of himself was left.

"I'm Joe Jammer. What dey call ya?"

Toby ignored the voice to determine what had happened to him and where he was. He could only recall coming down off the block and being rope tied, but couldn't recall more, or how long he had shivered beneath the strange blanket that covered him.

Once the buck could stay on the ox long enough to travel a significant distance, they moved on. By nightfall the next day, a larger-than-usual campsite, littered with a collapsed tent and dirt-encrusted cooking and eating utensils, appeared up ahead. Not distracted by the clutter, Jammer built a fire in the midst of it.

Toby shuddered beneath the covers Jammer bundled him in as he slipped in and out of awareness. Joe cared for his new stock as if he were a blood relation. He bathed the lad, nursed the whip slashes on his back, and hand-fed him from his own rations. Toby knew it was so, because he didn't smell himself and had no hunger pains when he was conscious. Such attention wasn't something he wanted but was too weak to protest.

Jammer perpetually yakked about his dream to build on the property his deceased pa left him. Said he wanted to put up a new cabin on it; build a barn, corn crib, and spring house; sell crops; raise cattle; and make money. It seemed Toby's new master wouldn't stop spitting out wants, except when he slept or the boy passed out.

One day when the lad squirmed to sit, Jammer got in his face. "Been better than two weeks now. Ya haven't said a word. Ain't no cause to fear me. Got no reason to hurt ya. I want ya on ya feet movin' lak a wild horse boundin' across a plowed field. I need ya, boy. Need ya to work wid me ta build up my farm and git us some wealth."

When Toby heard Us and Wealth, he knew trouble and death were about to snatch him for their own sakes.

"Speak whenever ya want. It's gonna be the two of us from now on. And, I need ta know what ta call ya."

Toby, certain the man spoke out of his head, feared he was going to slit his throat as soon as he closed his eyes to sleep.

Jammer sat on a log not far from the fire with his elbows on his knees and hands clasped beneath his chin. A lengthy piece of dry grass dangled from between his lips as he waited for Toby to say something, but didn't push for him to speak.

With a dry tongue and a tightness in his throat, the buck said, "Toby. They call me Toby."

"How old ya be."

" 'Bout thirteen."

"So the caller said, but I thought you were older. Tall fa ya age. You're young. Gonna change your name. It's time fa you ta move on from ya past."

"Don't want a new name. Just want my clothes back."

"Whatcha got on is yours to keep. Your other belongings are in da saddlebag. Ya been talkin' outda ya head since ya been layin' der. Who's Mary, Molly, Jake, and George Henry?"

"The girls are my twin sisters. George Henry's my little brother. Jake's my pa."

When Jammer picked up his riding crop, Toby covered his head prepared for the furious clobbering to what was left of his slight existence.

"Not gonna whoop ya. Jest movin' dis here away from da fire. Go 'head. Have yaself a piece of jerky. I done told ya before, got no intention of doin' ya harm. Ya'll learn my words be good. I stand by dem. From dis day on, ya be Zach. It's a strong name. And things gonna be different fa us. Get dat crop planted come spring. We'll have money by the end of the cooling-off season. I gotta feelin' we gonna have us a good partnership."

We. Us. Wealth. Partnership. And now, Zach. Toby sensed trouble he couldn't prepare for. For sure, he didn't want to have words, good or bad, with the man who bought him. He turned the back of his head to Jammer and hoped he wouldn't slam it with a fire log.

After being on the bloody trail from Bruce Humphrey's place in Kentucky to Tennessee, for what seemed a near lifetime, and being renamed Zach–not to Toby's liking–the two arrived at Madison, Tennessee.

"The farm's near," said Joe. After riding a short distance, Jammer shouted, I see it! Look there. Ya see it?"

Hardly able to stay on the ox, Zach was powerless to fathom distances–here to there or there to here. He strangled the ox's ropes to anchor himself for a lean forward to probe the trees ahead and ingest what might enter his vision. Eventually, the shanty emerged from its mess–a flung-back structure tipped away from their approach. Zach wondered if it could endure a severe whirlwind sure to cross the fields unannounced and ride rough over its meagerness.

One behind the other, they branched off the turnpike onto an untrodden, horse-wide path toward the shed. Although the cabin's logs were intact, its tattered roof sagged in places, bulged in others, and even disappeared from vision at times. Crooked railings, stretched from the buckled stoop steps to the ends of the cabin, seemingly unable to offer support. Surprisingly, the warped floorboards were in place, and the door was still on its hinges.

Before dismounting, they glanced at the fast-moving clouds overhead. When Zach did, his feet skimmed the earth and his knees crimped and bonked the ground. Jammer got him back on his feet, hooked the buck by the arm, and lifted his legs from behind the knees, one at a time, to ensure each foot cleared the steps. Inside, Jammer propped his hand against the wall while he purged a corner to bunch dusty hay he covered with patched blankets from an old chest.

Zach's eyes scanned the floors, walls, windows, and floor-to-ceiling debris. The cabin didn't seem larger or smaller than the one he lived in with his family in Virginia, but was in such disarray one could hardly decipher its worth in size. Nonetheless, it took his mind back to Virginia and caused him to pine for his folks and his old name. He mopped his tears when he heard Jammer's voice.

"Go ahead, sit yaself down der. Gonna fix us a fire. Ya be feelin' better soon. Night's comin' on fast. Darkness will be bringin' a chill. Always does up here dis time of year. Have yaself a piece of dis."

Zach, exhausted and shaky, couldn't catch hold of the dry biscuit tossed to him by Joe, who retrieved it and rolled the lad's fingers around it. Unable to hold himself in place, Zach's body slouched over. Jammer covered him with one of the linsey-woolsey blankets from an old cedar chest and tucked it around Zach same as the boy's ma did for him on cold nights. The gesture sent a streak of harsh lonesomeness through the boy, cutting his breath short. Laid on his side, the smell of dusty cedar and dankness caused him to draw his knees up to his nose. With his head resting against them, he mumbled the words Jake had prayed the day they waited to be auctioned, "Help us be safe from dem mean hands wid dem whips dat do us harm."

Jammer stoked the fire. "Hold on der. Won't be long 'fore dis here spits out a good dose of heat."

Zach didn't want to hold on. He wanted to die. Nonetheless, the warmth from the embers and their musical crackling forced him to feel a smidge better. The constraint his muscles had on him loosened. Unable to battle the comforting heat, he succumbed to the onset of sleep.

Hunger, cold, and dreaded pain woke Zach the next morning and tugged him back from his attempt to roll over. He noted his nakedness but didn't remember his clothes being removed.

"Take care. Dat fall you took is still troublin' ya. Travelin' didn't help ya hurts none. You be in such agony, I couldn't git dat nightshirt over ya head, so I let ya be. Seems it's gonna take time 'fore ya up in a steady way."

The boy clenched his teeth and dug his nails into Jammer's upper arm when he raised him to pull a bedgown down over his head. The lad couldn't remember such pain, not even as a tot when the master's big horse threw him and trampled on his leg.

6

St. Louis, Missouri

Early morning, the first Monday of July, Mrs. Piper visited the mulatto community, about a half-hour buggy ride north of the city, to interview a teacher recommended by a friend from Virginia's social circle. She knocked on the door of Grace Devine, who welcomed her in with a warm smile and an offer of tea, which she accepted. Miss Grace was a pleasant, slim person, neither tall nor short. Her dark, thick, wavy hair that framed her oval face was tied at her nape with a puffy yellow ribbon. She was nearly white except for heavy freckling splattered across her nose and cheeks.

Virginia later learned Miss Devine was the most influential and reserved governess in the mulatto community. She, indeed, was sophisticated, well-informed, and versed on the significant subject matters. Together, the two women sipped tea and enthusiastically planned the best strategy for the girls' academic life ahead.

"I highly suggest they study dance, proper dress, etiquette, French, needlework, piano, and speech," Grace told Virginia.

The following Sunday, Virginia sat in the pergola with the girls to appreciate the sunset colors as they escaped the heat of the day. With a snap in her voice, she blurted, "How would you like to start piano and French lessons?"

"Lessons? Like when you teach us?"

"Yes, and I've spoken with a governess about the two of you. She thinks you're ready. Mr. Piper recorded your birth dates as Sunday, September 18, 1842. You will be five years of age when the school year starts, and be able to celebrate with a birthday party and invite your new classmates."

The girls leaped off their seats. Jumping up and down they shrilled with delight.

"When will we start?" they asked.

"Tomorrow."

"Tipper," Virginia said as she entered the kitchen with the twins at her side, "Miss Grace Devine will be here in the morning to meet the girls. She is the governess who will teach them what they need to know to be proper little ladies. Have them ready and nicely dressed early."

"Yes, Missus," Tipper said and was left with two bouncing gals.

"Miss Tipper, we're going to have our own governess, a birthday party, and a celebration." Mary and Molly looked at each other and then Tipper. "We know what a celebration is. But what's a birthday party?"

"Dat's a time ta celebrate the da day ya be born on. Ya play games, dance, and sing wid ya friends. And dey be bringin' ya little gifts. I be bakin' ya a special cake."

"Whenever we saw another harvest, we were told we were a year older, but we didn't get presents or anything special. Don't remember Ma mentioning a birthday party." Alluding to their mother wilted their gaiety.

"Come. Come. Don't start dat pinin'. Ya got somethin' good ta be lookin' forward ta. And da missus sho know how ta put on a swell shindig. Ya gonna have dat party wid ya friends, play dem games, and eat lots of cake. But don't ya be figurin' on dat too much. Ya can git dem hopes to where ya be gittin' a good dose of hurtin' if it don't happen."

Tipper gave the girls each a chunk of twice-cooked pork half the size of their hands. "Dis here gonna temper dem tummies while I gits dem dresses ready ta wear ta meet ya Miss Grace. After ya done wid dat meat, git dem nightshirts on and git yaself on dat beddin' fa a good night sleep. I be callin' ya early in da mornin' and don't be wantin' no grumpy gals."

Too excited to sleep, the twins whispered and chuckled about what might happen when the tutor came and what she'd be like.

"Hush dem voices dat I be hearin'."

The next morning, before the sun showed, Tipper soft-stepped about the kitchen. Pleased, that her griddle and coffee pots were in place, she brewed coffee, scrambled eggs, and flipped pancakes on the hot griddle. Afterward, she roused the girls and washed their faces and hands. With extra care, she brush their hair to a high shine and tie on hair ribbons with faultless bows sure to impress any governess.

"Miss Tipper, what do you think Miss Devine will be like? Will she be pretty? Will she be nice? Will she be mean? Will she make us work hard? Will she . . ."

"Gotta wait and see. Now, let me git dat ham outta da oven 'fore it be burnin' and won't be no good fa eatin'."

After the girls enjoyed their meals, to keep warm, they sat in the pantry with the bedding pulled up to their ears.

"My, my! Look at ya. Be lookin' like two lil, big-eye chicks hatchin' outda der shells. Come, come. Let's git dem stockings and shoes on ya." Tipper gathered the leg coverings and pulled them over their toes and heels–up to their knees before she buttoned on their shoes and laced up their petticoats.

She slipped apple-red dresses scattered with cloud-white roses and white tucked bodices over the heads of the twins. Pearl buttons that trekked from waist to neck, were fastened in place with a small button hook. Taking her time, she held the girls at arms' length to examined their frocks. "Stand der. Let me see ya. My, my. Ya be lookin' mighty dainty. Pretty, too." She smiled proudly and very slowly turned the two for a better inspection.

"Dat be the door knocker."

Tipper moved her charges closer to the kitchen door where they could hear the missus' voice from the foyer say, "Please, come in, Miss Devine. Let me show you to the library. Have a seat there, I'll send for the girls." The girls giggled as Tipper pulled them back.

Virginia crossed the room to tug the bell-pull. It was only minutes before Tipper appeared with the twins in hand and waited to be recognized.

"Bring them closer for Miss Devine to meet."

With the girls in hand, the three crossed the floor. Tipper nodded to the new governess. "Good morning, Miss Devine. Dis here be da twins. Mary is da one wid da blue ribbon in huh hair. Dis be Molly wid da green one in huh hair." She nudged the two forward. "Go 'head, welcome Miss Devine."

Nimble-footed, the girls moved closer to Miss Devine, winged their skirts, and gracefully curtsied. In soft, shy voices they said, "Welcome, Miss Devine. We're pleased to meet you."

After the three-times-a-week sessions, the girls began to communicate more freely with Virginia and Lawrence.

"Good morning, Miss Virginia, how are you today?" theyasked.

"I'm fine. Thank you," Virginia replied, and leaned forward to say, "And you. And you?"

"Good," they said without stepping away from her.

At lesson time, Mary and Molly questioned Miss Grace about the blue sky, green trees, chalky clouds, and the icy snow. "Is the world everything we can see? Can we fly as birds do? Where do raindrops and our tears come from?"

Grace was astonished by her new students. She informed Mrs. Piper, "Those girls are beyond smart. They're fast learners and never falter on a question or assignment unless they're playing and not paying attention to instructions. I won't be using toys and trinkets to instruct them. Books, chalkboards, maps, and slates will be my tools. And, I recommend they start school this coming fall. They can skip preschool work and go straight into the second year of studies."

Toward the end of summer, the girls stopped taking food. They spent more time on their bedding. Tipper moved them from the corner of the kitchen to the more spacious linen closet. They didn't bother to squabble or bicker in their nonsensical language. Their faces were flush as they grew more fragile than the day they arrived nearly two years ago. Time and time again, they refused attempts to be fed various healing portions: pepper soup; cooked chicken feet; boiled, sweetened onions; and sassafras tea.

After nothing Tipper did seemed to work, Lawrence sent Num to fetch Dr. Smead. Before the day's end, the clopping of a horse's hooves announced his arrival.

"Good day, Mr. Piper. I understand you've got two little Nigresses who are ill."

"And so frail, I felt they wouldn't live to see morning and sent Num to fetch you."

"I'll take a look at them. How's the missus doing?"

"She, too, is deeply concerned about the gals."

"Take me to them."

Lawrence escorted Dr. Smead to the closet. With a studying eye, the doctor set his medical bag down. Squatting, he leaned in for a better look at the twins–entangled in the covers, not yielding to his visit.

Dr. Smead sent Tipper to fetch water and then turned to Piper. "After I examine them, I'll give you a report."

Tipper hurried to the kitchen sink, fetched the water, and brought it back to the doctor, sure the girls were sicker than she thought.

"Put it there. Tell me, what seems to be the problem? Bad stool?" Dr. Smead asked her.

"No."

"Troublesome stomachs?"

"Dey be rafusin' der vittles."

"Then, what do you think might be wrong with them?"

"Dem gals won't eat. Won't talk. Don't play none neither. When I give dem der dolls, dey don't pay dem no mind. Dey jes seem ta be fadin' away."

"I see. Get your master."

"Lawrence, I can't identify the exact problem. They're a little warm, but not showing signs of any diseases I can give a name to. Tipper's gonna have to keep a cool towel on their foreheads, encourage them to sip warm broth, and let this illness run its course."

Mewling and shaking, Virginia monitored the girls throughout that day and on, till she was beside herself. Eventually, her health faltered to the point she couldn't care for her own personal needs.

Again, Lawrence sent Num to fetch Dr. Smead. He examined Mrs. Piper and said, "I'll send Hattie to sit with her. She's the best sick nurse in St. Louis. She'll be instructed not to leave the missus' side before she's fully recovered from her sickness and her grief," he told Lawrence.

Virginia and the girls regained most of their lost weight, but neither Dr. Smead nor his colleagues ever determined the source or cause of their illness.

With his left hand, Lawrence was braced against the fireplace mantel. His right arm was behind his back, he recounted activities of the past months. Virginia noiselessly entered the parlor as he was venturing deeper into his thoughts. A chilly breeze that brushed his back compelled him to embrace more of the warmth hearth. His wife cozied next to him, looping her arm through his, hoping to temper his somberness.

"What has you peering so deeply into the flames that seem to have taken you from me?" she asked and arched her back with an indication for affection.

Lawrence accepted the summon for his attention and kissed her lips. "You're so special to me. Many days I feared I would lose you and the girls." With heaviness in his heart, he stared more earnestly at Virginia. His lips trembled as he pulled her closer. Peering into her intense stare, he said, "It teases my mind how they have become such an unintended part of our lives."

Virginia snuggled against Lawrence. Resting her head against him she said, "A good amount of time has passed and they've grown more adorable and alike when it didn't seem possible. Pure delights:

quiet, smart, playful, and above all, mischievous. Your gift of them has filled me with more joy than I can grasp."

Lawrence sighed, "To avoid error in identifying them, I refer to them as You-and-You or Mary-Molly."

Six weeks later, Virginia and the girls had returned to a more familiar routine, but their dresses sagged. Even after multiple alterations.

When the missus, along with twins, arrived at the Society of the Sacred Heart to enroll the girls, Virginia was directed to the school office. Mary and Molly were instructed to wait in the hall. Miss Johnson, the principal, was behind her desk chair with her hands clasped at the waist. Shoulders drawn back and chin tucked in, stern-faced and commanding. She nodded and asked Virginia, "Are you and those girls well?"

"Oh, yes. The doctor said they're back to themselves and ready for school. I'm perfectly fine as well. Just had an unusual bout of malaise. It was my fear they wouldn't recover that caused me such stress. My health faltered a bit, but I'm feeling chipper these days."

"What was the prognosis of the young ladies' illness?"

"Dr. Smead never determined what sickened them but has said they're fine now and can attend school."

"Mrs. Piper, I'm so sorry to inform you, we can't, at t his time, accept the young ladies here or at any academic program operated by the Society of the Sacred Heart. We have stringent rules concerning the health of our students and your young ladies appear unwell to me."

Back in the carriage, Virginia and the girls sat in an uneasy quietness. She gazed at the little ones in front of her, knowing they sensed something troubled her.

"Miss Johnson said you can't start school this session. Don't worry. We'll come back when the next enrollment starts. Meanwhile, you'll carry on with your studies at home."

Virginia's disappointment didn't slow the girls down. They moved ahead with their tutorial sessions with Miss Grace, whom they adored. Because the Catholic schools required Latin, it was added to the agenda, along with the other subjects.

The following January, Miss Johnson permitted Mary and Molly to register for the remainder of the school year. The start was without incident. The girls rose to the top in their classes. However, the cholera outbreak during the spring and summer months sickened the surrounding populations.

Virginia withdrew the girls from school and all activities outside the house and reinstated the services of Miss Grace. One afternoon, the missus ordered a tray of cocoa and cookies to be brought to the library for the four of them. Tipper placed the midday snack on the table and positioned chairs around it. She glanced at Virginia for approval. A smile and a nod let her know that she had done well.

Curious about the girls' progress, Virginia invited them and Miss Grace to sit with her. The twins hopped up on their modified chairs.

"I'd like to hear about your French lessons and know how you are progressing," Virginia said.

Shy-faced, the girls looked at Miss Grace and then Virginia. They said, "Miss Grace awarded us with sweet crumpets. She said we did especially well with our French lessons."

"Let me hear you recite some of what you've learned."

"Miss Grace, what should we do."

"Why don't you do the song and dance that you learned last week?"

"Miss Virginia, can we perform for you?"

"I'd love that."

Mary and Molly lifted the wings of their skirts. From deep curtsies, they raised up on their toes, swished their skirts left, and then right. They danced around each other as they sang in their most joyful voices:

Sur le Pont D"Avignon (French Version)	**On the Bridge of Avignon (English Version)**
Sur le Pont d'Avignon L'on y danse. L'on y danse Sur le Pont d'Avignon L'on y danse tous en rond.	On the bridge of Avignon We're all dancing, We're all dancing On the bridge of Avignon We all dance in circles.
Les beaux messieurs font Et puis encore comme ça.	The fine gentlemen go like this And then the again like this.
Les belles dames font comme ça Et puis encore comme ça.	The beautiful ladies go like this An then again like that
Les filles font comme ça Et puis encore comme ça.	The young girls go like this And then again like that
Les musiciens font canne ça El puis encore comma ça.	The musicians go like this And then again like that

Mary and Molly bounced up and down on their heels to the beat of the song not stopping until it ended. Before the girls released their hold on their dresses, they curtsied to one anther and then to Miss Virginia.

The madame hugged the girls. "That was wonderful. You did very Well," she said with a prideful smile.

7

Joe Jammer's Farm

Zach, downtrodden, but on his feet, waited for the command. "Go 'head. Step. Step high as ya can," Jammer prodded. "Ya, some better now. When ya git ta dat well, fill dat bucket and tote it back ta dis here stoop."

The boy trudged to the well. Leaning against the sharp edge of it, he lowered the bucket and collected water. His spasmodic arm and back muscles toiled to pull it up to the rim of the well, but he couldn't lift it. Before Zach dumped a good deal of the water back into the well, he gave Jammer a grim glimpse.

"Don't seem ya any good for hoistin' yet."

At the suggestion of his master, Zach eased onto the unsaddled back of Noble to freely venture about the property.

"Go slow. Take a look around. When ya done, come on back. I'll school ya about what ya saw. Meanwhile, I'm gonna do some mendin' and cleanin'."

Zach grimaced and rode off while Joe took a studying stance to assess the cabin. He entered the lean-to and gasped at the incredible heap of rat-infested animal feed; bolts of muddy, molded fabrics; crushed pots and pans; rusted bridle bits; a dry-rotted table; stacked planks; and a child's crushed, wheelless wagon. Most of what he saw wasn't around when he left after Pappy's death some time ago. His family never had such. Because he couldn't identify what he saw from where he was standing, he assumed sharecroppers brought it in while he was on the road working odd jobs to earn enough money to purchase a work animal and bid on a hand or two at the upcoming auctions. Scratching his head, he questioned himself about how to make the floor-to-ceiling rubbish vanish.

He kicked a stack of dusty cowhides aside and then gathered an armload of mingled litter that he hauled to the rear yard and set afire. Jammer returned to pick up an arm full of decayed wood when the pole of a tattered tent blocked his step, flipping him. He landed face down with his nose butted against a splintered chair. Animal-hair batting oozed from beneath its jade-green brocade seat covering. Sneezing and coughing, he raised his head to a hoard of blankets–some he recognized, most he didn't, but for sure they were a tattered mass of frayed quiltings. Nearby, a once white, cotton, lace christening gown, possibly worn by the girl child his mammy lost and spoke of in snippets, so slight, Joe could never make sense of her words.

Back on his feet, he scooped up a larger bundle of rubbish and headed to the rear yard again. Jammer continued the routine till the barricade of junk diminished and light and space emerged in its stead. When he crossed beneath the ceiling beams that divided the shack, not much was in the back half. But what was there, generated visions from his past life. Still in place and layered with mangled covers was the rope bed his parents slept on. The long-handled hoe from Jammer's childhood rested against the small platform bed Pappy built for him. He remembered how he used the hoe for digging as he walked behind Pappy's plow. Hands sore and legs aching, he wished instead he was leaning on it under the canopy of the oak tree off to his left.

Jammer felt ambivalent about being jerked back to the memories of his boyhood days, but he couldn't resist it: Pappy's beatings, severe hunger, unreasonable work demands, and Mammy's prolonged sickness till her death. Because the thoughts depleted his mental and physical energy, he considered sitting on the stoop to breathe in fresh air but, instead gathered his hammer, saw, and nails and reflected on how to best approach the repairs outside and started with the porch.

Done and delighted to laze on the now sturdy steps as he visually traced the land that followed multiple bends of the Kentucky-Tennessee River; he gloated over a larger section that turned southward. The acreage was prized: rolling hills, slight valleys, dense forests, streams, and deltas–every farmer's dream and was now his. A fact that weighted heavily among his thoughts that were difficult to decipher.

At the edge of the property, atop Noble, Zach pondered the river factors, wanting to cross it, not stopping till he reached Glory Land, but a twinge in his back tugged at him. For some unexplainable reasons, the desire to run was replaced by a strange attachment to the earth beneath him and possibly the lingering hope for reasonable living conditions. Zach had not felt such peace since he was a young boy seated at the feet of his missus, back in Virginia, as she strummed her harp.

Jammer spotted Zach paused at the edge of the riverbank, neck stretched, turning his head, seeming to scan and regard what captivated his senses. Joe leaped from the stoop, certain the boy was about to run. Just then, the lad yanked the horse's straps and started back toward the cabin. Jammer waved as if he were his best buddy returning home from an extended journey.

Zach grinned at the sight of the cabin: the straight railings; sturdy steps, though still sagging some in the center, were well-affixed; and the faulty floorboards replaced with newer planks.

"Hey there. Ya seem rung out and needin' a drink. When you come down off dat horse, take ya time."

The lad rotated his body across the horse's back, warm and damp from riding. He grunted as he contemplated the pain he was sure to endure when his feet grazed the ground. Leaned forward, the boy lifted his upper body, swung his left leg from over the back of the animal, and let his weight draw his limbs downward. Once on a dependable foothold, he snugged his wrap around his mid-section and hobbled toward the stairs. Jammer handed him a tin of well water. Sitting close, they fast-talked about what Zach had seen and his thoughts about the river.

With a slap on his back, his master said, "Let's go in. 'Bout time ta eat."

Zach was awed by the scope of the cabin. The rubbish, previously stacked to the rafters, was gone. With no wall behind it, the additional footage doubled its volume and created an airy space throughout. The absence of dank odors, cobwebs, and dust made breathing effortless.

"You'll be sleeping over there."

In a nook to the left, is where Jammer's childhood platform bed, a three-legged stool, and canvas bucket replaced the sleeping straw and mucky covers. If the boy stood on tiptoe, he could peer out of a small window above the bed.

Jammer's trail-dusty jacket hangs on the foot post of the footboard of the knee-high rope bed. The headboard was pushed against the back wall. On one side of the bed, a chair, catty-cornered to the right of it, has a narrow cane-bottom and adder-back. On the other side, a cedar chest that would consume a pair of good-sized men, seems to be sturdy enough to pounce on. Joe pointed to it. "Got clothes in there. Be the ones my folks had. Some should fit you. Use whatever you need."

Jammer handed the lad a hammer. Because the day was approaching its end, they nailed cowhides to the windows to block the cool night air and brightness of the morning sun. Afterward, the boy lay on his new bed. With his eyes closed, he heard his ma cry out his given name same as she did the day he was auctioned away from her. He struggled to adjust to the name given to him by Jammer. A good part of him rejected it. Nonetheless, he was glad to be away from the punitive hands of Bruce Humphrey along with the cold rains, snow, and ice, as well as the constant peeling, shucking, and plucking.

While his new hand reflected on a mix of thoughts, Jammer tended to the flames in the fireplace that had fresh logs stacked knee-high on both sides. From Zach's bed, the lad peered straight into the fire. Joe offered a cut of jerky with an invitation to share the heat that drifted from the hearth. Still harboring fear, the boy pressed his coat against his chest, hesitantly moved toward the hearth, and accepted the meat.

8

Banking & Land

Zach's days with Joe Jammer were preoccupied with how he'd escape his new situation. He knew it wouldn't require much with his access to adequate clothing–for hot and cold weather–and food to keep his gut satisfied, but he wasn't sure of his proximity to Kentucky, where he last saw his family, or St. Louis where the twins were supposedly taken. Now he was in Madison, Tennessee, wherever that was. One thing the lad was sure of was the Big Dipper and the North Star. His ma and Jake had taught him and his siblings about them. "Listen to dem songs dat come up out da dem fields. Dey tells when it be safe ta run. Den ya git on dat Underground Train. Follow dem northbound trails," they told them.

Zach would continuously ponder, plan, and pine without pause if it weren't for the interruptions from Jammer's jabbering about items on his we-gotta-do list. The good was, he didn't have a punitive hand, thrashing whip, or harsh words–only grueling farm work.

"Tomorrow, we'll collect papers saying I own dis here land outright we been workin'. And hopin' it's mine, don't want to plow too far in any one direction without knowin' fa sure. But Pappy say, 'all ya see will be yours one day.' We be livin' so poor, I thought fa sure he was talkin' out of his head. Den, he went on to his restin' place."

"Heaven or hell?" Zach asked.

"He didn't have no religion dat I know of. Ain't fa sure where his soul be restin'. But his body, it be next ta Mammy under dat tulip tree out back."

The next day, riding along side each other, as buddies do on a journey, Jammer and Zach entered town amid furrowed brows and baleful stares with mouths ajar beneath them. Zach tugged on Pub's ropes, retracting a horse's length. Townsfolk who maintained their invidious postures forced the boy to downcast his vision. Finally, the two dismounted in front of the Land Office.

Zach toyed with the reins. "I'll get the animals fed and watered," he said.

At a porch-depth, through the window, from where they stood, gentlemen dressed in business attire waited to be seen. They lounged on oak, ladder-back chairs with brown leather inserts and matching seats.

"Might take a while," Jammer said under his breath before mounting the office steps. "Come back when ya done. Wait fa me here."

Zach led Pub and Noble to the barn where he instructed Brit, the stableboy, before he returned to the Land Office. Side pressed against the building, he eased around its edge. Slow and sure-footed the lad climbed the steps one at a time till flatfooted on the porch with his back pressed against the facade. Not hurrying, he maneuvered his body weight toward the double-hung windows. Not raising his head, he meticulously rolled onto his left shoulder. With Jammer in sight, he prepared his brain to consume what he saw and heard, certain he'd be needed to interpret the language and papers when the two of them got back to the cabin.

Joe fidgeted with his hat as he stood behind the most massive desk in the office. Postured behind it, he offered a hearty welcome. "Good to see you, Mr. Jammer. I'm Mr. Brown, owner and manager of this here place. Have a seat there. I've been expecting you since I got word of your father's death. Please, accept my condolences," he said, as he spread the documents in front of Joe. "I prepared these title papers for your signature. Here's a pen. The inkwell is full. The blotter is there." He pointed to his left.

Joe dipped the sharp point of the long, elegant, brown quill pen into the inkwell and was about to sign the paper when a body slammed against the outside wall gave him pause. When Zach screamed, Joe rushed to see what caused the commotion.

"Hey! Whatcha doin' ta my darkie?" he asked a stranger who had a grip on Zach's shirt and a fist above the buck's head.

"Darkie's stickin' his nose where it ain't got no business."

"He's where I put him and told him ta stay. I suggest ya talk ta me 'fore ya go puttin' ya hands on my property 'less ya can afford to buy it. From da sight of ya, I be doubtful ya can. Now, take ya hands off of him, and let me get back ta my business."

Shaken by the incident, Mr. Brown blurted with shakiness in his voice, "Mr. Jammer, please, sir, accept my apologies. We don't normally have such disturbances during the workday."

Feathered writing tool still in hand and breathing hard, Jammer followed Brown back into the office. Seated at the desk, he shut his eyes to reclaim his calm and slow his rapidly beating heart. With the pen braced against his ring finger and clutched by the others, Joe positioned his hand on one of the documents. He toiled to create each letter of his name.

"Take your time, boy. No need ta rush. It's not often someone acquires so much at one time. You'll be okay. Keep in mind money or land that comes to ya quick can slip away quick."

Joe nodded his head before completing the task at hand. When finished, Mr. Brown folded the papers into a protective sleeve. He secured it with a thin strip of hide before handing the property deed, along with a copy of the Last Will and Testament, to Jammer. The young man proudly slid the documents into a deep pocket inside his vest. He patted it for reassurance before he turned to take his leave.

Standing in the doorway, hands pocketed and staring into the day, Joe rocked some and grinned a lot. The unfamiliar expression on his face caused Zach an uneasiness he couldn't find an expression for. With an anxious eye, he asked, "Are you all right?"

"Yep. Get the horse and ox. I be needin' a celebration drink. I'll meet ya at the barn in a bit."

Jammer handed Zach coins to pay Brit before he jaunted off toward the saloon. Shoulders back, he high stepped down the dirt road right through the middle of town to the tavern.

Jingling the coin in his pocket, Zach crossed the road to the barn and collected the animals. Long-reining them, he led both out of the barn just as Joe exited the tavern, scudding in his direction.

"I own dat land straight out dat we been workin' on. I can build me dat big house when da real money come in."

"Where do you plan on putting it?"

"On top of dat hill where we can see plum ta the other side of the world. I'm sure it's dat chunk of land I also be havin' papers on. Didn't know Pappy had dat much land or had so much money. We always live poorly. When Mammy went on ta be with her folks dat went 'fore her, there was no fancy burial gown, no stockings and slippers for her, or a proper wake and funeral. Pappy sung a song and said a prayer. It was mostly 'bout God watchin' over da land. Not much was said about Mammy, only dat she'd rest in peace wherever she might go ta."

Closed-eye, Jammer heaved and then peered at Zach. "But I done got des papers here. Dey supposed ta say I got plenty land and plenty money. If it be so, we gonna be livin' good. But, I still need to see a Mr. Miller, the Will officer at the bank, about da money Pappy done left me."

Jammer headed back to the saloon for another drink while Zach took the animals with him to visit Amos at the blacksmith shop. It didn't take Jammer long to drink himself sloppy, sling chairs, and hoot about how life had unloaded a chunk of luck on him. Gabe, the bartender, went in search of Zach but couldn't go far. Leaving a drunken customer unattended could fuel trouble.

Back at the tavern, Gabe confronted Matt, his lookout and guardsman, who slurped warm beer and didn't seem to hear the call. The bartender slammed his hand on the counter, sending a vibrating ripple he followed to Matt's space. Head to head with him he said, "Scat. Get the sheriff. Tell him ta come get dis here bum and lock him up before someone kills him."

Matt snatched his hat off the bar. Not wasting a minute, he hurried out of the cafe doors and kicked up a heap of dust with his clumsy gait as he made his way to the jailhouse. Sheriff Ray was on the stoop postured against a post, chewing on a half-smoked cigar clenched between his teeth. Matt blurted the bartender's message.

Coming down off the porch, the two fast-walked back to the saloon. Before entering, the law officer began to assess the rowdy situation. He called over his shoulder to Matt, "Go get his darkie. Tell him to come get his master."

Matt put his hat back on and turned on his heels. He hastened toward the blacksmith shop where he confronted Zach.

Panting, he said, "Ya master be talkin' out of his head. Says he be rich, gonna build a mansion on a hill and surround it wid all kinds of structures. Sheriff Ray say, best ya hurry and take him out of dis here town 'fore dey done killed him for dat wealth he be tryin' ta make dem folks think he got. I can tell ya, dem rustlers gittin' antsy." Not waiting for a reply, Matt whirled on his heels and rushed back to his beer.

At the suggestion of Sheriff Ray, Zach hitched Pub to the tongue of a cart used to haul drunks to the jailhouse. With a promise to return it early the next day, he loaded Joe into the back and tied Noble to the rear. At that moment, Zach knew how vulnerable his life was. He cringed at the thought of how such an incident could have left him to fend for himself against the knavish whites in town.

Filled with annoyance, Zach glanced over his shoulder at his senseless master before he raised the horsewhip and hollered, "hike," urging Pub to move on. It was a good distance down the turnpike before he turned off, aiming the ox toward the cabin. Sickened moans from Jammer snagged Zach's attention. His master hadn't regained full consciousness, but had disgorged his gut's content.

At the cabin, Zach secured the animals to the hitching post before he pulled Jammer's sloppy weight from the floorboard. He slung him over his shoulder, took him inside, and placed him on the rope bed. He disrobed the non-complying body, bathed the stench away, and wrestled his master into a nightshirt.

Emotionally exhausted from the day's ordeal, Zach stared down on Joe, which reminded him of his ma's saying, "Don't ya drink, boy. Dat be da one thang dat can snatch a man's life quick." Those intense words became a barrier to the bottle, even when Jammer insisted it was a cure-all for whatever ailed one.

At the foot of the stoop the next morning, Zach heard Joe's bear of a snore as he gave the borrowed cart a perusal before he flooded it with well water, washing away the foul residue followed with a scrub brush and lye soap. Afterward, he hitched Noble to it.

Entering town, Zach noted men up ahead roughnecking in the street. He held tight to Noble's reins and eased him into a steady trot to maintain control. With his elbows pulled close to his body, he kept his head faced forward to avoid unwanted attention. The slightest gesture–a tilt of the head or fling of the arm–could ignite a confrontation. As he approached the jailhouse steps, Sheriff Ray waved an acknowledgment. The lad returned the wagon with a sense of relief and left.

Back in the saddle, he galloped away from town with an insignificant degree of speed to not distract from the brawls he passed along the way. In front of the farm, Noble galloped straight to Jammer, seated on the stoop of the cabin with his head braced on his hands. Next to his hip, a stone weighted down the legal papers from the claim office.

"Believe I'm sick. Ain't gonna be much good today."

"No need for worry. Everything's planted and the animals are in the barn. I'll fix some pone and fatback with a strong pot of coffee to wash it down. You rest."

Jammer held up his papers. "I can read this. But cain't understand most of it. I need ta know what I signed. Can ya help me wid it?"

"I'm learned."

"Thought so by da way ya be talkin'. But how so."

Drawn into a state of solitude, Zach cautiously took a seat next to Jammer on the stoop. He deeply inhaled, taking time to ponder if he should answer the question which hauled him back to his boyhood. The lad always avoided bringing such memories to the surface, at least no more than necessary, and never about his education. It and slavery never existed conjointly. However, Zach was beginning to feel grounded in brotherhood with Jammer. In a low, quiet tone, near a whisper, he guardedly said, "When I was a wee boy, my missus took a fancy to teaching me. Said I was quick-minded and wanted to see how many facts I can consume and retain in snippets of time: Bible study, reading, writing, arithmetic, some science, geography, and philosophy. I met her expectations and never tired of learning."

Distressed, Jammer gazed sad-eyed at Zach. "Ya know, I never went ta school more dan six grades. And, not wid good attendance. Can read a fair amount, but not enough ta make sense of des here legal papers. Pappy kept me home helpin' him and takin' charge of Mammy. When I got ta a good size, he put me in da fields. Mammy passed before I got ta my eleventh year. She left Pappy wid no other child and me widout a brother or sister ta squabble wid. You be the closest I got to a brother.

"I didn't know her as well as I did Pappy. She be sickly most of da time. Scarce a word waft from behind her cracked lips. Three years after she passed, Pappy was gone. Now I own dis here land. When I takes note of dis farm and des here papers dat say I own da land around me, I's lucky ta be able ta sign my name. I be happy if you can look dem over. Tell me what dey be sayin'."

"Best we go inside, to do that," said Zach.

No white person ever asked Zach to read something crucial as a land deed or anything else other than during titular sessions with his Virginia missus. A simple task, yet, if known, he'd be blinded or hanged. Zach, unnerved but not surprised when asked, agreed to review them. His nervous hand collected the documents. Inside the cabin, he spread them on the table. His tentative eyes trailed the cursive, line by line, that crisscrossed each page.

"The deed refers to the property we've been working. It says, too, it's free of any bindings or liens. That means no one else has rights to it. But, you don't own the strip of land where you want to build your house on the hill."

"Ya sure dat's what it says?"

"I am."

Zach shifted his attention back to the legal documents. He gave the Will a firm tap with a confident forefinger and said, "This one here tells you that you have money in the bank held for a signature."

"How much?"

"$21,360.00."

Joe Jammer sighed a profound, "Wow!" as he fell off the chair. From the floor he muttered, "Dat be quite a lump. I's fearful da paper might be sayin' I owed it ta somebody and not be somethin' comin' ta me." He adjusted himself and got to his feet. He refolded the documents back into the sleeve and tucked them beneath the clothing and blankets in the cedar chest. He peered fixedly at Zach. "It don't make no sense. Got money and acres, but not dat hill I want ta build my house on. Got ta learn who be ownin' it."

From long days in the fields, Zach's muscles bulged beneath his darkened skin. His clothing tightened around his body and up in his crotch. He had slit his boots to ease the squeeze on his big-toe nails. Jammer had to raise off his heels for an eye-to-eye with Zach. For their serious dialogues, they sat.

"Ya nearly corn-harvest tall," Joe told him and pressed a new batch of clothes and boots between the boy's hands. "Make these last you a while."

Zach put the garments on the table as he told Jammer, "We need to be the first to get the wheat sowed and shipped north to beat the northerners to their market if we want to make money on it."

"How's such possible?

"After we harvest the corn in the fall, we'll plant winter wheat and cut it in the spring before the northerners do. It takes their wheat longer to mature because of the cold climate."

"But we need to plant more corn."

"Don't worry, we will. And we'll get the hemp in, too."

Jammer had little to no knowledge of farming but did an excellent job clearing the land. Since it wasn't forced labor from his boyhood, he enjoyed it. He and Zach, along with Noble and Pub, worked diligently to prep the soil and seed it. Not an easy job, but once done, it progressed to the wait-and-see period.

Near the end of summer, without excessive rainfall or droughts, it was evident a record crop would be up, ready for harvest, making way for the hemp, which Zach informed Jammer grew fast and didn't require much care. "The work's hard and dirty. White men won't do it, and Nigresses cain't. However, bucks are the best workers. They're strong and will make it quite profitable for you."

"What's the calendar like dat we'll be workin' on?"

"Get good help with fast hands, strong backs, and good legs. Get it planted by next May in well-fertilized soil; we'll be cutting stalks by early September, but will take till Christmas for the hemp to rot. Breakers will be needed then. Money from the corn will cover their cost, followed by the wheat money in the spring."

"How is it ya so learned 'bout farmin'? I's told ya were a houseboy."

"Was. But my pappy was a field hand who never stopped talking about crops, harvesting, and planting till I knew all he knew. It was as if I worked in those fields right close to him, holding onto the same plow. As a young boy, I came to understand what it was he told me."

A couple of afternoons after their talk, Jammer returned from town eager to discuss the farm work suggested. He urged Zach to move ahead with the development of the north field along the river, and he'd continue the work on the south strip.

"I noticed ya spending mo time in dat field than in the other sections of da farm. It's as if ya and dat strip's bonded. Sure 'nough, it's the best producin'. So much so, folks in town be jealous."

"Got my reasons, but not ready to speak them. However, when the corn is harvested, the hemp will be planted in its place."

"Since I brought ya here, ya ain't given reason ta not trust ya thoughts on such matters. Cash is already comin' in from earlier work. Gonna start buildin' da outstructures. Paid for da supplies today. Goods will be delivered soon. Wood's cut. It's bein' cured. The other goods can be loaded whenever we ready fa dem."

The sudden thunder of horse hooves rocked the cabin walls. Jammer opened the door to a yard full of young renegades wearing black dusters and work caps. Each carried a torch ready to burn down what didn't agree with them.

"Joe Jammer, it seems you and dat darkie been livin' under da same roof lak he's one of us. Dat ain't proper. Folks around here been complainin' 'bout it. We come out ta warn ya."

A front rider smacked his horsewhip at Zach. Snapping the poppers he said, "I can give dat darkie of yours a lashin' he'll remember. Can even skin off his hide fa ya if ya like me ta," he said.

"Dis here is my land. Dat's my darkie. I'll take care of him as I see fit. You and da rest can take leave. Now!"

Another front rider squared himself in his saddle, raising his torch with a straight arm, prompting the others to yank their reins. In unison, the horses neighed and kicked up their front legs, hoofing the space above their heads before being turned to gallop off at full speed, but not before the rear rider dropped his torch, igniting the cornfield that heaped up a mess of red-hot flames. The hooligans rode away, yapping and yelling hoorays which caused the blood to drain from Zach's face. So shaken by the incident, his gut knotted and his knees folded beneath him.

The flames rose quickly and licked at the sky as they rapidly claimed the best of the corn. But luck stood firm as the winds from the south bent the blazes northward. If they had come off the river like they usually did, little in its path would have survived the inferno.

Distraught, Jammer shook his head. With a weighted gut he said, "We worked too hard fa a handful of ruffians ta snatch our future."

The next morning, Zach assessed the loss from the stoop as he watched Jammer, head bowed, fade into the charred field.

Sheriff Ray galloped up to the cabin. "I understand you had some trouble last night. Where's your master?"

Pointing, Zach said, "Just entered the fields not long ago."

An hour later Jammer emerged soot-covered, cradling an armload of burnt corn.

"Morning, Sheriff. What brings ya out?"

"Come to let ya know your visitors last evening were . . . "

"If I had a shotgun, dey'd be dead."

"They were a bunch of young drunken ruffians out for excitement. Got 'em locked up. Will keep them there till they cool down some. But, like I done told ya before, townspeople don't take kindly to a white man whose got a darkie under his roof like he's kinfolk. Coloureds ain't equals to us. We all know them and us need to be kept apart. Folks been questioning your politics about such matters. I can't promise them hooligans won't be back."

Sheriff Ray tipped his hat, spit tobacco, and took leave. Joe and Zach lingered in the yard like lost puppies.

"I'll pitch a tent and sleep down by the north fields to keep an eye on things," Zach said.

"Not puttin' ya out. If it weren't for you, there wouldn't have been a crop to burn down. There's been money comin' in ever since ya recovered from ya injuries. Seems like God put you on this land to make it yield."

"When we get the next batch of hands, there needs to be forty to fifty of them" said Zach.

"Why so many?"

"To start, we're going to need breakers for the hemp, hands for the planting and plowing, and carpenters to build a ropewalk. Nigresses will be needed to cook, weave, and sew hemp bags for the cotton picking down south and bucks to make ropes and sails for the Navy, if we get a contract with them.

"And don't you worry about the burned-out fields. What comes up after a fire is miraculous. I know. I saw it happen when I was a boy. And remember, our plan for next spring was to rotate the corn with the hemp. Once the planting is done, the burned-out strip'll burst with seedlings that will get up to eight feet high, could be higher. We'll harvest the seeds from the first batch. The male plants will be cut out, and the females will be lopped off at the top forcing the plants to produce more branches. While the soil is still rich, we'll repeat the process."

It was a cool fall day when Zach and his master entered town. Unnerved by the glares, the lad kept his eyes minding the dirt-packed road as he slowed Pub at the front of Freddy's Feed

Store and tied him to the railing alongside Noble. The boy and Jammer tromped across the main road. The lad stood at his usual post under the bank's overhang while Jammer entered and tipped his dusty, worn hat to the clerks before sashaying across the room with a proffered hand to greet Mr. Brown. He took it as graciously as he did the first time they met and nodded with a slight smile.

"How you doin' with that property of yours? Heard you were roused for sleeping with a buck under your roof," smirked Brown.

"Don't know who could have told you such unless they were sleeping under the roof with me, making them ticks on the same deer's ass."

"We'll let that rest for now. What brings you in?"

"I want that patch of land butted against my property which slopes down toward the river. It belongs to Mr. Gregg and his old lady, Mag. I understand they want to sell it."

"It's two plots. Each is a good hundred and fifty acres. Do you want both? If so, can you afford it?"

"Want both and got money ta pay for them," said Joe.

He put down a fair amount of notes on the desk. Impressed with what he saw, Mr. Brown shuffled through files, flipping papers till he selected the appropriate deeds. He positioned them on the desk in front of Jammer, tapped the signature lines, and said, "Sign here."

Jammer dipped a glimmering blood-orange quill feather tip into the inkwell and drew it across the papers, creating slanted letters as if he were left-handed. He rocked a blotter over his signatures before handing the title papers back to Mr. Brown who enveloped the copies and handed them back to Jammer.

Outside, Zach walked a good distance behind Jammer to avoid upsetting the townspeople passed on the way to Hick's Merchant Store. Jammer went in alone, selected the building supplies and farm tools he paid for, and then noticed the rope Zach requested. He purchased it along with the supplies and came out of the store.

Not raising his head, Zach said, "I'll take the cart, collect the seeds from Fred's Feed Store, and go on to the blacksmith's shop to ask about local hands. Possibly, find out when the next auction's gonna take place around these parts."

"I'll get a drink and meet you there in fifteen minutes."

After the lad collected the seeds, he followed the sound of the blacksmith's hammer. Amos sweated over a plier-gripped horseshoe that glowed red, then orange, yellow, and finally white. The pangs throbbed Zach's chest and eardrums.

"How you doin', Amos?" Zach asked.

Amos' hammer never stopped when he said, "Same as most. Ready ta run. Things been rough fa me. Massa tie me up last night. Beat me 'til I nearly pass out. Said I work too slow."

"How would you like to work for us."

"Doubt Mr. Jimmy sell me. I be bringin' in money fa him. People round des parts be likin' my work. Pay good for it."

"I came to ask about the auction coming soon. We need a bunch of hands, could be twenty or more, and sho could use a blacksmith. I'll let Master Joe know that we need you."

Their heads bobbed when gunfire erupted. They glanced at one another and then dashed toward the street. In the distance, a brawl tumbled from beneath the saloon doors. With one man's legs around the other's, they wallowed in the mud, the same as pigs. Jammer finally stood up, but collapsed to his knees and fell on his face. The lad didn't recognize him coated in blood and muck, and raggedy to his toes. The other fella remained sprawled on his side.

Sheriff Ray rolled the body onto its back. The man hemorrhaging from his nose and mouth didn't move. "It's Jimmy Wells. He's dead. It was a fair fight. He threw the first punch." A boy with his mouth open studied the drunks. "Go tell his pa come get him," Sheriff shouted to him.

Zach turned to Amos. "Your master's dead. Seems you got yourself a problem. Wait here. I'll be back."

The lad hurried to get the ox and cart. At his signal, Amos leaped in with the goods and grain. Pub was steered through the middle of the crowd pulling the cart with Noble hitched to its rear. Jammer moaned from the pain of his injuries when loaded into the back of it. Amos held onto him and pressed rags to his head till they were at the farm. By then, Joe was senseless, didn't know where he was or how he got back to the cabin and put on his bed.

Still tucked into Jammer's vest pocket were the title papers, crumbled and bloodstained, but intact. The stench of blood mixed with sweat, whiskey, and fight coated Jammer. Zach disrobed and bathed the filth from his master before he tugged a fresh gown down over his body. Clean rags and a cold compress on the blue-black swollen-shut eye replaced the blood-soaked bandages.

Back outside, Zach checked on Amos sitting beneath the roof's overhang, face drawn worry tight, unsure what to expect now that his master was dead. He gazed up at the horizon and down at his feet.

"I wanna run. I wanna run bad."

"Things are gonna be fine. Soon as Master Joe comes to, we'll see about buying you. We need to learn who your owner is now that your master's dead. Then, an offer can be made for you. You can sleep outback without worry. You'll be all right. Let's walk some." Zach pointed out the special crops, listed their particulars, and noted those to be planted.

"You be knowin' a lot 'bout dis here place. Most like it belong ta ya."

"Master Joe, the horse, the ox, and I worked this land when it was only dirt and weeds. The spread over there was bought today when I was in town to ask ya about buying hands and the upcoming auction. The time's come to do more building and to clear more land. Some of the building supplies will start arriving soon. The lumber's cut. It's being cured and will be delivered later. We can use you to manage the ironwork."

At the suggestion of Zach, Joe Jammer bought Amos from the brother of the man he killed in the brawl. Not able to feed the buck, he was delighted to get the money for him and gladly transferred the ownership papers with a raggedy smile and handshake, for the few notes.

Joe delivered the news to Zach and Amos who were on the stoop before they went inside the cabin. Amos kept his chin almost tucked between his collar bones as he thanked God for removing him from his old owner and giving him over to his new one. Before the prayer ended, he was on both knees. Rocking, he moaned, "Many a day I clench my fist to keep me from killin' him and his brother and tossin' dem in dos fires."

Glancing up at Zach he said, "When I gits myselfs ta dat blacksmith pit, I's gonna work hard fa ya and ya Massa Joe. It be mighty good of him ta be givin' me food and a place ta rest my soul. Don't even make demands of me. I be takin' my orders from ya. Ya hand been mighty kind. God done blessed me. He gonna bless ya, too, Mr. Zach."

9

The Farmstead

It was 1848 when Jad, an aged, sickly neighbor and good friend of Jammer's father, shut down his farm and sold two of his slaves, Cass and Miles, to Jammer, who bartered $850.00 for them–the usual amount paid for a single male slave of their quality, plus the hogs for a few more dollars. Jammer later learned a sow was among the passel and was certain the sum negotiated was intended for a higher bidder, but he was pleased his bid prevailed.

"Pay me when you can. Ya pa was good ta me." Jad patted Joe on the back, sparking his spirits. "They be sent ta ya when I gits settled in town," said Jad.

In the meantime, to be neighborly, he sent Billy and Bob, his burly sons, to help finish the barn and get the smokehouse up for the slaughtered hogs.

It was weeks before Cass and Miles bounded up the lane high stepping.

"Hallelujah!" Jammer yapped and slapped his thighs.

Zach danced a vivacious buck-and-wing as the buddies joyfully sang out, "Let's get ta work."

No time wasted, Cass and Miles joined Zach and Jammer as they gathered the farm tools, bent their backs, and harvested corn till day turned to night and night to day. Jammer's heart nearly stopped when he saw neighbors approaching the fields. He knew they were sent by Jad, a welcomed gesture. With the additional hands, the winter wheat was planted on time and would be ready for spring harvesting. It was then that Jammer perceived all would be well. He put the farm in Zach's hands and left to negotiate contracts with the local distillers and whiskey makers for his maze and arrange to have the corn-distilled liquor bottled.

At springtime, with the cash earned from the early start with the wheat, Jammer had a clear advantage over the local farmers. The wheat was bundled and tied for shipment north to Greenville, Ohio. He accompanied it to negotiate sales before returning to the farm to focus on the next crop.

By summer's end the first hog sold at the market brought in a reasonable sum. Another was slaughtered and strung up in the smokehouse to cure and share with old-man Jad.

Two months after, the sow birthed a litter of eleven piglets; they earned enough money to pay off Jammer's debt with Jad, obtain feed for the farm animals, and purchase building supplies for the pigpen. Fred at the feed store and Mr. Hicks at the merchant store were delighted to establish accounts for Jammer.

Come fall, the corn harvest rendered a significant cash crop that prodded Jammer to ponder the river's activities to determine where to erect his lavish house and outstructures that he dreamed of.

By Thanksgiving, the cabin was cramped with a second footlocker, an additional rope bed, a dining table, and six handcrafted ladder-back chairs. A hutch stood proudly braced against the sidewall. The furnishings left little footing-about room but sitting and slumbering were considerably more comfortable. Amos had hauled part of the old furnishings down to the slave quarters.

Zach continued to spend his nights under the stars, only going inside when the weather was so inclement the white folks wouldn't come snooping. Most nights, Jammer joined him under the stars to sip whiskey and chat long into the nights till he passed out from his drinking or Zach fell asleep.

Cass and Miles fashioned a corral for the wild horses Zach herded till a stockade was built. One day when Jammer was admiring the animals, he nudged Zach. "Pick the one you want, and it's yours," he said.

"My horse isn't among them, but I've seen him. He's a wild one for sure. Dark as a slice of midnight with a coat slick as black ice. Got eyes clear, clean, and fresh as snow. He knows I'm coming for him."

"Got a name for him?"

"Onyx."

Zach bridled the brick-red mare that frolicked with Onyx before she was captured. He comprehended why she chose him. This stallion stood apart from the pack. Zach mounted the mare. Burdened with anticipation, he trotted out to the grove where he pointed the horse's snout toward the mound for a direct view of Onyx. At the sight of her, the coal-black stallion slung his head side to side and kicked up his hoofs.

Glad Joe remembered to purchase the lasso, Zach collected it from the saddle horn. He created a lasso he clenched as he called out to the stallion in a tranquil tone. Before easing closer to the wild one, he sat in quietness permitting the horses to consider one another.

"Gonna call you Onyx, boy. Came to get you. Not gonna hurt you. Just gonna take ya to the farm to start a new life."

Joe Jammer was ready to build his impressive mansion on the hill with an expansive view of his now-massive property, stopped only by the Kentucky-Tennessee River. The time had come to call on Pierre Beaumont, the most prominent builder around. His family migrated from France to New Orleans and eventually settled in Tennessee where Pierre generated wealth as a contractor and builder.

Poised on the portico with parted feet and chest raised, Pierre toyed with his handlebar mustache as he contemplated the dense air when a steamy breeze cloaked him. With a stretched neck and raised chin, Pierre recognized his good friend, Jammer, riding toward the house. He waved a hand, prepared to greet him.

Joe always enjoyed the companionship of Pierre Beaumont, although, by social standards, it was inappropriate for Pierre to have such a relationship with the son of a poor farmer.

"Come on in where it's a bit cooler. It's good to see you." Pierre said as he escorted Joe to the library. "Been a while. What broughtcha here in this heat? Got something on your mind?"

Walking and easy-talking, Jammer said, "Barn's up. Corncrib's up. Smokehouse and ice house are finished, and all are full. The loom house is near ready for hemp weaving. The fifth and sixth cabins for the hands can be occupied in a day or two. A seventh is under construction. Each will hold up to eight souls if necessary."

Joe checked his feet for steadiness and raised his slightly tilted chin. Making serious eye contact, he said, "I'm ready to build my mansion. You know, the one I told you about. Been dreaming on it for a good amount of time. The plans I have here came by carrier last week. From what I can tell, I'll be needing a good amount of lumber, stones, and cement along with equipment and building supplies. Got a substantial sum in the bank."

"Let's have a look."

Beaumont gathered scattered documents from the French writing table to clear space for the drawings. "Spread them here," he said, as he placed the papers aside.

Jammer's nervous fingers teased the drawings from their leather encasement onto the desktop. Beaumont unrolled the blueprints and positioned weights on the four corners. Not taking time to sit, he stood silently with an intensive stare, reviewing what lay before him. His index finger glided along the gridlines for a more deliberate study. Beaumont reiterated details of the two-story, symmetrical facade: a gable roof and cupola, gracious columns, matching palladium windows, balconies, and covered porches–front, rear, and both sides.

"This house generates a great deal of awe."

Beaumont turned another page, tapped it rhythmically as he admired the interior drawings. He dragged his finger from the main entrance to its exits, and then, circled the elaborate staircase. He shifted his sight to the friezes that inched along the ceiling line before it followed the descending stairs to a hall with a parlor on each side, wide enough to serve as a formal reception area. Toward the back was a third room for family gatherings.

With his attention now on the second-floor drawing, Pierre noted, "I especially like the ballroom and layout of the sleeping space for the family." He squinted at Joe when he said, "This is quite a structure. Impressive. Big. And complicated . . ."

"You see a problem?"

"The only problem I anticipate is the townsfolk bolted with envy. Come. Let's have a brandy while we deliberate about your project."

Pierre pulled a bell cord. Ola, a petite mulattress, who stepped so lightly she seemed to dance on clouds, entered the library. She wore a white shirt tucked into the waistband of a gathered midnight blue linen skirt supported by petticoats and layered with a stark white apron bowed neatly at the rear. A sure beauty, Jammer thought.

Ola nodded toward the guest. "Evening, sir," she said and turned to Pierre with a curtsey. "Monsieur, ya be needin' me?"

"Pour two good-sized brandies in those fancy cut-glass goblets and bring us two Lorillard cigars along with them. We got some celebrating to do."

"Yes, Monsieur."

Beaumont's penetrating stare followed Ola till she exited the room. "She's my wife's favorite darkie. Monique keeps her tight at her side. Never flogs her and never lets anyone close to her. You know the kind of disturbance that can bring on. Ya gotta take an unrelenting hand to those gals, and bucks too, at least every two to three days without fail. More, if need be. Keeps them in line and knowing who's boss."

"I believe it's the rule," Jammer said to ensure his friend that they had the same mindset. However, he knew he and Zach were the exception, but couldn't say so.

After a fresh round of drinks, the tension in Joe's body eased and the conversation shifted to the particulars of building an elaborate structure on a hilltop. Beaumont documented the supplies that would be needed. At the same time, they haggled over expenses–a lengthy debate. Before the brandy had a chance to inebriate Jammer, he bid a good day and departed with his dignity intact.

10

New House & Passion

The day the painters left, Jammer and Zach were at the base of the mansion steps, mesmerized by its wonderment. Jammer turned to Zach. “Move in whenever you like. Pick the floor you want to stay on. There are so many rooms we can roam a good while before we come face to face. I’m gonna find me a woman to begin a family with. One who can manage this house and supervise a staff. What do you think?”

“I think the town’s ladies will gloat from the delight of having a new neighbor adorn their high teas. But me in the house? The thought of such would collapse the hoops supporting their skirts.”

“Don’t matter. I can manage them.”

“No need for a fuss. You’re out of the cabin now. I’ll have all the roaming room I need and can keep my dark hide on me.”

The two laughed as they strolled down the lane to the cabin while Amos, whom Zach had flagged in the distance, went to get the cart. With his help, they loaded Jammer’s belongings into the back and hopped in with the load.

When Zach returned to the cabin to claim the space, he stood, feet parted, on the porch facing the door. He re-thought his wishes about the woman he saw across the road from the north field and hoped was more than a mere vision. She was put at the top of his list to be pursued for a wife and mother of his children, challenging the former top spot to find Ma and the rest of his family. Although it all seemed a stack of dreams ready to tackle, he started with the woman to establish her realness.

The cabin generated a sense of awe whenever Zach pushed open the door to step inside after a hard day in the fields. This evening, he lit an oil lamp, started a fire in the hearth, and easy-lifted the top of the trunk. Stuffed in a far corner were the old britches he wore on his auction day. Unrolled, he slowly drew his ma's skirt remnant from the back pocket and slumped against the trunk. Caressing it beneath his nose, he drew his eyelids closed. An unbearable feeling of loneliness conjured up a flood of emotions Zach was sure would not dissipate and lamented: *Ma, I know ya there. I know, too, ya been keepin' an eye on me. I miss ya, the twins, George Henry, and Jake. He'd be proud of the farmin' I been doing. I use everything he taught me.*

Ma, I'm gonna find ya and the rest of the family as soon as I can figure a way to. We gonna be together again. I won't stop thinkin' about ya and searching for ya till I die. I pray the Lord is keepin' ya safe wherever ya be.

It was at least a good seven days before Zach entered the new house, allowing ample time for Joe to explore all untouched surroundings. Once he made the first visit, he was in and out regularly. One day, Jammer leaned back in his brown leather-tufted desk chair. He didn't need to turn around in it to know Zach entered the office.

"How ya doing?" Joe asked as he swiveled his chair and waved documents at him. "Got something here for ya to read."

"Don't have time. Trapped a rabbit I'm cooking up in a stew. Just came to get a hand full of the spuds and onions we dug up yesterday."

"Ring the bell when it's done. I'll bring the papers when I come down."

On his way out of the house, headed back to the cabin, Zach gathered the vegetables from a wooden box near the rear door. After he dropped them into a canvas bag, he continued down the stairs. Halfway back to the cabin, he remembers he wanted something from the attic and returns to the house.

"You still here?"

"Forgot something."

Zach scaled the rear stairs two at a time. Standing in the center of the attic, he scanned the space for a small table he knew was there. The legs were barely visible from beneath a mound of leftover drapery cuttings. He wiggled the find toward him, kicked the cuttings aside, and shouldered the small table. He hurried back down the stairs. Out the yard door, he grabbed the burlap bags off of the step and was on his way again.

Amos' dark, muscular body moved effortlessly as he cleared the grounds near the cabin to place cut logs around the fire for sitting. Zach told him that the small table on the cabin stoop was for him to take back to his cabin.

Zach removed the pot from the fire but didn't need to ring the bell. The aroma of the stew announced itself when it was done. And Jammer was already coming down the lane.

"Couldn't work for thinking about that stew. When my nose got a sniff of it my stomach grumbled and my feet started moving me," he said with laughter in his voice.

Amos went on to his cabin, shared with Cass and Miles, while Jammer and Zach sat on the fire logs. They ate in the quiet of the evening. With content guts, they scooted from the logs to the ground and leaned against them to face one another. They started a tete-a-tete and hooted well into the night. When the talks settled down, Jammer gave Zach an update. "Talked to the Navy folk. They're interested in the hemp. Said they need rope and sails . . ."

"That'll mean adding another ropewalk along with more hands."

"No problem. Lumber for the walk can be delivered as early as next week," Jammer said.

Zach finger-thrummed his knee. When he glanced up at Jammer, he said, "We'll need at least a dozen hands or more to break hemp. The precise numbers will depend on the production of the last field being planted. As of now, we can barely handle breaking what we got."

"Good thing I bought the additional stretch of land when I did. Folks in town been talkin' about how things are getting better for me. Said my crop planting and buildings are driving property values up. Things are going to get even better, but I got these papers here that I need help in order to . . ."

With an unexpected suddenness, Jammer ceased jabbering. His personality assumed a demeanor with a quietness that encased him for calculable seconds before he said, "Remember, I told ya it's time for me to be taking on a bride. This place needs a woman. Maybe a few children chasing one another around the yard. I see myself with a little girl on my lap, clasping my neck and two others at my knees, each vying for attention while . . . ."

Jammer's eyes sagged and his speech slurred. The alcohol took over. Then the bottle slipped from his grip. Zach kicked it aside, lifted his partner, slung him over his shoulder, and took him up to the Big House. He deposited the slackened body into the desk chair, braced Jammer's head against the backrest, and crossed the feet at the ankles on the desktop.

Joe woke the following day to an unrelenting headache and a sore, stiff neck. Strong coffee and cold rags to the brow and nape brought him back to a state of somewhat sensibility. He gave his shoulder a solid rotation before retrieving the ledger and receipts from the desk drawer. He dipped an elegant quill pen, he had ordered from France, into a blue Victorian porcelain and brass inkwell with the intent of recording the profits, payments, and losses along with the month, day, and year, but his blurred vision didn't permit such.

The hemp was up and plentiful. After the third ropewalk was erected, Jammer hired the best hemp breakers from a hundred miles around. Production spiraled and trading was on target, thanks to Zach's knowledge of numbers and farming skills. The crop processed in the 135-foot long ropewalk generated enough material for the ropes and the sails Jammer had negotiated for with the Navy.

Around Christmas time, two gunmen entered Hick's merchant store threatening a customer into a state of fright with a persuasive pistol barrel at his head and the promise of a severe whipping if he didn't pay what he owed him for the wench outside. Jammer, there to collect and pay for his goods, took advantage of the situation by offering the chap a favorable price for his nigress. The stranger took the money, handed the ownership papers to Jammer, and paid his debt to the gunman. He pocketed the balance and scurried to avoid further harassment.

Not long after Polly arrived at the farm, Amos took a fancy to her, and soon afterward they became mates. He positioned a custom-made army cot large enough for two to sleep on, against the rear wall behind the carriage that created a private space. The following year, a cabin was built for them and their baby Issac.

Mid-August 1852, Zach, behind Pub, plowed the lower part of the north field not far from the turnpike. On the riverside of the road a mirage seen several times before appeared. It seemed smaller and more beautiful than he remembered it. If pulled close to him, he was sure she'd be shoulder-high. The vision vanished into the thicket. Without hesitation, Zach leaped over whatever was in his path. He pushed his way through a burning bush, knocking the small woman to the ground.

She glared at him with disgust-filled eyes. Back on her feet she hurled a swing-picking basket and clobbered Zach.

"No need for fright. I only wanna talk ta ya."

"Don't need ta be talkin' ta ya," she scorned.

Zach shivered in his boots as if he were a child caught with his fingers in the plum pudding. Tongue-tied, he muttered, "Don't be angry. I've seen ya come here before. I been watching for some time but could never catch hold to ya. I wanna know your name and what brings ya here."

From his sotto voice, she determined the young man meant no harm. She glanced at him and then at her empty basket. "My missus loves des here blackberries. Dey be da sweetest 'round des parts. I come on dem by chance. Be dis time last year."

"Isn't this some distance from the farm you come from?"

"Is. But I stops here Sundays on my way from hearin' what da Reverend Peters gotta say 'bout dat Glory Land, the Big Dipper, and dat man dey call Moses." She pointed toward the bank. "Down der at da river, I bathe and sometimes baptize myself."

"But, I haven't seen ya for a while," said Zach.

"Sometimes I walk along da bank. When da river be high, I take to da road."

"You get a day off?"

"Part of Saturdays. Most of Sunday after da breakfast meal be fixed."

"You treated well?"

"Der's times when thangs not so good. I be tryin' not ta think about dem days. If we gonna keep talkin', I gotta be pickin' or der won't be no berries or free time. "

"I'll hold the basket. We'll both pick."

The bush was heavy with fruit. Their hands were quick to snatch the blackberries.

"Stop. Dat be plenty. Too many and I won't be able ta explain dem. Gotta go. I never be away fa long and don't pick much. Missus wants des berries fresh when she be wantin' dem."

"When can we meet again?"

"Next time I come."

"When will that be?"

"When Missus be askin' fa dem berries."

She circled the blackberry bush and evaporated from his sight.

How could this happen? She was standing here nearly on top of my toes. Now she's gone. Am I here alone dreaming and the moment never happened? Wasn't real?

In mid-October, after harvest and when most of the work around the farm was done, Jammer selected the bags for his trip to New Orleans. "Going to get me that bride I told you about. The white folks won't know I'm gone till I'm gone. I told folks I hired you out for a couple of months. That way, they won't cause you no harm. By the time they do their figuring, I'll be back," he told Zach.

When the Mississippi Steamboat pulled away from the Tennessee shoreline, it traveled on to New Orleans where Jammer disembarked ten days later and hailed a coach at the levee which took him through imageries of intrigue: flower markets filled with roses; thousands of fish hung on hooks while others filled baskets; shoulder-to-shoulder houses, two and three stories high, with unique facades and balconies graced with ornate ironwork.

People crowded on the streets enthralled Jammer as they bustled about: dark brown nuns in black habits–each face encased in a swan-white bandeau and coif; old Nigresses in colorful garbs wearing bright *tignon* headdresses; and the half-dressed Negro lads with French and Italian accents frolicking along the pathways. His interest shifted to the pedestrians that teetered on the cobblestone streets along the way.

An African peddling a basket of colorful goods and leatherwork crossed Jammer's vision. He prompted the driver to stop the coach. "Give me a moment. I want to barter with that fellow standing over there for some of his goods. Jammer gave the trader a few coaxing glances from his left eye and then the right one. It was only minutes before he exchanged money for the goods. After his prideful performance and purchase, he hopped back into the coach.

At Mahir Beaumont's door on Bayou Street, Jammer raised the heavy, brass, fleur-de-lis door knocker and clapped it to announce his presence. To his surprise, a smaller door panel cut within a larger door opened. A good-sized Nigress in a bright guinea-blue dress overlaid with a stiffly starched, lace-trimmed, white apron and a red and golden *tignon*, smiled with a curtsy. With a strong French inflection, she said, "*Veuillez entrer, Monsieur*. I'll let my master know you've arrived."

Joe stepped over the doorsill into a lush courtyard. Rotating in a slow circle, he was wonder-struck by the blue-gray flagstone flooring, at least a fifty-foot depth and more width. A gushing fountain postured in the courtyard center was encircled with concrete urns overflowing with red, yellow, pink, and white blooms embellished the space. The faded green tint of the walls, which encased the house, exposed purplish patches, possibly indicating age. He mused at the green lizard that slithered across the face of it, guiding his eyes upward to a three-story ceiling supported with crossed beams. Near the rear-left corner, a narrow staircase ascended the structure's stories, stopping at one mezzanine to curve its way up to the next. From top to bottom, the railings were entwined with a wisteria vine speckled with delicate purple blooms.

"What do you think?" Mahir Beaumont asked as he entered the courtyard from behind a white wrought-iron breakfast table and two chairs with his arm extended for a hospitable handshake.

"Your home is impressive. There's nothing comparable in Tennessee. The differences are so profound they're beyond words." Jammer said.

Seated at the small table, the two gentlemen chatted over a French, midday meal and later a cognac prior to a New Orleans-style dinner. Afterward, Jammer retired to his bedroom suite on the second level, furnished with a highly polished Victorian bed, beautifully carved from mahogany. His fatigued body sank into a comfort he could never have imagined.

A knock on the door the following morning woke him from a deep sleep. Clara, who balanced a serving tray, placed the coffee, smoked salmon, eggs, and griddle cakes on the table. "*Bon matin, Monsieur*. Your breakfast is here. I was told to let you know

Monsieur Beaumont would like you to accompany him to his cotton plantation. It will be about a four-hour carriage ride from here. You should be prepared to depart immediately after you've had your noon meal."

The visit to Beaumont's property was all Jammer hoped it would be. Cotton, as far as the eye could see, skirted the impressive plantation home. After an extensive bartering for the best possible deal, Jammer got the contract he had hoped for. His farm would provide hemp bags for Beaumont's 500-plus pickers. Jammer felt prideful his mansion and its surrounding rounds were suitable for the highbrows and his hemp production substantial to meet the demand of a hefty business deal.

It's her. I'm sure it's her. Zach rushed down the lane, fumbling over his feet as he shoved his way through the red burning bushes. Breathing heavily, his chest bloated as he pushed his shoulder up to yield a more authoritarian appearance. He lifted the basket from the gal's grip, and without words between them, they picked blackberries till the basket was nearly half full.

"What should I call ya?"

"Ma name me Ola."

"Sounds like a flower. Ya pretty as one, too. Who owns ya?" Zach said to put her at ease.

Ola blushed and flirtatiously brushed curls from her forehead. "Massa Pierre Beaumont and Madame Monique. But Massa's away. Done gone ta take his niece back ta New Orleans after huh visit wid dem."

"What's ya missus like?"

"'Bout like da rest of dem. No meaner. No nicer. Gotta go. She be gittin' upset if I be late. It might be da next season 'fore she be lettin' me have free time again. Maybe da next, if she be vexed enough."

"Do you . . ."

Ola vanished. Only footprints from where she had stood seconds ago, close enough to be kissed, remained.

Several days elapsed before Ola swaggered down the dirt and rock lane again. She slowed her pace at the sight of Zach who stood at the entrance of the burning bushes, grinning and fiddling with the leaves.

"Been here every day. I wasn't sure you'd come. The blackberry have dried up for the season," he said as he parted the thicket. Hand-in-hand, they slipped through the bushes.

"Missus asked for the them not knowin' it be too late fa pickin'."

"How ya gonna explain the empty basket?"

"I put dem dried ones in it. She be knowin' dey ani't fit fa eatin'."

In a state of wanting for one another, they snatched what hung on the bush before, Zach put the basket down. He draped his arms over Ola's shoulders, layered them across her back, and pulled her close. Her heart thumped against his. Zach lifted her chin to lower his lips to meet hers that didn't fight his. Their knees bent till they touched the ground. Holding one another, the weight of their bodies tilted them onto their sides.

With her eyes closed, Ola pushed hair up off her neck and curls away from her cheeks that Zach kissed. With a tender touch, he teased her shirt away from her shoulders, caressing each as his lips found their way to her breasts: small, soft, and round with firm, dark-brown nipples. He bunched her skirt and petticoat, pushing them upward to gently lower his weight to blanket hers. She was damp and craving when he penetrated her with rhythmic lovemaking. She flinched, gasped, and tightened her arms around his back and legs around his hips, not wanting to let go. The two of them fell limp–embracing and then lying in their moments of fulfillment.

Without warning, Ola sprang up, shook out her skirt, finger-combed her hair, gathered her headwrap and berries; she was gone. Zach, still on the ground, clothes disheveled, wasn't sure what had happened. The blood on the front of his trousers frightened him. Had he hurt her? He wondered.

He crossed the road to the field where he worked, turning over the soil till the dinner bell rang. He ate, slept, dreamed, and woke sweaty and love-filled. He knew he wanted Ola to have and to adore forever.

While Joe Jammer was away, the two continued to enjoy one another's company. On Ola's days off, they fished, drank lemonade, and roasted a piglet in a dirt pit dug near the river. One day they spread a blanket not far from the blackberry bush on a clearing only large enough for the two of them. On their backs they thought quietly, not saying much. Overcome with feelings of love Zach took Ola's hand in his. With serious eyes that consumed all of her, he said, "I be mighty pleased if ya consider being my wife."

"Got no time fa bein' no man's wife. Missus keeps me tied up wid huh do-dis-do-dats. Can't think most times, mo less be a proper wife fa ya."

Zach moaned, "You sure, Ola?"

Depleted and rejected, he reclined on his back with his eyes closed. A moment later he sat straight up and inhaled deeply to ask Ola if she would reconsider his proposal, but before he spoke, she was gone. He was alone on the blanket with an empty hand and a pig in the pit.

11

New Lady of the House

Zach entered the yard door loud and sure-footed, just as Jammer bounded through the front to grasp his buddy's shoulder. Gloating and filled with delight, he sang out, "I've come home with a bride. Her name's Francine. She's a real beauty for sure: eloquent, quiet, polite, and the kindest person you'll ever meet. Can't wait for you to see her. And by the way, I got something for you. I'll bring it down later."

A piercing, high-pitched, French-accented voice ricocheted through the conversation. "Monsieur Jammer, you left me standing with *le chariot*," the new bride said with a stern huff in her voice.

"I'm so sorry, my dear. Forgive me. I was eager to see Zach. Come, let me intro . . . "

"What's a darkie doing in our house?"

"What darkie? "

With her head drawn back, Francine nervously flipped her wrist, aiming a fluttering index finger at Zach.

"Him!"

"I ask again, what's he doing in this house?"

"He lives here."

"What do you mean, lives here?"

"Don't worry your mind about Zach right now. Come along. Let me show you the rest of the house."

"You . . ." Francine took in an extra breath, ". . . can unload the wagon."

Shuffling his new missus along, Jammer said, "Luc will take care of that. Zach has business to see to. Please, let me show you to your *boudoir*. You can freshen up and rest a bit."

Zach left through the front door. Down the steps, he nodded at Luc, the coach driver who stood dutifully next to the wagon. The two got up on the wagon bench where Zach sat next to him and directed the boy to the slave quarters. They collected Cass and Miles; the three bucks were taken back to the Big House. The trio unloaded the trunks and household goods under orders to arrange and rearrange them till the missus dismissed them. Zach continued to the fields.

At the end of the day when Zach informed Luc he'd bed down at the barn till time for him to leave for New Orleans, the driver said, "Madame's father done give me ta huh fa a weddin' gift. Say I be stayin' on here."

"Welcome to Madison, Tennessee. Amos, the blacksmith, will help ya settle in at the cabin with Cass and Miles. Tomorrow, you'll work in the fields with them."

Each time Zach passed through the house, the new groom was drooling as he contemplated the exaggerated movements of his bride's hips as she fiddled with whatnots. Zach laughed to himself, shook his head, and went on his way with Francine's voice trailing him as she warned Jammer, "It's not fitting to have a buck acting as if he's your equal. It isn't at all proper for a Negro to have so much freedom. He has got to be banned from this house and somehow kept in his place. And, I expect for you to see to that. Now!"

"You sure about that, my dear? After all, Zach and I have lived on this farm since we were boys, shared everything. Keep in mind, the yields of this land and its profits are because of him, as well as this mansion you gloated over coming up the carriage lane.

"When I bought him, I could hardly write my name. He read the legal papers. That made it possible for me to expand this property and build on it as I did. He even taught me to read, write, figure my numbers, and do business the proper way."

Exasperated with his wife's attitude toward his comrade, Jammer left Francine standing alone in the expansive entrance hall with a slackened jaw. Quickstepping, he crossed the spacious foyer and bolted out the front door, and met Zach, skirting the house as he came from the rear yard. Joe sauntered toward his buddy. Their unspoken words and body language indicated a need to meet in the shade of the oak tree in the front yard. Postured against it, neither spoke. They knew the others thoughts.

Solemn-eyed, gazing at his friend, Zach said, "No need ta fret. I won't cause ya trouble."

Hands pocketed and toeing a rock, Jammer pensively, mumbled, "You know my feelings. We've lived as brothers. Shared everything. Never been a harsh word 'tween us. I tell you everything and trust you with my life, as you do me with yours."

They gandered up ahead for a stretched moment before Zach let Jammer know he knew the rules and now they must consider them, like it or not.

Jammer's friend turned to him. With a stern voice, Zach said, "I harbor a dream I don't want tampered with."

"Tell me what it is. If I can, I'll help."

"I've stumbled on something that has encased my heart."

"You smitten for someone?"

"I am."

"Have you asked for her to be yours?"

"I have."

"Whose property is she?" he asked.

"Madame Monique, the wife of Monsieur Beaumont, owner the construction business and lumber yard. Remember, he build this house and is the uncle of my wife and her father's brother. I might've seen her on my visits there. If her name's Ola, she's indeed a beauty."

"It is."

Jammer whistled a full breath and said, "She won't be easy to come by. It'll take some doin' and a good amount of money to get her. Keep them feelings to yaself. If it's known there's an interest in a piece of their property, they'll sell it to be mean-spirited, and you'll never see her again. I'll have a conversation about her with Pierre. We're on good terms."

The exchange of dialogue concerning buying and selling hands always dug a hole into Zach's gut and jerked his mind back to the auction day when he was separated from his family, a subject he and Jammer never discussed, mostly because neither brought it up.

Something in the distance, too far to know what it was, caught Zach's eye. Without thought, his feet took off.

"Hey, where ya off to?"

"Got to check on a few things."

Although the day was a hot, humid one, Zach moved from field to field, like the long-legged grasshopper his mother always teased him about being. On the fringe of the north field, a smidgen of red calico faded into the bushes across the road. He glanced again. Seeing nothing, he rushed to the spot, barged through the thicket, and bumped into a youngin, nearly knocking him to the ground.

"Who are you? What are you doing here?"

Speaking rapidly as he struggled to regain his balance, the stripling said, "I be Jimmy Boy. Ain't done nothin' wrong. Come ta catch fish and frogs and git a turtle, if I can. Ma gonna fix dem fa us ta eat. Massa done took our rations." Picking up his line and hook, the boy asked, "Why ya be tryin' ta knockin' me down?"

"Thought you were someone else."

By night and exhausted, Zach decided to bypass dinner and instead stretched out on the new rope bed for a full night's sleep, but the moment was disturbed by a boot thump and a rap on the door. On the other side, Jammer was slouched against the door frame. He gripped the neck of a whiskey bottle in his right hand and supported a package secured in his left armpit.

"Come on in. Don't stand there appearing lost."

Jammer flumped into a chair at the new dining table positioned across the front of the fireplace hearth. His unsteady hand placed the whiskey bottle that he clutched on the table, along with a crumpled newspaper-wrapped package secured with a skinny strip of cord. He raised his somewhat grumped face polished by the yellow-orange glowing flames. Staring at his confidant, he uttered in an inebriated tone, "How you doin' these days, Zach?"

"I'm fine. Ya self?"

"Fairing. My dear wife doesn't want Ola. Said we have enough hands around the house and don't need one more. Her father has sent her chambermaid. She'll supervise the house and the other hands. Name's Clara. She should arrive in the next day or so. I remember her from my visits there. Plump and jolly. Got a sweet smile and pleasantness about herself."

"And Polly?" Asked Zach.

"She'll stay on as house help. Francine likes having her around. Said her voice is musical, and she has a charm about her."

"Pleased she favors somebody."

Jammer tilted his head back and turned up the bottle. His eyes peered the full length of it till they met his friend's glare at the bottom.

"I didn't offer you a drink. I know how you feel about taking whiskey and what ya ma done told ya.

"Got something for you. Brought it from New Orleans."

Braced with an arm on the tabletop, Joe nudged the package toward Zach. "I think you'll like this."

In the slowest motion possible, Zach teased apart the knot and pulled back the wrapping. What he saw brought on such a rush of gratification that it widened his eyes.

"My goodness, I know the black and gold-threaded cloth this waistcoat is made of. It's called *Aso-Oke*. My mother had a *buba* and *lapa* from her village in Africa made of it. She told me many stories about it and the person who wore it. Most I've forgotten because I was so young. One day it disappeared from our cabin and she never spoke of it again," he said. Zach slipped both arms through the waistcoat and humped his shoulders. "Nice fit. I'll treasure this for sure."

"There is something more there."

Zach sorted through the packing material and found a rolled belt bound with red ribbon. "My. My. Never seen a thing like this before. And, the detailed handwork of this brass buckle is astonishing."

"I thought the two strong hands clasped together in unity represented us."

"I'll wear this every day."

"That's what I hoped you'd say."

Zach pushed back the fronts of the waistcoat and threaded the leather strip through the belt loops of his britches. Clasping the hands of the buckle seemed to validate the brotherhood he had with Jammer.

After he peeled and sliced an apple, buttered day-old bread, and broke a piece of pork belly into several chunks, they ate. Although the intention was to temper Jammer's drunkenness, it became a mini feast as they chatted and laughed about his New Orleans events. While Joe sipped liquor till his head thrashed wild as that of a newborn colt, Zach sipped from a cup of sassafras tea.

As Joe turned to get up, his body tumbled from the chair to the floor. Zach left him there to clear away the mess made by Joe's sloppy eating and drinking.

With Jammer's drunken body slung over his shoulder, Zach hauled him up the carriage lane to the Big House and kicked open the main door. Francine stormed down the front staircase wearing a pale-yellow robe winged by a breeze that lifted its panels. Her royal-blue bedroom slippers that thwacked each step reflected her aggravation.

"You should have gone around to the rear door and waited to be invited in, if ever."

"I understand, Madame."

Zach dropped the load with a whopping thud at her feet. Not wasting a moment, he turned and went back out the front door with a hefty degree of contentment in his soul.

"Come back here, you belligerent, obscene, Negro. You weren't dismissed."

Amos scudded after Zach with a horsewhip. He knocked on the cabin door before he entered.

"Ya be dapper in dat vest. Ya dressed fa a party?" asked Amos with a mischievous grin.

Zach ignoring the whip, said, "It's a gift from the massa."

"Well, ya missus done sent me ta thrash ya hide. Said, give ya 50 lashes and make dem heavy ones dat ya won't be forgettin' soon."

"Well, go on out back. Scream like someone's slicing off your hide. Then take dat whip to the chicken coup, cut off the head of one them. Smear the poppers with the blood. When you're done, take dat chicken to the kitchen and the whip to the missus. Show her you've done your job."

Zach shut the door behind Amos with the knowledge he wouldn't have to work for several days and took to thinking about Ola, while he recovered from his supposedly whip-lashed back.

12

Clara & Avida Maria

Joe Jammer and Francine had been married about two years when Zach stood in the yard assessing the grounds when a carriage came up the lane and stopped at the Big House. The door of it sprang open, permitting a plump, dark-skinned woman with a thick head of mussed-up, mixed-gray hair and broad hips to exit. She adjusted her stance, tied on a bright red and gold *tignon*, and raised her plump arms for her missus, who rushed down the stairs to be embraced by them.

"Clara! Clara!" Francine wept as she fell on the bosom of her chambermaid once her nursemaid. The two hugged and kissed as Francine looped arm and arm with Clara, pulling her along to climb the steps to the door held open by Polly.

"Missus, I'm not alone."

"What do you mean, not alone?"

"The baby, Avida Maria. She be sleepin' in da carriage."

"What do you mean sleeping in the carriage?"

"Madame, the convent burned down. The nuns brought her to me. Said I have to care for huh and to let you know. They gave me the small amount of money left in the account, but it wasn't enough to hire a scribe, feed the baby, and keep her hidden from your father who sent me to ya. He still doesn't know about the baby. I didn't know what to say to him, so I brought her along."

"Oh! My, my."

"Let's go back to the coach."

Dumbfounded, Francine stared down at the child curled up on the bench. "Let her sleep. And let me think. You wait here. I'll be back."

"Polly, we have guests. That's Mammy, my darkie from New Orleans. She has a baby with her. I want you to take them straight up to the nursery. Get them settled and fed. Do not disturb your master. Be quick and be quiet."

The brisk turnover of days conjured up a feeling of urgency in Francine who was not able to focus on anything other than how to introduce Avida Maria to her father. The time had come to tell Joe about his daughter. She knew she couldn't delay it any longer.

Francine had Polly prepare a pot of Mr. Jammer's favorite drink: roasted chicory coffee with cream and sugar. Then, she headed to his office, which she entered with a significant degree of grace. In her most gentle voice, she flirtatiously said, "Mr. Jammer, please consider having coffee with me on the front veranda."

"Of course, my dear, since I can't resist your charm. I'd be pleased to close the ledger and join you."

Francine swiftly left before he could utter more. She was seated in a white wicker chair when Joe took his place opposite her, at the three-footed oval table, layered with a stark white eyelet tablecloth and a small bowl of fresh-cut Queen Anne flowers.

Tay, a young gal gifted to Francine by her Aunt Monique to help around the house and in the kitchen, but couldn't handle significant chores, placed the coffee service on the table. Careful not to bump the floral arrangement, she partially filled the two cups with the aromatic, dark, chicory coffee that she sweetened with nips from the sugar cone and highlighted with sweet whipped cream.

When done, Tay curtsied. "Madame, der be anythin' mo?" She said and stepped backed to wait for the next directive. Francine flexed her wrist, dismissing the gal. She shifted her weight to squarely face Joe.

"Are you vexed about something? You seem uneasy."

"Not quite. But I must let you know," Francine lowered her eyes from Joe's stare to her hands wringing the napkin in her lap. "We have a child."

"A child. How could that be?"

"Do you recall your first visit to New Orleans and the night we strolled the quarters? Then, I hired a coach to take us to the spot where we enjoyed an extravagant Quadroon Ball. Afterward, we went back to the house for a sip of sweet Kentucky bourbon."

"I do. But, you never mentioned a baby when I returned to New Orleans for our unexpected wedding." Jammer tightened his shoulders and then quickly released them. Peering straight into Francine's pupils, he said, "And . . . " Joe slanted forward over his forearm, bracing himself on the table. ". . . there's been no evidence of a child since Clara arrived. Yet, you tell me my child is here, in this house. And has been here for nearly ten days."

"I didn't know how to present her to you and had her taken straight to the nursery. It's only now that I have accumulated enough courage to tell you. The baby knows Clara and is comfortable around her. She needs to know us. I can't keep her hidden from you any longer."

Francine, sniffling, said, "I, too, am a stranger to my child. It was the Sisters of the Holy Family who nursed me through the pregnancy. I stayed with them at their convent. After I gave birth, they immediately took the baby to the nursery. I remained in the infirmary. My postnatal recovery kept me on my back for several weeks. I named the baby Avida Maria Jammer and put money into an account for her care."

The nuns ran a school and orphanage for Negro and mulatto children that would be available to Avida Marie as she grew. It was easy to leave her with them because I knew her safety wouldn't be compromised and there was little possibility of her identity as a Beaumont being learned.

"Because we were unwed at the time; my pregnancy had to be kept confidential to maintain the integrity of the Beaumont family name and its reputation in the community."

Clara ushered Avida Maria out to the veranda. The nearly three-year-old ignored Jammer's dumbfounded stare and backed away from Francine's attempt to grasp her hand.

Jammer's eyes blinked with surprise. "Seeing her," he pushed back his cowlick and said, ". . . leaves me with no doubt that she's mine. The hair color. The cheek with the mole on it. Even the hazel eyes, same as Mammy's. My Lord, what's happened? What's next?"

"I hope you understand why I couldn't tell you about the baby."

Choked with uncertainties, Jammer, speechless, was unable to find an expression for his uneasy feelings. On his feet, he felt he had coffee with a stranger who was the mother of his baby that he never knew he had. With a profound need to escape the confusion bombarding his entire existence, Jammer headed to the cabin where Zach lazied on the stoop.

"Have a seat," said Zach, and waited for him to balance himself, fumbling to do so. "Seems something is tormenting your state of harmony. Let's go down to the river."

Seated on the bank, the partners sat and waited for the transitional period to bleed into dialogue. Jammer propped his elbows on his knees. With his head butted between his palms, he mumbled, "I don't know what's happened. I married a beautiful, frail flower of pure southern womanhood, filled with class and dignity: happy, cheerful, and nothing less than a delight. The next thing I know, I've got a cougar by the tail. What am I to do? I got a baby who doesn't know who I am or want to know."

"A baby? Let's start from the beginning. You went to New Orleans to make a hemp deal and find a bride. As I recollect, you came back with a deal and no bride."

"When I first arrived at the house, I didn't see Francine, who's Mahir Beaumont's younger daughter. She was away visiting her Uncle Pierre, the Beaumont who built the house. It was the following week that she returned to New Orleans. I was immediately smitten. Each afternoon, I offered my arm, which she took. We strolled through the most magnificent gardens of New Orleans. We watched the sunset that created a magnificent glow over her face.

"One evening after we had coffee at a *café avec terrasse,* she hired a carriage to take us to where an elaborate Quadroon Ball was underway."

"A cafe what?"

"*Café avec terrasse*. That's what she called the sidewalk cafe."

"Go on."

"When we arrived, we remained seated inside the coach. She dismissed the driver. 'Come back at midnight,' she told him.

From our position, we had a full view of the ball through

floor-to-ceiling palladium windows. My head was crammed with alluring smells, sounds, and music whirling from the mansion. I tell you, such glamour doesn't exist around these parts. Minuets resounded as young ladies waltzed about in magnificent ballroom gowns, belling in every pastel color that swayed gloriously. White pursuers escorted most of them. Some couples strolled along an enormous veranda, chatting and possibly sipping wines or cordials. So extravagant, I've never seen a thing like it before. "

"Where did those women come from?"

"They were the illegitimate girls of white men and their Quadroon mistresses, more often referred to as the daughters of joy. Some marry the girls, but most go off and take a white woman to be their bride. The mistress and children are left behind. Those gals are the most voluptuous I've ever seen–walk and move with the same confidence of privileged white women."

"How could that be?"

"The daughters of the wealthy men were convent bred. The nuns teach them their school work, needlework, classical music, and how to play the piano."

"And then what happened?"

"Around midnight the driver returned. He took us back to the house. Once inside the courtyard, I was told to wait where I stood. 'I have something to show you.'

"Francine collected a bottle of Kentucky Bourbon and two small glasses. 'Follow me.' We climbed the narrow staircase to the third floor where a small, quaint bedroom, tucked in the corner of the house, smelled of fresh-cut flowers. She opened the window and pushed back the shutters. 'Come see,' "she said.

"The boulevard below was intriguing: carriages coming and going; clowns dancing in the streets; lovers strolling hand-in-hand; young boys playing kickball and tag; and the sails of the ships docked at the pier shimmered with a special moon glow.

"We yattered and laughed at the nonsensical and shared the bourbon. Tipsy, we fell into each other's arms under the canopy of a poster bed. The soft, silky locks of her hair fell across my shoulders. Her luscious kisses, moist and honey-sweet, met mine. Her curvy, damp body begged for mine. My hands caressed the whole of her.

"After that, it was Clara gathering petticoats from the bed. She scatted out of the room and soon returned with a washbasin and pitcher of water. At the corner of her eye, she speculated about my disheveled clothes. I couldn't offer her an explanation. Francine was gone.

"After I left New Orleans, Francine wrote continuously about our relationship but never mentioned a wedding. Yet, she sort of did. But I can't recall making a proposal or her accepting one. That part's fuzzy.

"However, as you know, when I returned to New Orleans, nearly a year later, I was charmed into a magnificent marriage. I willingly strolled down the aisle of an amazing Roman Catholic Cathedral, so massive it consumed an entire block. Drunk on pomp and circumstances, I allowed her to lead me as if I had a ring in my nose. Now, I'm here with a wife who's become a stranger and a baby I don't know."

13

Ola

Clara, too drawn and feeble to work and care for Avida Maria, now a rambunctious four-year-old, has taken to her sickbed on the rear porch. The repugnant smells of her ailment permeated the entire house. Concerned about her own well-being and that of Avida Maria's, Francine heavyheartedly restricted Clara to the barn and instructed Polly to stay at her side.

Even after Clara was isolated in the barn to recuperate, the stench from her sickness and other fetid odors from the dirty laundry, rotten food, and overflowing chamber pots fouled the airflow. They weren't only inundating the Big House; the smell soared freely outside, stopping shy of Zach's cabin, except on windswept days.

Jammer sauntered down to the cabin after Clara's quarantine; he had finished a dinner with his wife that left fishbone words stuck in his throat. He knocked on the door and let himself into the space that always ensured comfort and a feeling of well-being. He sat with Zach who was finishing up a meal of beans and rice.

"Can I offer you something to eat?"

"No. I ate and had to get away from the house. Things up there are bad. My wife's making unreasonable demands of me. 'Clean this. Get that. Wash this. Scrub that.' Her words smack at me as if I'm a field hand at her disposal. Things are bad. I'm doubtful about what to do. Among other things, there're no clean clothes in the wardrobes or fresh linen in the pantry. When morning comes, I'll try again to persuade her to accept Ola. At this point, I don't think she'll resist."

After coffee and hoecakes the next day, Zach strolled to the Big House to check on his boss. When he heard the missus reprimand him about his drinking and allowing that darkie to come in the front door, uninvited, to drop his drunken body more than once at her feet, he didn't go any further. He stopped in the main yard.

With a raised voice, Joe clearly enunciated each word: "Don't concern yourself about Zach and me." He moved toward Francine. Gritting his teeth, he downshifted his voice. "I'm gonna approach your uncle about selling that gal, Ola. Pierre's told me she's a good worker, spoiled, but trustworthy. "

Francine didn't want Ola. Her beauty could be a concern, but she was desperate. With a sour face, she sucked in her bottom lip. Nervously twitching, she fingered unruly hairs dangling at her temple. She shifted a defiant hip before she asked, "Do you think Madame Monique will agree?"

"If I offer Pierre the right price, her concerns won't matter."

"Well. Get her and be quick."

Zach scatted to the barn and speedily saddled Noble and Onyx. He was soon back and waited at the offside of the front yard with the horses' reins in hand. Battle-worn and perplexed, Joe came out of the house, haphazardly descending the steps.

Zach led the horses toward him. "I heard most of what she said. If we leave now, I can ride part way with you. We'll stop at the bend of the road. I'll wait there for your return."

The two moved down the turnpike in a dubious state. Not sharing words like they usually did, but instead, staring straight ahead. They sorted their thoughts about Ola and her purchase.

Zach pondered: *What will I say when I see her? It's been some time since we last spoke or she picked berries. Will she still be wanting me? I know Joe Jammer is contemplating the price he's gonna offer for her. I hope it's one that'll persuade Monsieur Beaumont to part with his wife's most treasured hand.*

Jammer deliberated in his head about which approach he'd use to haggle with Pierre for Ola when the hook in the road appeared, prompting them to pull the horses to a standstill.

"Shouldn't take long," said Jammer. He adjusted his hat before he turned in his saddle to give Zach a quick glance. "Be back soon. Don't go anywhere."

"Be right here waiting for my gal."

After sitting for an extended period and feeling antsy, Zach dismounted to rest his buttocks and shake his legs. He scanned the roadside to decipher the healthiest wildflowers. As he harvested the blooms, he rehearsed his presentation: *How do you do, Miss Ola? These were harvested especially for you. One for each day we plucked berries together. This yellow one is special. It's for the bright momen*t our bodies first touched in that special way. Hope you like them.

Zach's heart stopped when he heard a horse's hoofs. Joe appeared from around the bend. Tight-lipped, Zach quizzically asked, "Where's my Ola?"

"Wouldn't sell her. Not today. They were entertaining out-of-town guests. Monique discouraged Beaumont from discussing business, at least not about buying and selling Negroes. Each time the topic surfaced, regardless of the source, she diverted the conversation. Have faith. I have an alternative plan."

"And my Ola? Did you see her?"

"She was serving the guests."

Seething by what happened, Zach squeezed the flowers till they bowed over his clenched fist. Unable to imagine a next plan, he let them drop. The burden of disappointment made the return trip arduous for the comrades. Back at the farm, they parted ways. There were no goodbyes. Jammer continued on to the Big House. Zach headed to the fields where he worked beyond exhaustion.

Under the light of the moon, slow-dragging his feet, Zach meandered to the cabin where he knew the spirit of hope had been sponged away, leaving a dreaded emptiness behind. Simmering with discontent, he didn't bother to eat. He lolled on the rope bed that he had no doubt would share with Ola when night came, only to find himself alone and fretful he'd never see her again.

At sunrise the following morning, Zach opened the cabin door to Ola's presence. She stood at the entrance of the carriage lane, but without a blackberry basket. She clinched a red muslin bundle in one hand and droopy wildflowers in the other. So engulfed with disbelief, Zach scurried barefoot down the lane to consume all of her in his arms. Squeezing her, he mused, "Are my eyes and arms being truthful to me?"

"Monsieur say, I be sold ta Massa Jammer ta be ya wife. And dat I should report to da missus at da Big House by noon."

With the thrumming force of his heart and sweaty palm, Zach held onto Ola as if she might sprout wings and take flight. They didn't go to the cabin. They crossed the road and slipped between the burning bushes to sit on the ground next to the blackberry bush where they had met numerous times before. Zach snuggled Ola close to transmit all the love he possessed for her. With his lips nearly kissing her ear, he said, "I've pined for you so deeply since the last time we were here. I wanted you to come back a powerful lot."

"Been thinkin' 'bout ya, too, Zach. I picked up des here flowers from da roadside thinkin' ya left dem fa me."

"They were for you. I tossed them aside when Jammer returned alone. I figured he wasn't able to buy you."

"When I's done servin', I went on ta my cabin. Ya master come back late in dat night. Dey be talkin'. It be near ta sunup. When Monsieur come ta da quarters, he tells me, 'git dressed, gal. Take your belongings . . . go on down to Jammer's place. You belong to them now,' he says."

"I asked my massa to buy you, that I wanted you for my wife. If you agreed and were willing to have me."

"Oh, my! I be mighty happy ta be ya wife."

After they recollected what had happened and the life they hoped to build together, time forced them to cease dreaming. Zach took Ola by the arm to help her up off the ground.

"Come. I'll show you your new home."

They crossed the road and followed the lane to the cabin. "That's it," he said putting an arm around her shoulders.

"It be beautiful. And, plenty big." Squinting her eyes she said, "Ya been livin' der alone?"

"Jammer and I lived under that roof till the Big House was built and he took a wife."

"Together! You'n dat white man?"

"Till a mass of young rabbles raised a fuss and torched the fields. Then, I slept outside. Didn't want to get hanged and didn't want to cause Master Joe any trouble. After he moved out, he gave the cabin to me."

"Gave?"

"Yes. And got papers for it."

"Madame know 'bout dat?"

"Doubt it. If she did, she'd reduce it to cinders."

Inside, Ola's jaw slackened by the things she saw: a big trunk, rope and platform beds, eating table, chairs, hutch, cooking utensils, food, and plenty of space. "I ain't got proper words fa what I be seein'."

While Zach sat at the table putting his boots on, Ola turned in a slow circle, embracing all that her eyes witnessed. Opening and closing the hutch doors, she imagined herself sifting flour and sitting at the table where she and Zach would dine. Without a word she quietly waltzed about the cabin as if she were box-stepping inside a dream. Zach lifted the lid of the cedar trunk to put her bundle in the corner he had prepared for it. The sack instantly disappeared among the contents.

Ola sipped the cup of coffee Zach handed her with a smile that revealed all he needed to know. With tentative eyes and a quivering voice, he said, "I'll sleep outside if you feel the need for time to adjust to me and your new place."

"No need. I be wantin' ta be close ta ya as much as I can. Ya gonna be my tall, lean, handsome husband wid dat head fulla dark curls. When ya turn ya back I be smilin' at dat butterfly on da back of ya neck."

The time passed like a breeze across Zach's face. He studied his bride-to-be, not wanting to part from her, but knew the time had come. To make the best of the minutes Zach took Ola by the hand. "Come. I'll walk with ya up to the Big House. I'd rather ya be a little early than a second late."

Ola entered the yard door, cautiously stepping, she eased down the hallway. Movement in the front of the house could be heard. At the parlor, Francine was braced against the back of an oversized wingback chair. She fidgeted with an expansive pile of smelly clothing which separated the two of them. Unsure what to expect, Ola stood motionless with her eyelids politely lowered.

"Come on in here, gal."

"Morning, Missus," Ola said with a curtsy and her meekest voice.

"Have you eaten?"

"No, Missus."

"Go find something and be quick. I don't want you to be sluggish because you're in need of a meal. When you're done, come back. You'll clean this room, collect the bedding, wash everything, hang it to dry, and then give it a good pressing."

Francine flicked her wrist, dismissing the gal who scurried out the door she came in, in time to catch Zach before he got too far down the lane.

"She tells me ta git somethin' ta eat. I'm not hungry, but I wanted us ta spend dat time tagether."

"So wise of you. I'll prepare smoked fish and eggs for us. That will hold you a good amount of time."

"How's it dat ya got so much? And ya can be movin' 'bout this here place wid no fear."

"Joe Jammer, who's not much older than I am, bought me when I was a lad, sickened and beaten badly by pattyrollers and the auction scum. On our way here, to Madison, Tennessee, I fell off the ox and badly injured myself. He cared for me.

"Later, I nursed him when he became ill, was delusional, and passed out. It was only the two of us. We shared everything: bedding, cabin, clothing, food, eating bowls and spoons, horses, and space. It was my knowledge of crops and my ability to read, write, and figure that earned him his wealth."

"Ya, read. And figure, too?"

"I can, but not for myself. You don't see any books or paper around here. Can't have evidence of my knowings. That can get a rope around my neck so quick I'd die and come back in the same instance."

"I don't know no learned Negroes."

With the last bite in her mouth, she reached for the dishes. Zach took her hands in his and kissed them. "I'll take care of these things. Today, your work is up at the Big House. I'm sure it'll be a long, hard day for you. I'll see you to the back door."

Ola paused and said, "Somebody in dat house be powerfully sick."

"It's Clara, the missus' gal. She was sent to her from New Orleans. As you know, the Beaumonts come from there. You might remember your master built this Big House. Soon after her gal arrived here, she started feeling poorly. The missus quarantined her in the barn, but the odors still linger in the house.

"How sad."

"No need to worry none. A hand is constantly with her."

Ola let Zach's hand go and vanished into the Big House. He trotted off to the barn to check on the folks there. He peeped at Clara who was lethargic and still flat on her back with a sunken and pale face that didn't show its eyes. It seemed as if she were fading away. The flab on her upper arms dangled like turkey wattles and the plumpness of her hips had melted.

"How she doin'?" Zach asked Polly.

"Not good. Gonna be sometime fa huh ta git back on dem feet of huhs. She don't speak none neither. Ain't takin' no note of me. She got a bad case of dat dysentery. Doubt she gonna make it. Missus sent us out here so she and dat gal of hers don't git it. She don't even want me ta be cookin' fa da family. 'Keep dat gal alive,' she tell me. Missus be plenty fond of her. She say she be her wet nurse when she a baby. Dat she growed up hangin' to huh tit and den ha apron strings."

Not tarrying longer, Zach hurried to the blacksmith's pit to chat with Amos who pounded on a horseshoe over a hot fire. His face took on a grateful expression when he entered the workspace and asked about his state of well-being. Amos didn't hesitate to express his profound need for help, "If only to sort nails," he said.

Putting down the hammer, he studied Zach with concern in his eyes. "Been keepin' an eye on baby Issac best I can. He be growin' a bit slow. He be needin' his ma's tit real bad. But by da time Polly's day done end, she be too wo out ta feed him." Amos' eyes teared when he said, "My Polly cain't hold on ta lil Issac or hep me none. Things be bad. Don't want ta be botherin' ya none, but I's scared I be losin' my baby. Maybe my Polly, too. Mr. Zach, I tries ta keep up wid my work. Don't wanta be makin' things bad fa us or fa ya. I tries my best ta not anger Massa or da missus."

14

The Blind Boy

Because Amos needed help, Zach searched for the blind boy he had seen on a trip to town earlier in the week. He felt confident the lad could do whatever chores his fingers and hands allowed him to. Little concerned Zach about taking him back to the farm. It was common knowledge locals had no interest in him. They considered him a pest to be done with.

Zach arrived in town, along with the first indication of daylight. Slumped, with his arms slackened at his side, he monitored both sides of the main road. He didn't want to generate a negative encounter with loafers or strays left from the fortnight's liquor brawl, fishing for trouble.

Up ahead, the sound of anxious feet seized Zach's attention. It was a gang of ruthless, rock-throwing boys, chasing the blind boy who scampered beneath the courthouse to escape them. The rowdies scatted when Zach approached the hitching post in front of the building to secure Onyx. He sensed the youngster wouldn't come out without coaxing, so he got down on his knees and belly-wormed beneath the stoop.

"I know you back up in there. Not gonna hurt you none. I only wanna visit with ya." Talking and squirming, he eased closer to the scuffing and smell of wet animal hair that caused an uneasy feeling. There was no voice from the boy or grunt from the animal.

"Ya there, boy?" asked Zach.

The quiet and smell continued to puzzle him. A low mutt sounding growl bounced off the underside of the building. He knew then the animal was only a puppy.

"I wanna help ya. Gotta job fa ya. Food. And a place fa ya ta lay ya head."

"Ain't got no eyes."

"Got jobs ya don't need eyes fa, but need a good pair of hands to do the work."

Rustling and sniffling pricked Zach's ears. It seemed the boy and the mutt were scooting deeper into the dark.

"I'm leaving. Be in front of this building. When ya ready, come on out."

"No! Out back."

To not cause trouble with the white folks, who would start stirring soon, Zach mounted Onyx and unhurriedly made his way to the rear of the building. Thinking the boy wouldn't come out and fearful about what might be perceived if the locals spotted him in one place too long, he turned the horse prepared to leave when finally, the lad showed himself along with a large-pawed puppy at his side.

"How ya be, boy?"

"Not so good."

"Stretch ya arm toward me. I'll catch hold of your hand. No. The other one. When I grasp it, be ready to throw ya leg across the horse's neck."

When Zach reached for the boy's slim, shaky hand, the puppy squatted, ready to leap at him.

"Not going to hurt ya young master. What's his name?"

"Partner. 'Cause he be my buddy."

The puppy relaxed when he heard his name. Braced between Zach's arms, the boy looped his frail limbs around them. They headed back out of town with Partner clopping alongside of them, not taking his eye off the boy. Once on the road that led back to the farm, Zach encouraged the boy to talk.

"Tell me about yaself."

"Got no tellin'."

"What about ya ma? Where ya come from? How did ya get here?"

Hardly able to breathe, the boy struggled with his words.

"Be still. We'll talk later."

The two rode in an uneasy quietude until they were a good piece from town and felt safe. Zach lowered the lad from the saddle. Soon as his feet touched down, he turned in circles, yapped and yelled nonsensical fears. Partner jumping about, tripped his young master whose arms lassoed his neck.

"Take me back. I's scared. Don't be knowin' where I be."

"I'm right here. Not gonna leave ya."

Following the sounds of Zach's boots against the ground, the boy caught hold to the stranger's leg. He butted his head against his thigh. His shaking eased and his crying softened to a whimper.

Although, the drop in temperature had relaxed Zach, he frowned at the slow-moving cloudage overhead. With his eyes on them, he dragged the boy along still clutching onto his leg while he pulled a couple of blankets off Onyx's back.

He scooped biscuits from the saddlebag, dropped them into his pocket, and hung a canteen on his shoulder. Taking the boy by the hand, they moved toward a far-reaching canopy of an old oak tree.

"We'll sit here."

The boy's sightless eyes searched for the source of the words. His hands, studying the space surrounding him, came upon the stranger's moist lips that he finger-brushed. Afterward, he meticulously palpated Zach's cheeks, chin, eyes, ears, forehead, and nose. He laid both of his hands on top of Zach's head and finger-combed through the hair with both hands. Since there was no protest, he explored the rest of the body: neck, shoulders, chest front, back, arms, legs, and booted feet.

"Ya slim. Tall. Be da son of a white man. Don't feel no evil 'bout ya."

"Can we talk now?"

"Not much ta talk 'bout. Don't be knowin' where I come from or how old I be. Nobody ever tell me dem things. I just be. Massa Jim take my ma's life. He be mad 'cause she sass him, den fight him. He locked Ma in da hole but not 'fore he beat her. I try ta protect her, but he knock me ta da ground. Next thing I knowed, I hear huh cries. When der be no white man's footsteps. No voices. I crawls ta da hole dey put huh in. 'Ya der, Ma ?' I calls to huh through dat metal grid. But she don't answer me none. I lay der on top of it. I know Ma done gone on. I smells huh death. Da next day, dey push me away. Takes Ma out. Drag huh ta where da dead Coloureds be put."

"Sip some of this."

The boy turned the canteen up, gulping till his thirst was satisfied.

"Hungry?"

"Naw."

"Then what happened?"

"Massa say he had ta go ta town. Want me ta go wid him. Don't be sayin' why. Jes say, 'You ain't good fa nothin'.' When we gits ta town, he tells me ta sit on dem steps and wait. He go on in ta da drinkin' hole. Gits him a whiskey. Be a long time 'fore he come out. Brought a chuck of bread and tin of water when he did, but he go on back in. I hears fightin'. He and another fella be yellin'. Den, dey tumbles out pass me. Didn't know what ta do, so I hides under da saloon. I knows both of dem be drunk. Dey fight. It wasn't long 'fore da sheriff come. He tell my massa, 'Git on ya horse. Ride out of here. Don't come back and take dat good for nothin' darkie with ya.' Massa grunt, but he never call fa me."

"How did you end up under the courthouse?"

"Der be no peace under da tavern, so I moves ta da next buildin' and da next. I gits ta da courthouse and likes da sounds I be hearin' under der, so I stay. Somebody knowed I's der. Dey leave bread and water fa me, sometimes beans and cornbread. When nobody 'round, I eats dem. When I gits Partner, I feeds some to him."

"How long were you under there?"

"Don't know. Ain't got no day or night in des eyes, but I's sure it be from when da time the town be hushed, den gits rowdy, and da quiet come back. Dat happen a bunch of times. I know, I don't be here long enough to grow none."

"And ya mutt? Tell me about him."

"Partner." The boy smiled for the first time. "Some men be arguin'. One say, 'You done killed my bitch and now her puppy's done run off. You owe me for dat dog. She might not have been any good, but she was mine.' Da other man argue back, 'Damn bitch bit me. Be glad I killed her and not you.'

"I hear gunfire. Den runnin' feet. Dis here Partner be da puppy dey lookin' fa. He be scared of dat man and come under da buildin'. When he hear his voice, he whine and butt down tight next ta me. I keeps him close. We be friends now."

Partner licked the lad's nose and mouth, knocking him off his seat into a roll-and-tumble playfulness. Instantaneously, the boy stopped. Partner–snout down, ears up–crouched against his young master, who looped his arms around his neck; they lay motionless.

"Sir, what ya name be?"

"I'm Zach."

"Mr. Zach. Is der any place ta hide?" The lad rolled to get on his feet, "Somethin' awful be comin'. We needs to be gettin' quick."

"There're hills over yonder with a pocket between them."

"Best we be gettin' der. No time ta waste," the boy said, raising his chin, turning his head side to side as if it were a lighthouse lantern.

"Ya sure. Weather seems mighty fine ta me. Clouds done moved on. Sun's out."

"Mr. Zach. We ain't got no talkin' time. We best be gettin'."

With Partner at their sides, Zach mounted Onyx and pulled the boy up in front of him. His new charge tightened his grip around Zach's arms. He quavered as if he had a bad case of chills.

Near the opening of the hill, a sudden darkness spooked Onyx. The stallion threw the two off of his back. Zach held onto the reins as he tossed a blanket over the horse's head to cover his eyes. The boy grabbed onto Zach's britches, twisting and yanking them.

"Damn! The opening disappeared. I can't see a thing."

Using the sound of the wind against the earth and its brush against the hills and through the trees, the boy amazingly led them in the direction of the hollow. Along with Onyx, they bore deep enough into the opening to be safe. Zach secured Onyx to a tree root with a tight knot. The boy leaned against Zach. He breathed easier, even though the eye of the storm created a severe clatter.

"Mr. Zach."

"Yes."

"Can ya git ya horse? We need ta be movin' from dis here spot."

Not far from where they sat, a rumble and crackling dislodged a section of the hills. The collapse of it caused Onyx to kick and buck something awful. Too small to reach the head of the horse, the lad stroked its shoulder. He gentle-talked him into a state of calmness.

The rain had such riveting force it stung their bare skin. Not knowing what might happen next, Zach mounted Onyx. He layered one of the blankets over the horse's head. With the other blanket, he secured the boy to his back. Partner was positioned across the front of the saddle. They headed home as the ferocious rain and wind, shy of a tornado, bent and uprooted trees. It lasted well into the night. Zach was due back in time for Friday's supper. Now he was doubtful about when he'd arrive, and fretted about Ola's well being as he was sure she was about his.

Saturday night, near to Sunday, they had reached the edge of the farm. Not as much as a candlelight could be seen in any window up at the Big House. Once at the cabin, Zach cleaned his muddy boot bottoms on the scraper, toed them down over his heels, and lined them next to the door before he let himself into the welcoming warmth of the cabin. The boy seemed to know not to make a sound. Zach led him toward the platform bed that had been placed close to the hearth for travelers who might have been caught in the storm. The boy and Partner curled beneath a cozy blanket. Before Zach removed his clothes, the deep breathing of the boy and puppy filled the room.

Naked, he slid into bed next to Ola, threw his cold leg over her warm body, and pressed his lips against her bare shoulder. In a state of disbelief, their arms wrapped around each other with a deepened passion. When he and Ola merged into lovemaking more than once, head-to-toe ripples scattered throughout Zach's body.

At daylight, they still hungered for each other. Zach entered Ola with passion and wanting as if the night before had never melted into day. When they released their holds and lay stretched on their backs, they revisited the events of the night before and that morning, wishing to continue their lovemaking till death parted them.

Ola buried her head in Zach's chest. "I's scared I's never gonna see ya again. Things be so bad Massa tell da hands ta stop workin'. 'Go on back to the quarters,' he tells dem. Trees come down. Some of da stock be lost. Fencin' be ripped away. The storm come quick wid no time ta prepare. Couldn't even git da cellar door up. I's sure ya wouldn't come back ta me or a standin' cabin.

"It was the boy who saved me. He knew the devil was coming before it showed itself."

Zach lifted Ola's chin, kissed her, and said, "I got the boy I told you about."

With the corner of their covering, Zach dabbed the tears swelled in Ola's eyes.

"Let's have a peep," he told her.

The two rolled out of bed and tiptoed toward the sleepers. When Ola lifted the covers, Partner growled and postured himself to attack.

Stumbling backward, she yelled, "Where'd dat beast come from? Get it out of here. Get it out now!"

Zach knew there was no use trying to explain that the mutt was only a puppy.

"Come on boy. You and Partner sit on the stoop. I'll come for ya shortly."

Zach gathered Ola in his arms. "No need ta be upset. The dog's only a puppy. He was protecting his young master."

"But he tried ta kill me."

"Let's have coffee and something to eat. I'll tell you about my trip."

After Ola started breakfast, Zach called for the lad to come in. In a state of confusion, the boy asked, "Partner?"

"He's fine. He'll be on the porch a while longer."

Satisfied, the lad felt his way to the table and clambered onto a chair. Partner whined to get back in but soon settled down. With his hands layered in his lap, neck arced, and eyelids lowered, he used his sensibility to monitor what surrounded him.

Ola flipped around the cabin singing her thanks to the Lord for bringing her man home. She danced around as she whipped up a breakfast fit for white folks: pork, eggs, and grits heaped on the plates. Zach ogled at all that his eyes could consume of his wife–glad the lad had no sight in his eyes to witness his lusting.

"Come. Let's eat," said Ola.

The boy devoured his food. When a hot biscuit was put on his plate, he grabbed it. Too hot to hold onto, he tossed it hand to hand to cool it.

"Stop! Got preserves fa dat," Ola said.

"Don't know what dat be."

"Ya mouth be tellin' ya. Jus ya wait."

The boy put the quick bread down and Ola spooned a glob of pear preserves onto it.

"Now. See what ya think?"

"I think I be wantin' mo."

Ola beamed as she doted over the boy with more preserves and biscuits and then wrapped his fingers around a tin of warmed milk. She put a cup of coffee on the table for Zach and dished beans and rice in to a pan. She cracked the door and pushed the pan of food out for Partner, who lay sad-eyed, staring at her.

Zach spread his legs and slumped in his chair with a courting gesture aimed at Ola, who bounded about the kitchen, pretending not to notice him as she tended to the food and fire. With a heavy wantingness, he peered over the coffee cup as he sipped from it. Her husband caught hold of her hand as she crossed the front of him. Ola returned the gesture with a playfully-stern look.

"Got no time fa dat. Der's work dat's gotta be done," she said and flipped a flirty hip at him.

The boy suddenly jumped from the chair, swinging his outstretched arms and knocking over his tin of milk. On his feet, he frantically searched for the wall. Patting it he found the door that he pulled open. He and Partner were down the steps and under the porch in a blink, scooting until they were deep into the darkness of the crawl space.

Joe Jammer galloped up to the cabin steps with his eyebrows pulled close and his mouth downturned. He shook his head. "When I assessed things this morning, I was sure I wouldn't see you again. The grounds, for as far as I can see, are a mess.

"Not going to stay and chat. Only wanted to check on you and your missus. Rest and enjoy the day with Ola. I know she's pleased you're back. Polly and Tay will take care of the kitchen today and tomorrow. We'll talk later. By the way, where's the blind boy? Did you get him?"

"Did. But he's a bit shy. He'll come around soon."

Jammer nodded and rode off.

"Come on out boy. He's gone," Zach said and went back inside the cabin where Ola was cleaning up the spill.

"Joe Jammerccc seems to be in a decent mood, which might give us more uninterrupted time together. The madame must have been shaken by the storm," Zach said.

"I hear something underneath da floor," Ola said.

"It's the boy. Let me take care of him. I'll be back for my coffee."

The lad stood in the yard, uncertain of his propinquity to the steps and the door.

"Over here," Zach said.

When the boy turned to face the voice, he realized he only needed to take in the breakfast smells seeping from the opened door to guide him back to the stoop.

Zach slapped the step. "Sit here beside me."
Partner was first at his feet for a pat on the head.

"He likes ya," the boy said.

"I think we're going to be friends. But I need to know what name they gave you."

"Didn't. Massa call me whatever come ta mind. Don't belong ta him long enough ta be named."

"In that case, you will be my boy."

"Dat mean I be Will?"

"Don't see why not."

"And you be MyZach?"

Zach picked up a few stones. With the boy's small hand in his, he placed them on his palm.

"Which of these feels special to you?"

"MyZach, I be likin' des here one. It's smooth. Lays flat in my hand. And got three smooth edges."

"It'll be your lucky stone. Stuff it in your pocket. Toss the others. If you get into trouble, send that stone to me. I'll come get you. Now, let's find a good stick for searching."

They walked a while before Zach stopped and pulled a small branch from a tree and snapped off the twigs. "We'll take this up to Amos, the blacksmith," he told the boy as they made their way up the lane. With a hearty introduction, he turned the lad over to his care.

"This is Amos, he'll be teaching ya ta sort nails and do other chores around the shop. You'll work with him during the day and come back to the cabin in the evenings."

Zach left the two, who quickly bonded. With a smile on his face, Amos seared down the juts on the walking stick. Each morning from then on, Will woke early, dressed, and ate a plate of ashcakes washed down with milk, water, or yesterday's tea. With Partner at his side, he tapped his way up the lane to the blacksmith shop, stepping most like he was sighted.

15

Lust

Anchored against the cabin post, captivated by the impeccable beauty of the farmland, Zach strained to consume the attributes of its lushness. He struggled to draw a proper breath as his skin wept and dripped profusely. The air, at least fifty miles around, was dense and steamy. Provoked by the same torridness, overseers on nearby farms, raised mean whips and unconsciously thrashed the backs of field hands who struggled to meet the unreasonable demands.

Songs entangled with hurt emerged from the pits of each enslaved soul. Lyric after Lyric reflected sorrow as the field hands pleaded and begged for faith, hope, and freedom. Ears that caught snippets of the musical cries, no matter how sedating the sound, knew blood spilled from the gashes of bent backs.

Up at the Big House, Táe stood in the corner of the portico and pulled the punkah fan cord stretched across the ceiling. Avida Maria created a make-believe world next to her. The little missus served her porcelain dolls from a tiny bone china tea set with gold trimmed cups and saucers slathered with pink apple blossoms.

Joe and Francine lazily rocked beneath the golden panel that gracefully swayed to and fro chasing pesky flies and the heat of the day. The couple hoped to capture a breeze that might drift up from the river.

Except for the extreme humidity that day, one summer evening wasn't different from the others. Francine enjoyed a goblet of spring-cooled tea as she advanced her needlework; Joe sipped his barrel-aged Kentucky Bourbon that he prided. The two chitchatted to the euphonious sounds of the riverbank creatures. But on this day, the kitchen door slammed shut behind Ola as she bounded for the quarters, bouncing foot to foot as if she were dancing.

At the sight of her, Jammer clumsily slid forward and reached for a pillar. Grasping it, he tugged to stand. Supported by the column, he stretched his neck till his mouth drooled and his chin pointed at what captivated his senses.

"You're lusting for that gal. Your eyeballs have nearly rolled onto your cheekbones. There's no doubt you're in a state of pure wanting. No sense denying it. Anyone with a fair set of eyes would be able to witness your risqué behavior without any effort on their part. And by the way, the type of observation you're displaying should be avoided in the presence of a proper lady, not to mention your young daughter. Try being a bit more discreet. If you're in doubt, I can let you know that your wife disapproves of your behavior."

Joe gazed over his shoulder at Francine. "Best you keep your eyes on your needlework and your thoughts to yourself. Then you can leave mine to me."

"You're a drunken fool."

"So, I am."

Francine huffed, put her needlepoint down, and sprang to her feet. She snatched Joe's rolled-up sleeve, spun him around, and peered fixedly at his bloodshot eyes. In a strident voice, she said, "Enough has been spoken about that gal. You know God doesn't take kindly to vulgar fools and has his way of managing sinners. The next time you disrobe that wench with your eyes and your hands, you might end up explaining your behavior to the Devil as he carts your soul to Hell. I'll leave you to your choices, Mr. Jammer."

Entering the house, Francine swished her skirt with a snap of disgust and let the door bang shut behind her to denote a degree of annoyance that Jammer wouldn't forget.

Nodding with contemptuousness, he sneered, "I shall heed your words."

The following morning, Ola didn't light the oil lamp or make a noise when she slid out of bed and dressed for the day. She struggled to pull her shoes on over her swollen feet. Her stiff fingers, unable to fasten them on, stuffed the laces inside the cuffs. She hurried out of the cabin and up to the mansion to stoke the fires and add fresh coal and logs if needed to warm Madame's chamber. Afterward, Ola continued out the yard door to the kitchen where she would ready breakfast for the Jammer family.

Although her pregnancy showed a good amount, Madame, in her perpetual state of meanness, refused to take note and didn't permit any of the hands to assist Ola, not even to lift large cooking pots or sharpen knives when the missus knew Zach waited to take them to Amos to be put against the spinning stone.

Ola lit the cooking fire and moved, as best she could, to get breakfast started: frying pork belly, boiling eggs, and stirring grits. Bread slices were toasted and jam spooned in a small bowl to accompany them. When done, she poured boiling water over ground coffee and placed the pot on the tray with a pitcher of cream. She carried the load up to the pantry at the Big House. The food was transferred to a silver serving tray and the coffee and cream were poured into the china serving pieces. She could hear Polly and Tay in the dining room chattering as they prepared the table for the family meal and the credenza for the service.

It wasn't long before the family was seated at the table. The mood wasn't entirely pleasant, but better than usual. Francine shared her plans to attend a tea party while Jammer would be away for business meetings.

After breakfast, Ola returned to her workstation to start the noon meal. She bounded from the kitchen, collected her basket, and raced to the garden to harvest stewing vegetables. While she was out, Jammer slithered into the kitchen and concealed himself behind the door. When Ola returned, not noticing him, she hurried to the sink and was startled when he barged toward her. She dropped the vegetable-filled basket into the sink that she grasped hold to. Joe planted his feet, one on each side of her, and pushed her over with his forearm braced across her shoulders. He thrust his body against hers, grinning his pelvic against her buttocks as she held steadfast to the rim of the sink, praying beneath her breath, "Lord, don't let dis here foolish man touch me dis mornin'. Done had a 'nough of him and his pesterin'."

Breathing a hot, pesky, whiskey breath on her neck, Jammer dislodged the headscarf that fastened her hair in place. He sloppily kissed her neck as he drew his fingers through her hair, down over her shoulders, baring her breasts. His probing hands dislodged the ties that expanded her skirt as he cupped her bulging belly before aggressively shoving his hands between her legs and groping her with penetrating fingers.

"See why Zach got such a fondness for you. You got that kind of beauty and grace a man can't resist. Or should I say, keep his hand off of," he gabbled in her ear as he manipulated her where she didn't want to be touched by him. Ola never raised her eyelids, moved, or spoke in response to Jammer's gibberish.

Her lower body tightened as she fought to hold onto the sink, determined to remain footed and not to let fear take her to the floor for the worse.

Distracted by the sound of a horse's neigh, Joe scampered out of the kitchen. Struggling to suck back her fears and tears Ola collapsed to the floor. Joe, nor the horseman saw Táe enter the kitchen from the side of the structure.

"Miss Ola, I's sorry fa what da massa done ta ya."

Táe swiftly moved toward Ola. Squatted next to her, she adjusted Ola's top back into place; tied her hair up, as best she could; and fumbled with the ties on the skirt. Not knowing what else to do she caressed Ola and stroked her brows. With quiet words, she whispered in her ear, "It's gonna be all right, Miss Ola."

In a raspy voice, Ola muttered, "Ya go on back ta da house. Don't tell what ya saw."

Táe rang a wet kitchen towel and pressed it against Ola's bruised eye and cheek. Ola patted the hand that held the towel.
"Go on now. Git. I be all right," she said and took charge of the kitchen rag.

Feeling hesitant, Táe backed away from Ola, not wanting to leave her. At the cookhouse door, she turned and ran back to the Big House.

Ola willed herself up off the floor and steadied her body against the sink. She pared the vegetables and added them to a pot of boiling smoked pork pieces. She felt a barrage of anger as her fingers squeezed the cornmeal mush for the fried cakes. If only it were his throat, she thought.

When the lunch was ready for serving, she took it up to the Big House and left it for Polly and Táe, glad they were assigned to serve the meal. Since she didn't need to stay, she spun on her heels and took leave without announcing her presence.

After the mid-day meal was over, Polly checked on Little Issac and Amos. "I'm gonna go see about Ola and deliver Missus message ta huh about huh work. Amos, she be lookin' mighty sickly ta me today."

Polly sauntered to the kitchen where she delivered the message to Ola, who cut up chickens for dinner. She seemed unusually tired, limp, and visibly sickly, but in Polly's mind, not baby sickly. She explored Ola in detail. What she saw worried her.

"Ya don't be well," she said.

"I'm not. . . cain't say mo."

"It be massa. I seen him runnin' off. He's a beast. I know his ways. He's ripped my clothes off when I be with child."

"Look at me, Miss Ola. Madame done sent me to tell ya, ya gotta tend da dinner. She gonna send Táe and me to da fields. We ain't goon be able to help ya. But I help ya now, long as I can. Make yaself a pallet in dat corner. Ya rest. Sleep some. Don't want ya losin' dat baby. I git dem chickens fried and the potatoes mashed. Missus thinks I'm in the da fields. Mr. Zach sent a hand to do my work so I could be here wid ya."

Polly finished the food preparation and Ola served the meal that evening, but not without challenges. Jammer continuously eyed her. From beneath the table, he put his hands on her each time she served him. When she attempted to fill his goblet with water, he demanded she put another piece of chicken on his plate. When she reached to get chicken from the platter, he grasped the inside of her thigh, high up near the baby. Startled, she dropped the meat shy of his plate. Madame hurried from her end of the table with a raised arm. She backhanded Ola, whacking the side of her head. The blow sent the gal to the floor, grabbing hold of her ear and spilling the pitcher of water.

Avida Maria dashed from her seat. Kneeling on the floor, she hugged Ola's arm to help her to her feet as best a small person could.

"You, little lady, get back on your chair.

"And you, clumsy fool, clean up that mess, and let us finish our meal without another incident."

Avida Maria heaved, and then, screamed loud as her voice permitted. "Mommy, you're being mean to Ola. You can see she's tired and sick. And you won't let Polly or Táe help her." Avida Maria bounded out of the dining room, sprinted up the staircase to her bedroom where she slammed the door and turned the lock.

Ola put the chunk of chicken on Jammer's plate and mopped the floor with rags. Afterward, dumfounded, she stumbled backward against the wall and braced herself next to the buffet. She stayed there trembling till time to serve the coffee and cake. After dinner, without assistance, she began to clear the table.

From behind her head, Ola heard Francine scoff, "You'll be washing those things and putting them away. Polly and Táe have other chores to do today. And, Clara's still sick. I suggest you hurry and be done soon."

By nightfall, overwrought with anxiety, Ola curled her body around a pillow on the rope bed and buried her bruised face in it. She reeled and rocked as she whimpered. Unsure what to do, Zach gently stretched her somewhat-resistant body out on the bed. He rubbed witch hazel oil between his palms. With a faint touch, he massaged her feet and legs. The pungent vapors stung his eyes and flared his nostrils but didn't phase Ola. She adjusted her weight and lay on the side of her bruised face. Not moving, she drifted into an uneasy sleep.

The following morning Zach pulled Ola back to bed. "Why are you up and about so early? It's still dark," he said, attempting to delay her.

"Madame say I gotta start dat fire 'fore dat crow cries. Say, she don't want ta be gettin' up ta no chill."

"You're with child. You weren't well last night. You can't keep working at such a pace. It worries me."

"I takes care. God be knowin' what ya dream be. He gonna gives ya dat baby boy ya be yearnin' fa."

Ola twisted her hair into an oversized red and purple paisley hanky that held it in place at the back of her head. She pressed Zach's hand to her belly. A simper appeared on his face.

"I'll be back 'fore dark. Madame be visitin' with huh friends dis evenin'."

Something Zach couldn't define about Ola's persona troubled him. His eyes trailed her waddle that hampered the usual swift pace of her feet. He struggled not to be overbearing, but songs coming up out the fields some nights ago revealed that her cabin-mate from Beaumont's farm was beaten and raped, possibly by Pierre, and later found dead behind the corn crib. Zach's mind flashed back to a time when he and Jammer were on their way to the barn as Ola came out of the yard door. Joe leered at her in a manner that caused concern. Zach knew his wife's safety might be compromised if there were no eyes to monitor Joe's drunkenness and wandering feet.

Zach sighed; despair rumbled in his gut. The matchstick in his hand trembled as he lit an oil lamp to search for his britches, entangled with the bedding. He pulled them on with yesterday's wrinkled shirt and stuck his feet into the socks kicked to the corner of the cabin, the night before He seized the boots nested next to the bed.

After a breakfast of coffee, fatback, and cornbread, Zach snuffed out the wick and stepped outside. He was awed by the treetops that blushed with a blueish-purple tint topped with a hint of pink gossamer, something he was rarely up early enough to experience.

Will and Partner, disturbed by the commotion, came out on the stoop. Standing close, he said, "MyZach."

"Good morning, Will. Got a job for ya. I want ya to clear the big stones in the alley to create a smooth walking pathway for ya Miss Ola."

"I clear 'em." Will picked up the first stone and turned his ear toward Zach, "All da way ta da kitchen?"

"She'd like that, but don't stop till ya at the yard door. Then, go on to the barn to help Amos."

Will joy-stepped up the alley. He dragged his walking stick side to side, tossing protruding stones aside as he moved along , all the way to his nail-sorting station. By then, Zach had reached the north field where a steady rainfall the night before had soaked the ground, making the day's fieldwork effortless. Cass, on the back of a work wagon, barked orders to the field hands, as others sorted for tools in the back of it. Others waited their turn to collect a tool or receive a customized directive.

Zach prompted Onyx to swing right. They rode back and forth between the fields but stopped when he heard Will yell his name. He spotted him swinging his stick as he ran toward him. Zach jerked the horse to a stop.

"What troubles you, boy?"

"It be Miss Ola. I past da kitchen. She be painin'. I go ta check on ha. She be doubled up on da floor. Say, gitcha and . . . "

"Get up here."

Zach caught hold of Will's arm and lifted him off the ground. The boy straddled Onyx's loin muscle and hugged his master's waist.

"Hold on."

Giving the bit a sound tug, Onyx reared up, kicking his front hooves. When they dropped, they were off with the speed of an owl snatching prey. Ola's moans pierced Zach's ears before he neared the kitchen door. He dismounted and curled Will's fingers around the reins.

"Go find Amos. Tell him to bring the cart."

The boy pressed his knees against the fenders of the saddle like Zach had taught him and did as he was told. Partner trailed behind Onyx and Will.

Zach stepped in Ola's blood as he crouched at her side, gently scooping her into his arms. She tried to clasp hers around his neck. Too weak to hold on, her body slumped into the folds of his arms.

When Zach came out of the kitchen carrying her, the wagon was at the door. He lay her on the floorboard, hopped in next to her, and tenderly placed her head on his lap. To jar Ola as little as possible, Amos slowly guided the cart to the cabin steps. Will on Onyx came afterward. At the cabin, the lad and Partner nested together on the steps, butted against the post.

"Come on, boy. I'll take ya and Partner ta da barn wid me," Amos said.

"Naw. Gotta stay. MyZach be needin' me."

"Will!"

"I's here, MyZach."

"Bring me a bucket of well water and then sit outside till I call again."

Zach didn't hear Will come with the water or leave. Nevertheless, it was there when needed it. He carefully slid Ola's shoes off her feet one at a time and rolled the bloody skirt and apron down her legs and over her feet. Using his pocket knife, he split the soiled shirt and peeled it away from her torso.

Bathing her from hairline to toe tips, he didn't believe he could sink lower in despair; but the sight of Ola's swollen face drew him further into it. He wondered when it happened and why he failed to notice the blue-black eye and swollen cheek that morning. But then he remembered, she undressed in the dark that night, and kept her back to him. Zach layered fresh covers over Ola's naked and weathered body, now empty of its new life ,which compounded the depth of what had happened to her.

Zach didn't answer the tap at the door. It sounded again. This time Polly opened it. "Come to help ya," she said and embraced Zach with a comforting arm across his shoulder. He fell against her and wept like a child.

"It's gonna be all right. God's wid ya. Go 'head. Take yourself fa a walk. I sits wid Ola. If she gits weaker, I send Will ta fetch ya."

With the backside of his hand, Zach blotted his tears. Heavy-footed, he headed up to the Big House. So consumed with rage, his heart raced and his head spun with dizziness. He could hardly take in a decent breath before he attempted to ascend the steps leading up to the entrance to the Big House, but Joe Jammer came out with a buoyant jolliness about him.

"How you doing, Zach?" he asked.

"Not good. We gotta talk."

"Wait here. Let me get my hat."

By the time he returned, some of Zach's anger had settled, but not nearly enough.

"We've got to go to the river."

Without an utterance, they started down the carriage lane to the turnpike. Zach's aura was so drawn and dissonant, Joe

Jammer knew it was best to hold his words and not encourage dialogue with his friend. Growing into manhood together afforded them a closeness few brothers had. For no particular reason, they hesitated at the big oak tree near the carriage lane entrance, like they did in their earlier days, to debate what needed to be attended to around the farm.

"Follow me," said Zach.

They crossed the turnpike. Both sets of hands pushed through the burning bush to where Zach and Ola frequently spent time together. Zach's finger detected a bit of red plaid broadcloth snagged from her shirt. He quickly pocketed it and continued downhill to the riverbank to bare his soul. Zach pointed to the ground, indicating for Joe to sit.

"I can tell it's bad. Whatever it is, you gotta tell me."

The comrades sat side by side as they did from their first times together. Only this time, Zach's heart was strained.

In a more concerning tone he said again, "We need to talk,".

"It's serious?"

"Is."

"Say what ya gotta say. Be straightforward. We've never shied from the truths, not even the hurting ones."

"I try not to intrude with what goes on under your roof. I let you live your life up there, while I live mine down here. But your Madame has breached our brotherhood."

"How so?"

"She nearly took my Ola's life. She didn't. But my baby's dead. Ain't no secret I wanted it a powerful lot if it made it to this world alive. You knew it as well as everybody around these parts."

"I can attest to that. I was in town yesterday. Folks asked about the new baby coming. I never knew a time when white folks asked about Coloureds having babies, but they were carrying on about yours."

"Joe Jammer, your wife has taken too much from me for too long."

Joe studied the ground as he pushed his boot toe around in the soft dirt before he glanced up and asked in a concerned voice, "How so?"

"She works Ola excessively. Today she looked as if she'd been to war. Battered and beat up. My wife's in the kitchen before the crow calls and is still there long after the owl hoots. Your Madame insists she stands when she can sit. Such insensitivity has got to change. She keeps her up at your house when she should be down at mine, in bed with me. I don't want Ola to lose another baby. It hurts too much. Don't know what you're gonna tell your wife, but I'll tell you, mine won't be back to the cookhouse till she's well and the treatment she gets is promised to be better."

"I didn't know it was that bad. I'll have a word with Francine as soon as I'm back at the house. Things will change. I promise. No need for Ola to rush back. She can take whatever time she needs to heal."

Jammer seemed more concerned about his business than Ola when he said, "If you don't mind, later, I'd like to bring papers down for you to look over.

"By the way, Mr. Brown complimented me. Said I'm doing business like a well-informed businessman and talking like one, too. I can thank you for teaching me to speak, read, write, and figure like I'm educated. But these legal papers are still troublesome."

Jammer shifted as he stared at his feet. "I'm truly sorry for what's happened," he mumbled.

He was lifeless, and more humble on his return to the Big House. He shrugged his shoulders with a profound sigh as he entered his office. With the flat of his foot, he kicked the door shut behind him and seized a bottle of whiskey from the sideboard. He flung it down on the desk. Disgruntled, he pondered the neat pile of legal papers, most recent on top, while he reflected on witnessing a part of Zach he'd never seen before.

In the parlor, Francine postured near the window to take advantage of the natural light that filled the room. She set and sorted quilting squares, until Jammer entered, with such a rush, she vaulted to her feet, dumping the content of her lap onto the floor.

"So, you're back, Mr. Jammer."

"I am and we need to have a few words."

"My! You sound unusually sober."

"You've got to find help for the kitchen. Ola's sick."

"Oh!"

"Seems you've been harsh to her. Even after my warning, you're still being overbearing with the house hands. I know you don't want an out-of-control household. However, a hand whose death is caused by your carelessness won't be replaced. It's not certain how long it will take Ola to recover. She's bad off. Lost her baby and a lot of blood. You'll have to make do without her for a while. And it might be a long while, so don't go near their cabin. Let them be."

Francine grumped, "I'll bring Polly in from the barn. She's slow, and her meals lack flavor. She's not like Ola, quick and everything she prepares is tasty, but she'll do for now."

"What about Clara?"

"Polly will check on her during the day and before she snuffs out the candles in the evening.

"Is she better?"

"Some days when I go out to the barn, she's sitting up. Bat an eyelash and she's flat on her back again."

"You should have considered your situation when you ordered Ola about with such punitive demands."

"One would think she was your mistress rather than your slave."

"Best you take care and mind your tongue."

When Francine spun around, she whacked Jammer with her crinoline cage, wanting to put him on his knees. He, instead, fisted a bunch of her skirt and yanked it. She stumbled, fell against the quilting chair, and clipped her cheek against its armrest.

"Take care if you want to keep wearing those fancy hoops."

Francine got on her feet, drew her trembling lips tight as she reached for his throat. Her glare prompted such a bitter taste in Joe's mouth, he gripped her shoulders, shaking her till her vision doubled and her neatly parted coiffure graced smooth wings over her ears and a twisted braid at the back of her nape fell apart. The combs that held them in place tick-tacked as they hit the floor.

"Stop! You're hurting me."

Pulled closer, Jammer's hot breath buffed Francine's face as he practically shouted down her throat, "But not as much as you hurt Ola. Before you climb those stairs tonight, you might want to have a few words with Polly about her new chores."

Holding her bruised cheek, Francine sobbingly said, "I'll do that later."

When she stooped to collect her combs, Jammer bumped her when he pivoted to leave. She was back on the floor–this time, weeping into a fist-full of quilting squares.

"Joe Jammer, you've been mean to me. You're a belligerent monster! I'm gonna let my uncle know how you've treated me."

"Do as you please. But don't forget, Ola was their favorite hand. Remember, too, Monsieur did not want to sell her, and

Madame did not want to part with her. I wonder what they would think if they saw Ola lying in her blood-soaked bed wailing with pain for the loss of her baby. And, by the way, don't think about locking the bedroom door. If you do, it will disappear from its hinges."

"You're a hateful beast, Joe Jammer."

Back at the cabin, Zach dismissed Polly and crept about as he put a pot of water on the hot coals, unsure why he did, but it generated a sense of calm. He stared deeply into the flames as he contemplated what he had experienced with his friend at the riverbank before he prepared a cup of coffee for himself. He glanced at Ola, who rested in a light slumber and hadn't realized his return. From a hearth-side jar, he fingered out a chunk of meat and sat outside to nibble on it, but didn't taste a thing. Jammer's foot steps caused him to flinch when he came around the cabin.

"Sorry. Didn't mean to startle you. Got these legal papers I mentioned to you."

"Quite a stack you got there. Wouldn't be able to read them this evening. Got to take care of Ola and there's work in the fields to finish. I'll review them tomorrow or the next day."

Jammer placed the documents next to Zach and mumbled a few inaudible words as he took leave.

"You, all right?" Zach asked.

"I am."

Zach's eyes trailed the gloom of Jammer as his body shrank into the distance.

Things around the farm settled down. Jammer somehow persuaded his wife to let Ola be. By mid-April, the hemp was in and the corn soon followed. Weeks later, both crops sprouted. Clara was back in the Big House cleaning and supervising the laundry. Avida Maria had grown accustomed to following her mother about and staying within her vision.

Zach was busier than usual, managing the double-crop and the extra hands hired to harvest it and break the hemp. Ola was lethargic after losing the baby. She was never overworked again. Zach tried to cheer her with her favorite dish of smoked pork skins and funny stories about when he was a young boy and fell into the river trying to catch a fish with a knotted at the end of a line. She didn't perk up, not even a bit.

Will moved around on his own with Partner, no longer a puppy, but still faithfully at the boy's side. They monitored Ola's movements and reported anything out of the ordinary.

On one of Jammer's infrequent trips out to the fields, Zach flagged him toward where he supervised the field hands.

"Sure glad you came out. I was going to send for you. I won't be in the fields tomorrow. I'll be spending time with my wife. So, you will need to keep yours engaged to not be tempted to pester us."

"I've planned a trip to town to do some shopping. I'll take her along. You can rest assured she will not intrude with your plans. You two got something special. Wish I could conjure up such with Francine, but she's got her ways. Most, I don't understand."

16

Trauma & Death

After being granted permission to sit on the front steps and eat candy, Avida Maria maneuvered a black horsehair chair against the huntboard and crawled onto its seat. She straightened her four-year-old legs and plucked several pieces of sweets from the crystal candy dish. Counting one to six, she let them fall into her pinafore pouch and then jumped down from the chair. She bounded out the front door, plopped on the top step, and adjusted her skirt to sit in a lady-like manner taught to her by Clara. She fished two nuggets from her pocket, fingernailed one, and licked the particles of sugar from her fingertip.

With Partner at his side, Will marched up the carriage lane tapping his searching stick, singing *Little David Play on Yo' Harp*. Avida Maria, wide-eyed and elated to see Will, sprang to her feet. With a candy in each hand, she beckoned to him. Her girly high-pitched voice called, "Will! Will! Come see. Got some sweets for us," she said, waving the candy pieces as if he could see them.

She bustled down the steps to meet her buddy. In a fit of excitement, her foot was caught on a protruding tree root. Flipped, she tossed the candy pieces as her body slammed the ground. She expelled a piercing yelp. "Will! Will! I got a big hurt."

"Don't cry. I be comin'."

The lad dropped his stick. Down on his hands and knees, he patted the grass as he followed the wailing sound. Finally, he slid his hands beneath Avida Maria. Panicky, she hooked her arms around his small neck and squeezed it. "I hurt Will," she cried as he straightened his back and legs to stand. The lad held his armload secure while he assessed the zephyr to determine where to put her down.

Hearing the shriek of Avida Maria's voice, Clara rushed to the main door held open by Polly. The missus dashed past her, knocking her against the door frame. Standing on the portico, Francine heaved deeply and held her breath. When she let it out, she yelled in her most vulgar voice, "Take your filthy hands off my child! Put her down. Put her down now!"

She lifted the front of her dress to hurry her feet. At the base of the steps, she plucked a fist-sized rock from the flowerbed and grasped it till her knuckles whitened.

Dazed with pain, Avida Maria clutched tighter to Will's neck. He pivoted in semi-circles, left to right, as he struggled to decipher where and how to put his buddy down. The harshness of Francine's voice caused him to be disoriented and unable to determine a suitable surface other than the earthy patch his feet palpitated. Benumbed, he ceased all movement.

"I said, take your filthy hands off of my child!"

Gesturing and bellowing obscenities, Francine raised the stone above her head. Without hesitation, she repeatedly bashed Will. Blood spewed from his eyes, nose, and mouth. Still clutching Avida Maria, he collapsed to his knees and fell over with his head rested in her lap.

Partner lunged at Francine. A gunshot stopped him in mid-air. Whirling and whining, the hound dragged his weight to the base of the yard tree. He crumpled, shallow breathing, with his tongue dangling from his mouth.

Joe Jammer holstered his pistol as he struggled to make sense of what had happened: his daughter clutching onto Will; the boy, small and frail for his age with a bloodied face; and the dog, always at his side, never trouble for anyone–now shot.

With a rebellious grip, Avida Maria held firm to Will. At the same time, her mother tugged at the boy's overall straps, trying to pull him off her daughter. Perturbed, Francine sucked in a deep breath. Between her gritted teeth, with a low agitated tone, spitting, and shouting, she said, "Let go of that darkie!"

"Stop! Mommy, you're hurting Will. He's bleeding badly, and my leg hurts."

Avida Maria laid her face on the side of Will's head. Her blood-saturated tears bathed his cheek. With hushed words, she whispered in his ear, "Say something, Will."

Francine snatched the boy's arm, "Let go of him."

The girl turned an angry eye toward her mother and then quickly back at her playmate. She smoothed Will's brow and in a hushed tone called his name again. He didn't flinch or answer her.

"Mommy, you killed him. He's dead."

"He's not dead. Let him go!"

Irritated, Francine forcefully yanked the limp body from the girl's grip and let it drop. Before her daughter could react to the gesture, Jammer scooped her into his arms and pushed the young buck aside with his booted foot.

Wiggling and screaming, Avida Maria hollered, "Pappa, Stop! Stop! Put me down. You're making my leg hurt. Help Will, Papa. He's bleeding bad. I think he's dead."

"He'll be all right, my dearest. Let us tend to you. And I promise I'll send someone to fetch the lad."

Francine brushed at the blood splatters on the front of her bodice as if they were removable flakes. "Hmm," she said in an undertone. With an arrogantly straightened back and still yelping obscenities, she scurried behind her family.

Clara submissively held the main door open as Jammer quizzically glanced at her before he said, "Go tell Amos to saddle up and fetch Dr. Brim. Alert him that my child's badly hurt and to come quickly. Hurry. Be on your way, gal."

"Papa, what about Will?"

Jammer raised his voice. "Then, go tell Zach to come see about the boy and bury dat hound."

"Papa! Clara didn't hear what you said about Partner. She was running before you finished your saying."

"Don't worry, sweet dear. I'll see to the mutt myself if I have to."

Clara wasted no time delivering Massa's message to Amos before she skirted the hemp crop to find Zach. Hardly able to feel the earth beneath her feet, she pondered how she would deliver such a message. Her heart thudded and her breaths were a challenge to take in as knots churned in her throat.

"Zach. Where Zach be?" Her voice cracked.

In the distance, she heard. "Up at the north field. Can fetch him fa ya? If ya be wantin' me ta . . . "

Clara turned and followed the crop rows as she yelled for Zach. He emerged from behind a section of sky-reaching hemp.

"Over here. What troubles ya, gal?"

"It be Will."

"Will? Where is he?"

"Up at da Big House. He be layin' not far from da front steps."

A whistle brought Onyx galloping in his direction. Within seconds, on his bareback, Zach grasped a mass of mane and jockeyed him to the main lawn where the boy lay clumped on the ground. Consumed with concern from what he saw, he eased off the horse. Wilting to his knees next to the lad, Zach sat on his heels with his back curved. Angry and trembling, he turned the boy's body. His sightless eyes, bloodied and swollen, faced him. With fingers spread, Zach eased his trembling hands beneath the boy's frame, heaved it against his grief-stricken chest, and slowly rocked it. Will's fragile arm fell limp over Zach's forearm. The lucky pebble he didn't have a chance to send to Zach, slipped from his hand.

"You gonna be all right, boy. I got you in my arms."

Zach retrieved the stone, put it in the boy's pocket, and got on his feet. He brushed past Onyx as he guardedly hurried down the carriage lane to the cabin where he shifted Will to one arm, cleared the platform bed with a swoop of the other hand, and stretched the boy out on it. The lad never in any way indicated that he was aware of his surroundings.

Left behind in the hemp fields, Clara ran the distance to the cabin. Rested against the doorway, she panted and mumbled, "He all right?"

Zach humped his shoulders with uncertainty, trembling he mumbled, "Can't detect a grain of life in him. Ain't moved a hand to explore the darkness in front of him. Who did this to my boy? How could anyone do such a horrible thing? What happened?"

While wringing her hands, Clara caught Zach's stare; barely taking a proper breath, she said, "When I hears the Little Missus scream, I rushed ta see what da matter be. Missus 'bout knock me down goin' out da door. She be plenty upset 'cause little Will pick up huh gal after she done fall in da big yard and hurt huh leg. She tell him, 'Take your filthy hands off of my child!' Next thing I be knowin', she clobbered him wid da big rock. He bled a powerful lot in da face. Dat's when Massa shoot Partner. Den he send me ta tell Amos ta git da doc and den fetch ya."

Zach turned his stricken face to view Clara's. "Get some water and put it here next to me," he said with a frightening calmness.

She eyeballed the cabin till she took sight of a large mixing bowl on the dining table. She corralled it and snatched up a handful of rags from a burlap sack next to a wooden bucket filled near to the rim with water. She ladled some of it into the bowl and moved close to Zach. In a difficult-to-decipher voice, he told her, "Take care of the boy. I'm going to get Ola."

Onyx was at the porch railing where he'd typically be tied. Zach mounted him but didn't gallop away at full speed to enable his mind to sort the words needed to tell Ola what happened to Will.

As he approached the Big House, before veering off to the kitchen, he scanned the grounds where the weight of Will's and Avida Maria's bodies had crushed the grass. Something goading Zach's vision prompted him to wander closer to the spot. It was Will's searching stick and the blood-smudged stone. The images conjured up anger so severe it blurred his vision and twisted his gut. He picked up the stick and coiled his fiery fingers around the gory rock. Heavy-heartedly, he headed to the kitchen. Ola's eyes twinkled at the sight of him coming from the lane. Her spoon stopped stirring the hocks and vegetables to shake the crumbs from her apron. She pushed hair up off her neck and broadened her smile.

Zach ambled in. He gruffed, "Got a rag?"

Noting his sour face, Ola ladled up cool water. "Have yaself a drink." She offered with one hand and a piece of kitchen cloth with the other. “What done brung ya up here so early in da day wid a scrunched face?”

Zach wrapped the rock and shoved it into his pocket. Mumbling, he said, “Got bad news.”

“Somebody’s done run and got caught?”

“No. It’s Will.”

“Will?”

Ola dropped the ladle that walloped her big toe. The sharp pain made her jump back and kick it aside.

“Whatcha mean, Will?” She said, stepping up to Zach.

After noticing the lad’s stick, she gazed more intently at Zach’s sweat-coated face accentuated with downcast eyes that peered deeper than usual into hers.

“He’s been hurt. Hurt real bad.”

Ola submerged the tail of her apron into a water bucket, rang it, and pushed it against Zach’s eyes with tears that nearly spewed over their bottom lids. With her other hand, fisted, she pounded her chest and moaned, “Our Will?”

“You gotta come. Be quick.”

Ola gestured to Táe with her bottom lip. “Tend dem fires. Shouldn’t be gone long.”

“Go on, Miss Ola. I mind dem pots ’til ya gits back.”

Ola snatched off her apron, hung it on a rusty wall nail, and followed Zach. From atop Onyx, he looped his arm around his wife lifting her off of her feet. She sat sideways in front of him.

“I think he might have gone on. When I collected him from the yard, he didn’t move, not an eyelash or eyelid. Never seen him so still . . .”

“Hush, Zach. Things might not be dat bad. Reverend Peters always say, ‘Pray,’ cause da Lord be listenin’.’”

At the cabin, with their feet back on the ground, the wailing on the other side of the door revealed a grim happening.

Ola grabbed Zach's arm. When the two entered and approached Will's bed, Clara leaped to her feet. Patting her chest, she wept, "Done all I could. But he done gone on. Be wid da Lord."

Ola stood pensive next to her husband, no longer the boy's protector. Choked up, in a difficult-to-manage voice, she peered at Will and said, "What devil cudda pack such meanness ta hurt our boy?" she asked of no one in particular.

Clara grasped Ola's hand. "It be da Madame."

Ola crouched next to Will's platform bed. She stroked his blood-caked brow and marveled at the sweetness of his young, innocent face.

"Why she do such a thang? He can't even be seein'. Never hurt a critter. What could'da cause dis?" Ola asked.

Clara put a comforting arm across her friend's shoulder. "Missus be upset 'cause he put his hands on huh gal to help huh when she fall. I's so sorry fa ya pain. I knows how ya be lovin' dat boy"

Ola sobbed, "Der be no evil in him dat 'llow him ta harm dat gal. Dey always be laughin', and talkin', and playin' der games dat make dem happy. Seem like dat gal didn't know he got no sight the way dey frolic and play."

The sound of crushing gravel interrupted the talk. Zach went to the door to see who was there.

"How you be, Amos?" Zach asked, going down the steps.

"Got Partner in da back. Dragged himself ta da barn. Don't know how he did. Been shot bad. Ain't sure he gonna live. Be doin' mighty poorly. Wouldn't even lap da water I be tyrin' ta give him. Cain't stay none. Massa say I gotta git da doc quick fa his gal. Say she hurt bad and . . ."

"Amos."

"Yah."

"Will's dead."

"What! Can't be. Jes seen dat boy. He was singing and tapping his stick. What done happened ta him? What be goin' on? Will be dead. Da dog been shot. Massa's gal hurt." Amos shook his head and leaned to stand.

"Stay put. I'll get Partner out of the wagon. You go ahead and get Doc. We'll talk more when you get back."

Soon as Zach pushed his hands beneath the mutt, he knew he had gone on not to leave Will behind. He placed the hound against the big tree in front of the cabin that he and Joe Jammer leaned on to laugh, talk, and build fires underneath its canopy to warm themselves during their nighttime chats.

After Amos returned from town and delivered the doctor to the Big House, he went back to the cabin where Zach greeted him. "I need you to take Clara back up to the Big House. She'll tell you about what happened to Will."

Clara supported her weight on the wagon wheel with one foot to boost herself up. The other was braced on the toe board. She clambered into the wagon box and plopped down on the seat next to Amos. Her eyes drooped when she looked back at Zach. "Ya take care now. I be back. Be prayin' fa ya."

The horse lunged as it headed up the carriage lane toward the Big House. Clara spoke over the clatter of wagon wheels into Amos's ear to recall the horror of the day.

"What's goin' on 'round here? Not long ago we bury Cass wid a chunk hacked out da his scull by da missus wid dat ax 'cause she say he tugged huh skirt dat was hung on a bramble. Now ya tell me, what buck got dat kinda nerve dey gonna touch a white woman's skirt in da bright daylight wid folks around? He'd be out da his mind ta even think of donin' such. And his grave still be soft."

Amos squeezed Clara's arm. "We gotta keep prayin', Clara, 'cause dat woman be a evil one. Ya step easy when ya git back at da house," Amos said and encouraged the ox to move on.

Zach pulled Ola to her feet, embraced her, and kissed the top of her head. "I don't want you to be away from the kitchen too long. That might give the missus a reason to put her spiteful hand on you. I'll bury Will and take care of Partner. Onyx will take you to the barn. Let Amos know to bring down the wheelbarrow. Then, keep on to the cookhouse."

Filled with anguish, Zach tugged Will's overall down his legs. The lad's lucky pebble was spit from the pockets and bounced across the smooth earthen floor. Zach retrieved it but didn't immediately drop it into the pocket of the fresh trousers Will would be dressed in for his journey to meet his new keeper. Instead, while holding the pebble, he peeled the tattered, blue plaid shirt away from the frail body. Rubbing the stone between his palms he heard Will's voice claim in his head: *MyZach, dis here shirt be feelin' mighty good on me.*

Zach put the sone in the pocket of the fresh pants as he ruminated about how he would start to prepare the body for burial. After a prolonged sigh, Will's MyZach bathed the motionless body. Unhurried and light-handedly, he made sure there were no signs of blood or dirt on it. The lad's feet were scrubbed twice so as not to leave a trail of dirty footprints when he trotted around heaven.

Zach towel-dried the small body with the softest rags of the lot. When done, he maneuvered the Will's thin, limp legs into the clean britches that he drew up to his waist. A yellow and blue calico shirt was buttoned on the boy and then tucked into them. With a freshly cut piece of hemp cord, he secure the shirt and pants. Afterward, he collected Will's coverlet from the platform bed and swaddled his body in it.

Zach opened the cabin door to check for Amos. The wheelbarrow was at the foot of the steps with a shovel, spade, and pick inside of it. He knew his friend had left them and rushed back to the barn not to be away from his station if he were sent for. Zach propped the cabin door open with a stray brick and then retrieved the corpse and walking stick.

Down on one knee, he elbowed the shovel aside and carefully positioned the body alongside the other digging tools. Over his shoulder, he peered at Partner. Filled with a deepened misery, he picked him up. His hind leg dangled from its torso as it was placed next to its young master.

Latched onto the wheelbarrow handles, Zach agonized as his steps moved him up the carriage lane, passing several cabins before he made his way between two of them. Paused on the hilltop, his eyes scanned the Negro burial grounds to determine where to dig Will's grave when a bright ray of sunshine lit a portion of grass beneath an oak tree. Sure it was God's cue, he guided the wheelbarrow down the bumpy face of the hill.

Tightening his grip on the handles, he reeled it to the center of the sunny spot where he started the arduous task at hand. Each scoop of dirt deepened his despair. He wept painful tears same as he did from his family separation and now for his God-given son. The disbelief of what had happened hung onto him as he labored with each shovel full of earth, one heavier than the next.

Grieved, Zach situated Will's lifeless body in the dark, damp hole with the boy's jacket pillow-rolled beneath his head and his feet north, ready to take him to God's Glory Land. A smile stretched across Zach's face when he positioned Partner next to Will, his head resting on the boy's shoulder. He knew his boy would never be alone again. The two souls melted beneath the earth tossed on them till the dirt formed a heap. Playing a rhythmic marching tune, the shovel firmly packed the dirt. Zach heaped heavy rocks on the grave to deter beasts tempted to unearth it.

With angry hands, he stabbed Will's searching stick into the ground and anchored it in place. He wished instead, it was piercing Madame's heart. Exhausted from the burden of sorrow, Zach genuflected next to the grave and prayed: *Will, you're going home too soon, but you got your best friend with you. And you'll be with your maker. There's going to be nothing but friendship and happiness surrounding you from now on. Partner will always be at your side. Ain't gonna be no more hunger, no more cold, no more mean hands to touch you. And no harm will come to ya and Partner again. Rest. It's gonna be all right. You're in the Lord's hands now.*

17

Stolen Dignity

Nearly half a year later, Zach knelt next to the rope bed. He nested his head on the sweat-wet pillow with Ola's. Grimacing, she snuggled her head against his, best she could. She pushed back hairs layering his ear. Her limp hand soft-stroked his cheek. "Listen ta me good. No matter what happens ta me . . . ," Ola shifted her eyes as she coughed and continued to say, "Ya know dat a Negro woman can be taken fa da wrong reasons."

"Your words trouble me. Shake me inside and out," Zach wept.

Ola coughed again. Wanting to hold tight to Zach, but couldn't. Clearing her throat instead, she said, "My heart'll always belong ta ya 'til der ain't a breath fa me ta be takin' in."

"What's put you in such a way? Your lips are moving, but your words are coming from a spirit that doesn't belong to you. They're too strange to decipher."

Zach cuddled Ola's hand to his cheek. He knew she was with child again but never expressed happiness about it. When he leaned to kiss her cheek she slipped from consciousness. Fearing she was dead, Zach rushed to get cold, wet rags that he dabbed on her forehead. Gradually she came to, moaning as she whimpered his name.

"Don't leave me, Ola. You're my life. The baby's coming and will need you. I will need you. Please! Please! I beg you, don't let death steal you from my arms. You're safe here. Joe Jammer always sees to what I want and what I need. He knows how I feel about you. He'll make things better for us. I know he will. Remember how he did before?"

"Life don't care none about dat."

Ola's involuntary contractions pushed the unborn forward. The baby's head crowned.

"It's coming, Ola. Don't give up. Hold on."

Her screams didn't ease the pain. The baby's tiny shoulders pushed, till they appeared behind the head. The rest of the body connected to its umbilical cord emerged, followed by the bloody afterbirth.

Amos was headed up the carriage lane on his way to the barn when he turned on his seat. The agony-filled voice that bellowed from Zach's cabin filled him with uneasiness. Without thought, he tugged the reins to turn the ox and cart toward Zach's cabin where he brought it to a halt. He leaped from the bench to rush up the steps and knock on the cabin door. After no answer, eased into its damp, dim-lit space.

The dense smell of sweat and lifeblood was more than a childbirth usually produced. Amos, hardly able to move, slowly eased, heavy-footed, closer to the bed. Ola lay in a tranquil state on blood-soaked bedding with lifeless eyes peering into space.

A tuft of blood-clotted blond hair that capped the crown of the baby's head made Zach scrutinize the bluish-gray body, barely larger than his hand, that lay between Ola's legs. He turned the flaccid body over on its back. A black, fuzzy, pencil-point-sized mole, below the earlobe on the left cheek, sprouted three hairs from it. Infuriated, Zach trapped the tiny thumb-size feet between his fingers. Lifting it from between Ola's legs, he let it dangle at his side with its afterbirth attached.

Startled by his actions, Amos sucked in a quick breath he couldn't manage and quickly back-stepped into a nervous stance. His eyes popped. Not knowing what to say, chewing his words, he asked, "She g-g-gonna be all right?

Zach's flesh tightened and tingled the same as it did when he was snatched from his family to be sold, and then watched them auctioned away. Now he was about to bury Ola because of a white man's punitiveness–another throbbing humiliation to bear in the face of life.

Amos peered into his buddy's taut stare as the friends stood flummoxed in heavy silence, each wishing with unspoken words that what they witnessed wasn't so.

Zach gulped to loosen the obstruction in his throat, but couldn't cough up words to express his embedded rage. In a deliberate manner, with anguished tears standing in his eyes, he said, "I say to myself, this cannot be, but it is." Those same eyes scoffed at the infant, created by a nefarious act.

"Zach, dat hate in ya face be scarin' me. Dem veins in ya neck be bulgin'. Ya eyes . . . dey be showin' da kinda meanness dat can take down a stonewall. Ya gotta take care. Des things happen. We be knowin' it. Jes cain't speak it."

"He took my Ola from me and my dreams of a happy future with her, supposedly, bringing forth a life that would have been a part of me. Me! I say me! "

"Let it be or it'll drag ya down to the pits of Hell ifin' ya don't."

"I'll pay any price I must to make sure Joe Jammer doesn't live a moment of peace till I do. My Ola won't breathe again. She's been taken from me and the baby we lived and planned for."

Zach toed the chamber pot from beneath the bed, kicked off the lid, and released his hold on the stillborn that sank into the depths of the waste. In a done stance, he pushed the pot aside with his foot, knelt by the bed, and meticulously brought the blood-stained bedding up around Ola's chin. He pondered her face, kissed her lips and eyelids, and unhurriedly pulled the coverlet over her head.

Crammed with hurt and sadness, he said, "I'll dig her grave under the weeping willow she loved. It's not far from Will's grave. We rested against its trunk on warm summer days and held onto each other as we fantasized about our hopes for the future. Ola and I planned what we were going to do and how we would love the baby. We'd call it Clarissa, after Ma, if it was a girl, and Jake, after my pa, if he were a boy."

"Ya put Ola in da cart. I'll take ya and da body down ta da tree and do dat diggin' fa ya."

"Don't want help. This'll be the last time we'll be together. Don't want to share those moments. I'll carry her in my arms, dig her grave, and dig it alone."

Amos came from the foot of the bed, positioned himself next to Zach. He compassionately laid a reassuring arm across his friend's shoulders. "I'll take care of this. No need fa ya to fret," he said and picked up the slop jar.

"Leave it be. Let it rot."

"If we don't take dat out of dis here cabin, dat baby'll swell and smell of death."

"Then dump it in the pig trough. Be done with it."

Zach balanced Ola in his arms. He took his time easy-stepping to the graveyard back of the slave quarters. Amos put the digging tools and the slop jar in the rear of the cart and followed his friend to the weeping willow tree. He got off the cart and placed the shovel at Zach's side. He lingered till his friend cried through his initial mourning.

When Zach started digging, Amos continued to the other side of the burial grounds, where a cluster of Atoz flowers captured his attention. He put the potty jar down near it. Spade in hand, he dug a grave about an arm's length across with the same deep. When he tilted the slop jar, the tiny corpse coated in bloody sickness and slime splashed in the bottom of the hole. Amos filled it with dirt; he packed it with slams from the spade, and then capped it with heavy stones. There was no marker or prayer. The unwanted baby was left to return to dirt.

Amos ambled back toward the mourner. He left a comfortable space between them as Zach continued to dig and curse in throaty words whose meanings were clearly understood.

"What's done is done, but my anger is too raw to lay eyes on Joe Jammer," Zach said and headed to the wagon.

Amos hollered after him, "I let Massa know 'bout Ola and da baby. I leave da ox and cart wid ya. I need ta walk and think. I come fa it later."

Amos knew Massa Joe wouldn't be pleased with such news and might not like the fact Amos brought it to him. Measuring his pace afforded him time to decide what to tell and what not to tell, sure Jammer knew he might have had a hand in the conception.

At the Big House, Amos raised his hand several times before he knocked on the yard door. When he finally did, he was glad Polly answered to let Jammer know he was there. He felt unprepared to answer questions Joe might quiz him on. While waiting, he nervously picked at a thready tear in the side of his britches. He was startled when Massa, larger than life, appeared at the door.

"What can I do for you, Amos?"

Backing down the yard doorsteps, he answered, "Sir, got bad news. Ola's birthin' didn't go well. She had a hard time. Huh and da baby both be dead. It be a boy. I done took care of him. Zach put Ola ta rest. She gonna be under dat willow outback of da quarters."

Without another word or question, Jammer turned and left. He seemed to be headed toward his office but stopped. With an afterthought, he said over his shoulder, "I'll record the deaths."

Jammer penned the date and time of Ola's demise in the ledger, along with the baby boy, but didn't give him a name. A churning and shamefulness knotted his gut. He surmised the baby might be his doings. "These things do happen," he said to the void in the room, justifying his lewd behavior.

Back at the cabin, Amos tapped on the door and let himself in. Zach was cleaning up the blood and rolling the soiled beddings into a bundle to bury or burn.

"Massa say he gonna record da deaths."

"Let's go. Got to get my mind off some things," Zach said.

He rode in the cart with Amos to the fields where the hands tended to the corn. He stood in the back of it and waited for them to assess the depth of his pain

Zach took in a deep, tear-filled breath and mumbled, "Got something to say. My Ola died only minutes ago. I buried her under our wishing tree. My heart's sickened with fear and loneliness. Got a tightening in my chest that's challenging my breathing and my speaking. I can't say more right now."

Zach, back on the bench with Amos who tugged the reins of the ox, prompted it to trot toward the barn. The field hands followed, marching foot to foot. With each step, they sang in a low mourning tone:

Ooooh
Nobody knows the trouble I've seen

Nobody knows my sorrow
Nobody knows the trouble I've seen
Glory hallelujah

Sometimes I'm up
Sometimes I'm down
Oh, yes, Lord
Sometimes I'm almost to the groun'
Oh, yes, Lord

Ooooh
Nobody knows the trouble I've seen
Nobody knows my sorrow
Nobody knows the trouble I've seen
Glory hallelujah . . .

Jammer took his family to town to shop for household needs and fabric for Francine and Avida Maria's dresses to meet the fashion demands of upcoming events. Clara decided to take advantage of the opportunity to visit with the hands down at the quarters. Because the weather was warm, she knew they were gathered to enjoy lunch and laughter–something impossible when the Jammers were on the property.

Once the carriage pulled away with the family inside, Clara sprinted the full distance from the Big House to the quarters. A robust smile consumed her face. "How ya be doin' today?" she asked of the gang and took a seat among her comrades.

Amos' jolly voice said, "We be good 'cause da massa be away. Got time ta rest. Time ta sing. And time ta dance. Can even gripe ifin we want ta and not worry 'bout no ears."

"How things be up at da Big House?" Amos asked.

Clara's face saddened as she told about the going ons with the Jammers. She lowered her eyelids and said, "Things not good. After all dis time, da little missus. Well, she still be plenty upset 'bout Will's and Partner's death and be scrammin' dat dey hurt Ola, kill Will and Partner. Most like it was yestaday. She done stop wetting huh bed and tearing up da linens and coverlets. Good thing 'cause I done 'bout run out of sewin' thread tryin' ta keep dem mended. But most evenings I be cleanin' up huh food off da floor dat she done throwed down. She don't talk much ta huh ma and pa. She be settin' in da corner of da parlor, facin' da cornor most all day, playin' wid huh dolls and huh tea set. Talks to dem 'bout huh hurts. Den she lock haself in huh bedroom. One day, she cut huh self on da hand and smeared da blood on huh ma's face.

"It be only da Lord dat knows what gonna become of dat family. Dey all be tore apart. Be spattin' all durin' da day. At night, too. Dar ain't no peace in dat house. I's glad dey gone even if it be part of da day."

"We be so, too," Amos said,. They all had a laugh.

With a stern eye, Clara said, "It gonna take the Lard, all da saints and all dem angels to hep dem folks."

Feeling free, without eyes on them, everybody got on their feet in a fit of celebration. They juba danced back and forth across the yard as they sang praises to the Lord. The women swayed their hips and flipped their skirt tails as they spun in circles. Backs arched, the men high kicked as they crooned, asking the saints to shield them and their families from punitive hands. Everybody begged for protection against the evils that couldn't be seen but lurked about, except Zach. He sat alone, whittled, and watched the hands frolic about.

18

Revenge

Enveloped in a dreary calmness, gripping the neck of a burlap sack, Zach reflected over the farm's layout and the sunset-brushed structures that glowed a golden-purple hue. He mused at the lush green corn and hemp coming up strong and predicted to be record cash crops with great profits at harvest time.

When daylight evaporated, constellations lit the skies in its stead. Awed by the transition, Zach came off the porch, descending under the brilliance of the moonlight. He defiantly placed one foot at a time down. With Onyx attached to the pulling bar of the ox cart, he clambered up to the bench, placed a burlap sack on the bench next to his hip, and slapped Onyx on the rear with the reins, encouraging him to move on. After entering the Negro graveyard, Zach took his time, dismounting with the burlap sack in hand He visited Ola's and Will's resting places. He laid a flower on her grave and visited a while before he moved on to place a bone on Will's for Partner. He spent a significant amount of time at Cass's grave to say goodbye and prayed he'd help with his endeavor.

Back on the cart bench, Zach drove it, till it was in front of the double doors of the barn that stood open. He unloaded a hefty bundle from the floorboard and stretched it out just inside the barn. He collected kerosene cans stored in a back stall and loaded them into the cart. Outside, around back, Zach drizzled a thread of fuel from the first can across the baseboard. More significant threads were looped around the other structures and each cluster of crop. Afterward, the cabin was doused with a hefty dose of the remaining paraffin. Satisfied, he returned to the barn where the empty cans were positioned in their original spots and the wagon was maneuvered back into its usual place.

Atop Onyx, in a near trance, Zach trotted back down the carriage lane to the turnpike. Once at a safe distance, on the other side of the road, not far from where he and Ola entered the burning bushes to spend hours together, he tied a fist full of kindling to a stick that he lit and tossed across the road. A thread of flame snaked its way to the cabin, exploded into sky-reaching flames, and then zigzagged up the carriage lane till it forked, following one tine to each outstructure, while the other looped the fields. The blazes thrashed everything flammable as they rumbled and tumbled along. Zach knew the locals would gossip about the devastation. He envisioned newspaper headlines that might read: *The Jammer Conflagration Sets a Record.* He moved on, putting his life with Jammer behind him.

The strong smells of burning grass, animal meat, and wood roused Amos from his sleep. He tripped over his feet as he scampered out of bed. On his hands and knees, he searched in the dark for his work boots and pulled them on over his bare feet. As he exited his cabin, choked by smoke, he raced up the carriage lane to the Big House, shouting, “Fire! Fire!” and banged on the yard door till his fist ached, and his voice couldn’t bellow another smoke-laden word.

Master Joe and Madame, with Avida Maria, who refused to let her father pickup her up, was at his side. They all staggered as they came out the portico door. Their jaws dropped as they grappled with what they saw. Jammer struggled to calculate the damages of the fire.

Feeling disoriented, Amos left Joe and his family to their disbelief and scurried back to the quarters where his family and the other hands were in a state of fright as they moaned and spun about the yard. Disbelieving mothers wept as they cradled crying babies. Some hands collapsed from smoke inhalation.

Jammer lamented at his amassed wealth being diminished to ash and cinders. He stumbled barefoot down the portico steps.

Choked on the smoke, he yammered, "What's happened? How . . . ?"

Forced back by the heat of the flames, he marveled at the blazes' breadths. So broad, field hands couldn't douse enough water on the fire to make a difference. Nonetheless, the intense glow seen from town brought firefighters with their water-weighted lorry to the property, but they, too, could do little to temper the blazes.

Rufus, the fire chief, took time before saying, "Mr. Jammer, this is a big one. Biggest firestorm I ever seen in des parts. From my experiences, I'd say, I don't think dis here fire's gonna leave much behind, if anything at all."

It was noon the next day before Jammer and Amos were able to get close enough to view what was left of the barn to explore its damage. They stepped over what was, without a doubt, Zach's charred body. Both men recognized the waistcoat and belt buckle with the clasping hands that Jammer had gifted to Zach. Unnerved by what he saw, Joe became perplexed. Nauseated, he vomited and reeled at the sight of what was once his brother, confidant, friend, and partner in life and wealth-building.

Sobbing, he cried out, "How will I live without Zach? He made me what I am. Without him, I can't go on. Don't want ta go on. My life's ended."

"Massa, he be knowin' ya care about him. He be tryin' ta save ya barn. I take him on down ta da graveyard and bury him next ta his Ola."

Fraught with dolefulness and guilt, Joe lumbered back to the house while Amos carted Zach's body to the Negro cemetery where he spotted an empty grave. Sure it was Cass's, he went straight to it and meticulously laid the corpse at his feet. When he did, the hat tumbled off, exposing a hole in its skull. He smiled, stomped his foot, and slapped his thigh. "Hallelujah!" he shouted, and eased the dug-up body back into its resting place. Down on his knees, clasping his hands, Amos sent up an apologetic prayer: *Lord, I be knowin' ya understand. Don't be angry wid Zach fa diggin' up dis here body. Amen."* Amos peered down on his friend's carcass: *"Mr. Zach be sorry fa rootin' ya up, but he be needin' ya help and he be knowin' ya be wantin' ta givin' it. Rest in peace now. Ya ain't gonna be bothered no mo.*

Using his hands, Amos scooped most of the dirt back into the grave with the intent of returning with a shovel, if it wasn't destroyed in the fire. He hurried back to the Big House to report the burial and his observations around the farm. He called for Jammer from the yard door and was answered with a sickly, drunken voice, "Come in."

Amos sauntered, at a tortoise pace, down the hall to the office and hesitated at the door before he knocked on it. Flagged in with a weak gesture, Amos entered the office that reeked of dense-whiskey smoke. Jammer offered an invitation for Amos to sit, but he remained on his feet, not moving closer to the desk than necessary.

"Massa, I jes be wantin' ya ta know I done buried Mr. Zach and from what I be seein', things don't be good around da farm."

Joe nodded for him to continue his telling.

"Da kitchen, carriage house, corn crib, smokehouse, spring house, wash house, loom house, and da icehouse, dey be gone. Dem rope walks and dat hemp be gone, too. Ain't nothin' left standin' but ya Big House and da quarters. Even Mr. Zach's cabin be gone."

"And the animals?"

"What ain't dead from the smoke, be burnt badly or done run off."

Jammer followed Amos out the yard door. Amos went on back to the quarters and Jammer sat on the steps with his elbows on his knees and his palms bolstering his head. "I'm where I was the day Pappy died," he slurred,

Drenched in heavy silt and weak from a painfully empty gut, Zach clawed his way along the riverbank, not stopping till daylight to hide. It was the third morning when he moved into a thicket where a bur oak tree, full of acorns, protruded from a hillside, leaning northward with a canopy large enough to cover a hundred good-sized bucks. Zach rooted between it and the slant of the hillside.

Curious about what was above his head, he clambered up the slope to explore. The jabber of passersby made him duck. He drew his head back and raised it just enough to peek as best he could and quickly pulled it back. Cackling schoolboys walked along a narrow dirt road. He knew he wouldn't be able to travel on it, even though he had hoped he could for a faster footing come nightfall.

When the footslogging stopped, Zach heard one lad ask another, "Did you hear something?"

"Yeah. Sounded like twigs breaking," he said.

"But what made them break?" another asked.

"Over there by that big bush standing alone," his mate laughed with a stiff arm and pointed finger. "It's a wild turkey," he said. The boys snickered, joked about it being fat and good enough to eat if they had time to catch it, but couldn't and hurried, probably, not to be late for school.

Once the stepping sounds bled into the distance, Zach scooted soundlessly from behind the tree. He lowered his feet to the ground with an eye on the turkey and another on the sky. He squatted behind tall grass and gradually extended his arm with an open hand. He made a low gurgling hen call taught to him by Jake. In his head, he heard his pa' words. *Don't move 'til ya ready ta catch dat bird. Can take some time, but dey come ta ya. Jes ya be quiet and be still.*

Sure enough, when the turkey nearly stepped in Zach's hand, he clinched the fowl's legs and snapped its neck in the same moment. Startled by the speed and strength of his hands, his fingers sprang open. Bouncing erratically and flipping and flopping, the bird's wings swept up debris till it laid motionless. Zach dragged the bird to the tree, sitting with his back rested against it, he checked the game for disease.

Because the tom turkey would be troublesome to haul, he peeled and diced it into walnut-sized chunks with a hunting knife pulled from his waistband. Zach fashioned a small cooking fire heaped with dry twigs and Y sticks on each side of it. He skewered the turkey pieces on a sharpened twig that he gradually rotated over the hot flame while thanking the Lord for the tree's canopy that camouflaged the smoke.

After eating, Zach squirreled the remainder of the meat into his tote, anchored himself again behind the tree, and waited for night to come. Exhausted but well-fed, he settled into an uneasy slumber invaded by running feet that seeped from the thicket and came to rest six feet from him. In seconds, five darkies stood in his vision, gawking at him as he leaped to the ground.

A tall, lean, ebony buck about twenty-five years of age reached out and rocked Zach's shoulder with a glad-to-see-you hand and friendly inflection of, "Where ya be from? And, where ya be goin'to?"

"Tennessee. On my way to St. Louis."

"Dey call me Guy. What ya called?"

"Zach. But my given name is Toby."

"Den, we be sayin', Toby. And ya call yaself dat from now on. Ya got no mo need for dat white man's name.

"We's comin' from Virgini. Goin' on ta St. Loui. Be wantin' fa work. Done been told dey got plenty fa us folks. Say, even dem free Coloureds got work fa us." Scrunching his face, Guy tilted his hat-covered head, searched Toby's eyes, and asked, "Ya got folks der. Or, ya be searchin' fa work?"

Toby took a moment to recollect before he said, "Searching for my twin sisters. I hope to find them there. Some years ago, the day we were auctioned apart, I heard a fellow say they were taken to St. Louis by a businessman."

"Ya be educated. Can tell by da way ya be talkin' and usin' dem fancy words. Ifin ya don't be knowin' da way, come along wid us. Seem like I be smellin' meat cookin' 'fore we come on ta ya."

"Caught me a wild tom. Charred him good. Got some I can share."

With a happy sigh, Guy said, "Be pleased ta be havin' some. We heard voices and movement comin' down from da road. Decided it be best ta hide a spell and wait for night. Dat's when we turn under dis here tree."

Toby gave each a fist full of turkey chunks that they enjoyed. Come night, the group was on their way again. Toby's weary body forged along behind them as they moved at a grueling pace.

Guy glanced over his shoulder at the gang. "Daylight's comin' up fast. Gotta find us a hidin' place," he said staring at the horizon. "Dat sun ain't up yet, but it be gittin' der soon. Can see a sliver of dem sunrise colors. Best we be gittin' out of sight. Folks start stirrin'. When darkness comes back and dem stars show dat dipper, we be movin' again." Worry-faced, Guy said, "Sky be clear. Night should be, too."

"You seem concerned. Expect trouble?" asked Toby.

"Jes thinkin' 'bout dem folks dat don't take kindly ta us Coloureds. Dey show up when ya don't be wantin' dem ta." Smacking his hat and putting it back on his head, he said, "Got ta keep da good eye watchin' fa dem."

"How much farther is St. Louis?" Toby asked.

"Based on what I done been told, three, maybe mo, weeks. Cain't rightly say yet. Ain't seen da sign yet dat let ya know ya movin' in da right direction. Or be on da right path. But whichever day we gits der, we don't want ta be gittin' near before dem city lights come up. Be too many white folks still roamin' dem streets."

Come night the freedom seekers were back on the trail guided by the light of the moon. Guy grabbed one of the darkie's. Pointing, he jabbered, "Over der wid da moon at his back. Dat horse been followin' us fa better den two days now."

"It be most like a shadow." Straining to see the silhouette better, he said, "Damn! I believe it be such. Shadows don't be movin' like dat."

Peering intently, Toby monitored the vision to determine its structure. Sure enough, it was a horse but was it the one he thought it might be or hoped it was. The horse's gait was too familiar to him. He whistled; the animal raised its snoot and neighed. Shocked and delighted, he whistled again. The horse galloped his way.

Toby's voice resounded with elation. "My God, it's Onyx! He followed me. But how could he have? I was not able to cross the river with him and was forced to leave him on the bank."

He locked his arms around Onyx's neck. A flood of tears washed over his thick matted mane. Toby's brain was inundated with thoughts and ideas about how his horse made it to this point. He gripped the unfamiliar bridle and led it along.

The day he ran, they could only go as far as the Ohio River. Onyx must have been put on a skiff, swam, or was taken to the west bank and set free. But who, Toby wondered, could have done so. Perhaps he was trailed when they left the farm. Too overwhelmed with hurt and running when he was parted from Onyx, he didn't think to note possible followers. Now he pondered about the spirit behind what might have been.

"Go ahead, ride him. Go on up ahead. See if der be a hidin' place fa us to use come daylight," Guy said.

In a good distance, with the brightness of the moonlight, Toby eyed what seemed to be a tight cluster of fallen trees with adequate space between them and a hollow in the hillside deep enough to conceal five darkies, the horse, and himself. He turned Onyx around and headed back toward the group.

"I'll take you one at a time to the hideout. The others can continue to hike along. By the time everyone is transported to the new spot it will be full daylight and we can rest there and wait for nighttime."

Once settled into the new hideout, Toby took out the rest of the turkey chunks, sorted them among the gang, and suggested, "Divide them into three portions. Munch bits at a time to temper your guts. It's gotta last three more days. That'll give time to set traps and hopefully catch a few critters."

Fed and feeling some contentment, the group knew they'd need more to eat and laced twigs into small cages, disguised them with leaves, and sat quietly in their thoughts. Some slipped into a state of slumber.

The croaking and squealing sounds roused everyone. Saggy-eyed, they retrieved the camouflaged traps and smoked the frogs, turtles, a rabbit, and a squirrel over a washbasin-sized flame. The catches were divided equally among the six of them while still hot.

"It's not much, but it'll spare the turkey. Git yaselves some rest. Be some hours 'fore we can run," Guy said.

As soon as the first star glittered, the group was on its feet and moving westward toward St. Louis. Toby again rode ahead to scout the area, only this time, he returned with a bright yellow rag that was doubly knotted on a low branch to secure it in place. He waved it above his head.

"Do you think this means what I think it does?" he asked the group.

In unison, their voices gleefully sang out, "Dat be da sign."

"Means we be on da trail ta St. Loui. Won't be long now," Guy said.

Toby walked along with the group to give Onyx, who wasn't trotting at his usual 4/4 rhythm, a rest. When daybreak came and they stopped to hide and relax, Toby rubbed his horse's legs with cool, wet grass cuttings to soothe them. To not stress the animal, he didn't bother mounting it and went alone to explore possible encounters up ahead. A twinge of guilt twisted Toby's gut when he left Onyx behind with the other freedom seekers, still sleeping, to venture alone, on foot, to scout what was up ahead.

Toby trekked for better than a day before he came across another clue tied to a bush that his anxious fingers fiddled to untie. The knotted piece of filthy cotton fell loose in his hand.

It was nearly dark when he arrived back at the camp where the group prepared for the next leg of their march. The five bucks gathered around Toby to learn what was ahead of them.

"The walk ahead of us is going to be a challenge. I don't think trackers and their hound dogs will be on our heels. What appeared to be a trail is badly overgrown. The shrubs and vegetation are dense and tight. I got caught up in a bramble along the way. That's going to slow our pace, but keep us safe. However, it'll make trotting difficult for Onyx. I probably won't be able to ride him for a good amount of the remaining distance. But the good news is, I came across another piece of rag. I feel it will be the last. When I reached the bush it was tied to, I saw what I think were city lights in the far distance, blurred by the early morning fog. They seemed to be a several-day walk away from where I discovered this rag. We'll know better when the fog lifts."

As the gang moved on, Toby returned the pieces of raggedy cloth to their original post to help guide any freedom seekers who might follow after them. A sigh of relief was heard from each soul as the trail widened and opened to a clearing. However, the trees and vegetation prevented any significant depth of vision.

Toby and Guy sat together to discuss how to forge ahead. Both noted that the trail had widened, but what appeared beyond it was a mystery.

"I'm sure hoping I can sit and rest a spell, eat, and catch a breath. And, give Onyx time to graze when I get there," Toby said as the two canvassed the sky to calculate when to move on.

19

St. Louis Search

It was a blistering July day and too early to enter town. Gathered on the outskirts of St. Louis, the darkies contemplate their next moves. From the position of the sun, it was nearly 9:00 p.m. They held back and waited for the oil lamps to light the streets. They never exchanged names, except for Toby and Guy. After everyone expressed adieus, they scattered in different directions.

Toby and Onyx walked a considerable distance before his nose detected stable smells and a blacksmith's hammering that drew him toward a barn down the road a piece and around a corner. Feeling rescued from a pending disaster, he poked his head inside, glad when he saw several Negroes moving about, too busy to notice him. Onyx needed substantial equestrian care so he called to them. "Pss, pss." After no response, Toby hissed a bit louder. "Psss, psss." Still no answer.

He ultimately pushed the door open and stepped inside, leading Onyx. A dark-skinned, pudgy man slightly balding with graying sideburns greeted him in a soothing voice.

"Don't believe I've seen ya around these parts before, young man. You and that horse of yours are mighty beat up. What can I do for ya?"

"Got to town about an hour ago. Come from Tennessee."

"Ya runnin'?"

"Am. From there to there, in search of my identical twin sisters."

"They shouldn't be too hard to find. Aren't many look-alikes around town, especially identical ones."

"I need my horse taken care of: fed, shoed, and groomed. Don't mind working for the service and a little food if you need help."

"What can you do?"

"I'm learned. Can read, write, and figure as good as any white man. And know about farming."

"Dat so?"

"It's so." Toby, hankering for a good dose of rest and sleep, shyly asked, "Mind if I sit?"

"Go 'head. Rest yaself on that bale of hay over there," he said, thumbing at it. "You mighty scratched up. Like ya been fightin' with a bear."

"It was the trail. Parts of it were overgrown with brambles and prickly weeds."

"Well, I'm Ezra. Dis here is my barn and your lucky day. When you're rested, Lee, my blacksmith and helper, will take you to the house where you can clean up. Frida, my wife, will help you take care of those cuts. She'll fix ya a plate of grub, get you some clean clothes, and settle you in. Ian, here, is my groomer and stableboy. He'll tend to ya horse."

Lunchtime the next day, Ezra seated himself in front of Toby at the kitchen table, gave him a once over, and said, "You seem a heap better. Your horse is outside. Had himself a hefty bucket of oats along with a wash down followed by a good salve rubbing. He's got a new set of horseshoes, but his hoof walls are cracked and the soles and frogs got a good amount of damage. He'll be back to his fit self, but you'll have to take it easy with him for the next few months."

Reaching into his pocket, Ezra drew out a thready bit of rag. He handed it to Toby. "Ian found this braided in his mane. Thought it might mean something," he said, and laid the snippet on the table.

Toby snatched it for a closer exam. Surprised at what he held in his hand. He glanced at Ezra. Choking back tears, he mumbled, "This is the answer to so many questions that have taunted me since I ran. This is a cut from the shirt my friend Amos frequently wore. It's letting me know he helped Onyx somehow cross the waters, enabling him to find my trail and reunite with me out there in the hinterlands."

"Dat's quite a story."

"I got money to pay for your services."

"Keep your money. You gonna be needin' it. But I got a plot of land on the skirt of town where I planted a crop that's not fairing. I was gonna harvest it, but it's got a strange look to it. Know about wheat?"

"I do."

"Well, let's get movin'."

Ezra hugged Frida. "Won't be gone long," he said and the two men headed straight to the fields.

Ezra remained still as Toby surveyed the crop. In a short time, he was quiet and contemplated some before he said, "Mr.

Ezra . . ." he paused and shifted his weight. "You got yourself a problem."

Toby moved closer to him to express his concerns and was quickly repelled by a glare that implied an invasion of Ezra's personal space.

Ezra drew his head back and gruffed, "Problem? You clearly stated you could help me. Could even work for your food and stable services. Done took care of you and dat horse. Now you seem to be saying you can't take care of my wheat."

"Sir, I know my farming, and it seems you don't."

Ezra's eyebrows arched a bit higher. He had never been spoken to so pointedly by a young buck.

"Well then, tell me, what do ya think?"

Leading the owner into the wheat field, Toby flung his arms, palms up, and said, "That's a bad crop. The fishy smell and chalky white appearance of the stalks are a concern, as well as the leaves speckled with orangish-brown rust spots."

Toby gathered a handful of grain heads and squeezed the kernels that easily broke apart and puffed out a blackish powder. "This indicates trouble, too. It won't be possible to bring this crop back even though it's near harvest time. Your only recourse is to burn it out, prepare the soil for a new crop, and seed it in the fall. That gives you a couple of months to ready it."

"Burn? All of it?"

"It's best that you do, or the disease will continue to spread and nothing will be gained."

"When will I have another cash crop?"

"It'll be the summer of next year."

The day Toby torched the wheat field, he mused how it was the third time he watched a crop go up in flames. First, it was the young hooligans that burned down Jammer's first corn crop.

Then it was the fire set to Jammer's wealth-building crops, and now Ezra's wheat.

They cleared the land with the help of a few hands hired to work alongside the two of them. It took some time, but eventually, the field was plowed and fertilized.

Toby and Ezra worked extended hours, right through the summer months that finally cooled off, allowing fall to raise its head. Each evening after dinner, with time to spare, Toby walked the streets in search of indications that the twins might be in St. Louis.

One evening, at the kitchen table with Ezra and Frida, Toby revealed a plan to till and fertilize the land once more before sowing the seeds. He told them, "The soil is ready and the day is near. If you want a good summer crop come next year, the seeds must be in by October, no later. We'll need additional hands again. And this time, at least two mules with plows."

Ezra filled the requisition. Lee and Ian kept the barn open and operating while he was in the field with Toby. Together, with the help, they took turns behind the plow. The group toiled days preparing the soil. By mid-September, the seeds were in and Toby was back, patrolling the neighborhoods. He walked the streets at night till his legs were weary, and the cold evenings forced him inside where he read, scribed for the other Negroes, and did odd jobs around the barn–even sorted nails that made him reminisce about Will.

Slumped against the wall, exhausted and feeling defeated, he squeezed the wad of fabric snippets in his pocket and called to Clarissa.

Ma, if you hear me, life has depleted me. Everything I lived for and cared about has been taken from me. I hold onto you in my heart as I caress your garment piece, luckily ripped from your skirt. Along with it, I weep into the thready, thumb-sized piece from Ola's skirt, too small to hold my tears for her. Ma, she was my wife and my life. You would have loved her as much as I did. She's gone from me. I pine so deeply for her, I cain't find words to tell you how much. Ma, it doesn't stop there. Onyx, my horse and companion, had to be left behind when I ran, but we've been reunited. My dear friend, Amos, got him across the river with a bit of his shirt knotted in his mane, which I still have.

If you're living, Ma, I'm in St. Louis searching for the twins. I feel I'm gonna find them. Then we'll find you and the others. I don't want bits of clothing. I want you, Ola, my family, and my friends. I had a boy, too. He wasn't mine by birth, but I loved him as so. His name was Will. His dog was Partner. Hug them if you're in heaven and see them. Let your spirit watch over me. I'm tired of hurt. Real tired, Ma.

It took weeks before the weather warmed enough for Toby to plot his return to the neighborhood. When he did, he trekked streets to street, executing his search.

One evening, postured under a tree on Perry Street to rest, he struggled to determine if the time had come for him to leave town and move on. That's when he glanced at a big house not far down the road from where he hid. A carriage pulled in front of it that gave him pause when a woman and two young ladies bounded from it and hurried up the steps to where a door sprang open for them.

Several sundowns later, Toby returned at nightide to the same spot and again witnessed a carriage slow to a stop in front of the same house. This time a gentleman with three ladies stepped down from it. Two of them, tucked inside black hooded capes, could be twins, but their faces couldn't properly be seen. However, they walked and swayed the same, even stepped as one. The two bustled up the walkway and ascended the stairs to an oversized door they disappeared behind. A plump darkie, dressed in gray Negro cloth, could be seen pulling the drapes closed in an upstairs window.

Toby flinched when a carriage up the road moved in his direction. He fixed himself between clustered bushes and a red maple tree to not be seen. After it passed him, Toby hurried around the corner to where a small cargo wagon always parked. He cozied up to it to guard against the chill of a swirling wind. After drawing his hat down over his ears, he tugged his coat tighter and stuffed his hands inside the pockets, intending to return to his post, but the weather grew more dismal, forcing him back to the barn.

At dawn the following evening, although emotionally depleted, Toby was allured back to Perry Street. He easy-walked along the avenue to his viewing point. The wagon usually parked nearby wasn't at its customary place. The carriage approaching the house, that stopped at its entrance, evoked a restlessness in Toby.

The plump hand of the servant seen in the upstairs window opened its door. The mature, well-dressed gentleman in a top hat who stepped down from it was followed by a woman. The carriage door that closed behind them caused Toby's head to swirl. When he gandered once more, two young ladies clambered out, and the house door opened a second time. The same hand collected their bundles.

Toby saw no more of the girls than he had at other times when they bounded from the coach. Bewildered, he turned and walked in the direction he came from, till the crackling of slow-turning buggy wheels caused him to fall back into the shadows. When the sound was closer, he saw it was driven by a darkie and called out to him with a whispering voice.

"Sir."

"Ay. Someone der?"

Toby rushed forward. "Please, sir."

"What ya doin' out here in dis nighttime. Wantin' ta git yaself caught and whoop ta near death? Folks 'round here don't take kindly to darkies out at night."

"I came to town in search of my twin sisters. I know they were brought here after they were auctioned from the block in Louisville, Kentucky. Better than ten years ago. At that time, they were near four years old."

With an arm stretched and a finger pointed straight ahead, the darkie told him, "Go on down three corners. Be der when I turn it. Git, now."

Not needing further prompting, Toby hurried but not too fast and stood back in the darkness at the assigned corner.

"Ya der?" the coachman asked.

Toby stepped into the road. Another step put him closer to the buggy.

"Whatcha ya say ya be needin', boy?"

"Trying to find twin girls that are identical. Pretty and quick. At least the last time I saw them. The young ladies I see coming and going from the big house back there might be my sisters. If so, I've come for them."

"What names dey got?"

"Mary and Molly."

Not saying more, the driver's head jerked. Without obvious prompting, he announced, "Gotta go. Be here at dis corner da same time tamorrow."

Not two minutes later a horse-drawn carriage rolled into the same spot.

"Boy," a white man's voice exploded with a frightful tone, before he said, "Whatcha doin' out here dis time of night? Does your master know where you are?"

Toby, frozen in place, couldn't speak. Couldn't move.

"Mackabee, let dat boy be. We got business ta take care of. If he wasn't supposed to be out here, he'd be runnin' scared and we'd be right on his hide with a whip and a pistol. Let's move on."

Toby was at the corner three more nights before the buggy returned and slow-rolled to a halt in front of him.

"Hey der, boy." A voice sang like it came up out of the fields back in Tennessee.

"I'm here." Toby eased out of the shadows. "I didn't think you were coming back."

"Massa sent me ta fetch packages two towns over. But I got news fa ya. Ya might not hav'ta go no further. It seems dem gals ya lookin' fa be right der in dat big house on dis here Perry Street. Least dey be twins. Be fittin' da description ya give 'bout dem bein' pretty and all. Folk 'round here be knowin' 'bout dem. Say dey be fancy raised by der missus. Dat be all I got ta tell ya."

20

Determination

It was a month later when Mary and Molly came out of the house unescorted, strolling down Perry Street toward Toby's nook. They're mere visions, he thought, till they stopped barely two feet from him. Not looking in his direction, they called, "Sir, don't come out. We'll speak to you from here. We're being watched. Word came you wanted to speak with us."

"Yes. You might be my sisters. If so, I have come to take you back to Kentucky with me to find our mother and the rest of our family."

"How will we know you are our brother?"

"Can I follow you to where you might be going?"

When a wagon pulled along the side of the road leading up to a neighboring house; it, along with the trees, blocked the view of anyone who might glance in their direction from the upstairs windows.

The twins checked over their shoulders to note possible followers before they continued toward the corner, past the streetlamp. They called to Toby, "Follow us," they said.

Squat-walking, Toby came out of hiding with presentation words he had hoarded in his head for many years. Crouched at the hems of the girls' skirts, he muttered, "If you're indeed my sisters, you were four years old when put on the auction block after me. On that day, I heard from a distance that the gentleman who purchased you was a businessman from St. Louis. As soon as I could free myself, I come for ya. I don't know where Ma; our baby brother, George Henry; or Jake, our pa were taken to. I only know what I heard at the auction."

Toby pulled the indigo-blue remnant from his pocket. "This is all I have from that day."

"We've gotta go. Be here tomorrow at this same time."

The twins fled like spooked hens before Toby could establish a relationship with them. He brooded, *what if I don't see them again*?

Back at the barn, weary and confused about his experience with the girls he hoped were his sisters, he sat in a corner with his head bowed in prayer. He pleaded with the Lord for the outcome to be what he desired.

The next evening when Toby was on his way to meet his possible sisters, a sudden blast of thunder and a pelting hail storm bombarded the area. So harsh, he was forced to return to the barn.

Well into the next day, the storm subsided and left the sky a sunny blue and the air cool and crisp. Ezra was elated that his part of town survived the harsh weather. Because the farm's topsoil remained in place, he'd be able to reap the cash crop he dreamed of come next summer.

Toby was back on Perry Street that evening where he was certain he had seen the silhouettes of the twins in a third-floor window. He moved on, not stopping till he was camouflaged between the hedges and his hideaway tree.

Later, the girls appeared on the sidewalk, strolling in his direction. As before, they continued to the corner, not stopping till the same wagon as before pulled up at the nearby house. Toby trailed behind them at a distance. Without making a sound, he stayed in the shadows of the trees close to the fencing.

"Sir, if you're there, we have something to show you."

Toby eased forward with his eyes on the girls, whose faces he still could not see.

Gazing up ahead, they said, "We're pleased you survived the horrid weather and weren't harmed by it. We want to let you know, Tipper, the darkie who took care of us when we were first brought to this house, kept these hidden for us." They extended their hands that held remnants matching his. "She said these were inside our bloomers. On our thirteenth birthday, she gave them to us. She said she felt they might mean something. Told us to keep them hidden, and we'd know when to bring them out."

"I pray you, same as me, want to find Ma and the rest of the family."

"Oh, yes, we do. But, serious eyes are kept on us. Walking out a few minutes in the evening is the only time we're alone, but only long enough to walk a couple of blocks and back. We gotta go."

"Come back in five days. I'll have a plan," he told the girls.

"That's Sunday. It will be late when we return, and we won't be permitted to leave the house."

They were gone without another word. "I'll come the following day," Toby said, wondering if they heard him.

The day he was to return to Perry Street, it was misting, and before he knew it another catastrophic storm system, more severe than the first, pelted the area. The sudden gust of deafening winds and rush of rain forced Toby and Ezra out of the wheat field, running to a work shed to escape winds so severe they ripped off doors and roofs, overturned wagons, and flooded fields and the city streets.

While waiting for the turmoil to subside, Toby crouched in a corner with his back to Ezra, deflecting conversation that might be encouraged. Toby had something to say to him but didn't want to speak till he was confident the words transitioning through his thoughts would convey what he wanted them to when they came out of his mouth.

Ezra shook his head in disbelief. "Never seen such weather like dis 'round des parts before. One storm, then another. I pray something's left standing when it leaves," he said.

The system finally quieted enough for Toby to say what consumed his core. He turned to Ezra, deeply sighed and then said, "Been pondering awhile. Got something serious to say."

"Go 'head, boy. Say what's on your mind."

"The wheat's come up strong and hearty. You'll be able to harvest it by early spring. My help's not needed any longer. Time's come for me to move on. I haven't decided the day, but the girls I've been monitoring are indeed my sisters."

"How do you know for sure?"

"I don't know when, but at some point my ma stuffed pieces of her skirt into their drawers." Toby tugged the rag from his britches. I ripped this from Ma's skirt when I was sold. It matches theirs."

"You've done well by me. Getting the crop I've always dreamed of to come up bright, green, and healthy. My crop is more than I ever thought it could be. You were God-sent. And, you never asked for nothing, not even ya pay. I want you to know I've been taking note. You'll be paid handsomely for what you've done. Should be enough to get ya and dem gals to where you need ta be gettin' to."

It was April when Toby and the twins met at the corner. And, as promised, the Perry Street buggy driver returned with his master's carriage.

"Git in. Be quick."

They hustled into the carriage and were taken straight to the dock where tickets, purchased by Ezra, awaited them at will-call. For the first time, in daylight, Toby saw the twin's faces framed by their hoods. Indeed, they were as pretty as he thought they would be.

The three glanced at one another–each knew the rules. The girls were sophisticated travelers. Toby, with Onyx, was the faithful servant who stayed a respectful distance to the back of them and only spoke or moved when ordered to do so.

Two gentlemen, afar, watched and debated, "They are. They aren't."

One approached them. "Good evening, ladies," he said and tipped his hat with a bow. "We fear you might be in the wrong line. Negroes are back there," he said and nodded toward a group standing off to the side, awaiting permission to board.

"Monsieur, we decided to keep our darkie with us until boarding time. Might you be the ones in the wrong boarding line?" Mary asked.

Molly gaped at the gentlemen steadfastly and asked, "Are you sure we are the persons you want to question about our darkie?" she asked, with a French accent, as she removed her glove to expose perfectly manicured nails. Her pretentiousness was one only a refined white woman could generate. Mary discreetly pushed her hood back. She revealed a professionally designed traveler's coiffure.

"Mademoiselle." He bowed to Mary. "And Mademoiselle." He nodded to Molly. "I hope you'll forgive me," he said. With his eyes averted, he backed away, shame-faced, from his faux pas. The girls rolled their eyes as they prompted Toby to follow them to the boarding plank.

"I'll take Onyx with me and join the other Negroes in the quarters below deck."

"What will you do with him?" Mary asked.

"He'll be secured at the end of the planks."

Running through the house panic-stricken and hysterical, Virginia sternly questioned Tipper. "Where are those gals? They're not in their room. It seems they didn't come back from their evening stroll. What could have happened to them?" Filled with an uneasiness, Virginia bounded room to room. Not seeing them, she screamed once more, "Where are they?"

Lawrence caught hold of Virginia and asked her. "What are you saying?"

"They're gone. The girls are gone. Someone has kidnapped them. They've never been late returning from their evening outings."

To calm Virginia, Lawrence said, "I'll check the streets. They don't go more than a block or two before returning.

"What were they wearing?" Lawrence asked Tipper.

Ringing her apron, she said in a worrisome voice with her eyes downcast, "Dey in dem long black velvet capes wid dem hoods."

After walking the blocks, plus some, and not seeing the girls, Lawrence sent Nam to fetch Sheriff Wilford who came promptly and began an interrogation.

"Have you searched the house? Is anything missing? What time did they leave the house? How long are they usually gone?"

Lawrence sent Tipper to check their room and to report back to him. Smiling to herself, she took time to mount the steps to the third floor. She entered their room, twirling about, knowing what wasn't there and not needing to tally their belongings. When she had spent ample time with the inventory that didn't happen, she returned to Massa's office where Virginia wept uncontrollably.

"Sir," Tipper said.

"What did you learn?" asked Sheriff Wilford.

"Dem capes I done told ya dey be wearin', dey be gone. Der travelin' clothes and dem good shoes da missus jes bought dem be missin' as well as der handbags and large travelin' totes."

"It seems those wenches have run," said Mr. Piper.

Lawrence stood discombobulated. His face was blood-drained, lips scrunched up, and angry eyes that stared at the sheriff from where Lawrence stood next to the empty desk drawer. Squeezing the sides of his head, hardly able to speak, he said, "My entire payroll and the profits from this year's fur sales are gone."

"All of it?" Virginia asked.

"There's not a cent to be seen."

Shocked and infuriated, Virginia stammered, "The moneys are gone." She turned to Tipper. "How could this have happened You were in charge of them."

Enraged, she lunged at Tipper, grabbing her by the throat, slamming her to the floor. She beat her so savagely Tipper collapsed. Virginia took in a breath, far down into her lungs, clutched fists full of Tipper's hair and smacked the darkie's head against the floor.

Sheriff Wilford, slow to respond, said, "Hey, hey. Let that darkie be. Ya gonna kill her if you don't."

Not hearing his words and too exasperated to stop, Virginia shook the senseless gal till her arms ached. Then Virginia rolled over into a heap, wailing and kicking.

Once onboard the Steamboat Missouri, Mary and Molly were escorted to their stateroom. The girls ordered a tea tray with sandwiches and requested Toby be sent to their cabin. Both arrived promptly.

"Come. Eat yourself a good gut full of food. We've been told it will be about nine days before the ship docks at Louisville."

Seeing Toby's arm bruised through the rip in his jacket, the twins asked, "How are you being treated?"

"A bit rough, but I'll survive. I think it's these fancy clothes you dressed me in. However, I've surely experienced worse."

Toby returned to his quarters below deck while the girls summoned the commander.

"Mademoiselles, did you ring?"

"We're concerned about our hand, who's being mishandled below. We'd like to have him sent to our stateroom to stay at the door. We plan to sell him in Louisville to a horse owner. We've been offered handsome money for him. He has extraordinary knowledge of equitation, but he must be delivered in impeccable condition–unmarked and unmarred."

"I understand, Mademoiselles. I will have him brought up immediately."

Toby lets the twins know that as unescorted ladies, it won't be a comfortable part of their journey when they disembark in Louisville, Kentucky. "We'll have to be very discreet. You'll rent a carriage, request a ride around town, and ask where to dine and board. I'll chat with the other drivers to determine if there are pattyrollers around town in pursuit of runaways. We'll meet back here on the pier, and I'll follow the carriage on horseback."

After a night at the DeVoe Hotel, the same driver collected the twins. Toby tied Onyx to the rear and sat on the bench with the driver. The horses were urged to move southward down the turnpike, headed to Goodwin, Kentucky, where they hoped to find their family. The carriage stopped halfway to permit them to stretch their legs, have a snack, and take care of their needs before continuing on. Once on the move again, they didn't stop before they were in front of Ben Muller's farm. By then, the horizon was graced with soft blues of the sky underlined with a tangerine mist.

"Dis is da place," the driver told Toby.

"How do you know your way around so well?"

"I's hired by Dr. Lilly whose farm is behind dis here one. He hire me ta drive his trolley back and forth 'tween Louisville and Goodwin Springs. When da harvestin' and pickin' be done, da hands ain't needed so much. I be takin' dem from here ta Louisville fa hirin' out. Be gittin' to know da Negroes and da white folks around des here parts.

"Cain't be helpin' ya no mo. Massa be needin' his carriage soon. He let me be drivin' some ta git a little money now and den. Dat's how I be at da dock. I's glad ya hired me. And ya pay me good. It be mo den I be askin'. I be wishin' ya and dem gals da best. If ya come ta town and be needin' a coach ride again, my name be Jarvey. Ya holla, Jar. I come if I'm der.

"Best ya be gittin' down dat hill. Ya don't wana be seen on dis here road," Jarvey said and turned the carriage around and was gone.

Toby, the girls, and Onyx worked their way downhill to wait for daybreak. At sunrise, there was no stirring about on the turnpike or the farm. Only the sound of a blacksmith's hammer could be heard.

"Stay put," Toby told the girls.

He scaled the hill. Keeping low to the ground, he scurried across the turnpike. Hunkered down to not be seen from the Big House, he inched along an s-shaped stone wall that stretched near to the barn. He studied his position before dashing to its door. The deafening sound from the hammering diminished to a steady ping.

A deep voice said, "I know ya der. Don't needs ta be seein' ya. Den, if dey come askin', I say I ain't seen nobody. What ya be needin?"

"Lookin' for my ma, Clarissa. Baby brother, George Henry. And my pa, Jake."

"I only be knowin' ya ma and da boy, George Henry. Der whatin' no Jake wid 'em. I be Little Bo den. My pa be Big Bo. He da blacksmith when ya family be here. Dey cut off his hand. Say he pounded out messages dat help da Negroes ta run."

"Was it true?"

"It was. Ya ma was the last one to hear da message."

"Is she here?"

"Ain't. Huh and da boy, dey run when dey got da message. Der ain't never been no word dey's caught. Some say dey gone on ta Canada. Believe it be London. Dat be where some folks 'round des here parts got ta, 'cause dey got word from der kin. I ain't sho 'bout what happen ta Miss Clarissa and George Henry."

"When did they run?"

"Not sho 'bout dat neither. But I know da boy, he be 'bout nine harvests. I can tell ya, ya ma was my ma. I love huh like she done birth me. I cry fa huh many nights. If ya fine huh, tell huh what I done told ya.

"Best ya be gittin'. Folks be stirrin' soon. Follow Goose Creek on da other side da road. It be flowin' north ta Louisville. When ya gits der, der be Negroes dat know about skiffs and ferryboats. Dey help ya git ta da other side of da river. Ya be on da Underground Railroad den and on ya way ta Jordan."

As Toby and the twins started footslogging back to Louisville, they saw Jarvey's carriage up ahead.

"Git in. Decided since I's goin' back ta Louisville and dat ya might be needin' a ride and ya took good care of me wid what ya done pay me. I waited some and come back fa ya."

At the boarding house, the twins ordered meals they took to their room. They cleaned themselves up while Toby boarded at the barn with Onyx.

The next morning when Toby checked on Mary and Molly, they were strolling along Main Street to pass the time. He hastened his feet toward them when two white men harassed them about being unescorted. He rushed to their side."Pardon me Mademoiselles, I be beggin' ya pardon. Mr. DeVoe, he ask me ta fetch ya. Say come quick. It be importin'."

The men quickly lost interest in the girls and moved on. Toby, along with the twins, hurried back to the hotel.

"Get your belongings ready. At sunset, we'll follow the river west. The two of you will ride on Onyx. I'll walk alongside you. Won't take more than a couple of hours. When the river curves north, about two miles west from here toward a town called Portland, Kentucky, we'll wait there for a conductor to take us across it to New Albany, Indiana," Toby said.

"Conductor?"

"Yes. When we cross the river, he'll put us with the Underground Railroad. The journey might take a day or two. It'll take us to our first station at Bethel African Methodist Episcopal Church not far from the riverbank. That'll be New Albany, Indiana. From there, the train will move along till it gets to the Detroit station at the Second Baptist Church on Fort Street. Before crossing the Detroit River to journey to Ontario, the station masters will give us food and warm clothing. When we board da train again, we'll be taken to Amherstburg, Ontario, Canada."

Because the weather was warm, the girls rolled their hooded capes and stuffed them into their totes with the other clothing and the food they packed to stave off hunger. Canteens of water were strapped across their bodies and Toby's. With his help, they mounted Onyx and held on.

21

River Crossing

Toby and the girls worked their way into the thick undergrowth along the bend of the riverbank. They sat on vegetation flattened by previous freedom seekers. While huddled together to wait for the conductor, Toby jabbered about the warm fire in the cabin in Virginia that they occupied as youngsters. The twins cringed when he described the day there was a ruckus outside the cabin. "It was a cold wintery night," he told the girls. "We were forced out of the cabin, put in the back of a covered wagon, and taken on a frightful journey to Louisville, Kentucky, where we were put on the auction block because our owner couldn't pay his gambling debts."

Hearing their whimpers, Toby knew their faces were drawn to sadness and quickly shifted his recalls to the times their missus played the harp for them and how they curled at her feet in the most tranquil sleep.

At nightfall, he left the twins camouflaged in the shrubs to meet the conductor at the riverbank.

"How many der be in ya group," he asked.

"Three of us and a horse."

"Cain't take da horse in dis here skiff. He be too heavy fa it. Ya gonna hafta git him across on ya own."

"I was told there'd be a ferryboat."

"Couldn't get one fa tanight."

"Is the water deep?"

"Not so much at dis here point. But further out, cain't be sho. Ya jes gonna hafta try and see."

"Take the ladies. I'll ride on my horse. He's a swimmer."

The twins, with their food and totes, plus three other bucks who bounded from the thicket, piled into the skiff. Toby followed on Onyx with a concerned eye on the girls. He glanced skyward, pleading with the Lord to ensure they all reached the bank unharmed. Midway across, a turbulence shoved him off Onyx into the path of a bear-sized driftwood. One piece snagged his shirt while another dragged him along. With his eye and nose barely above water, he gaped pointedly into the darkness that devoured Onyx. Not seeing him, he wept into the river waves that bathed his face. Another rapid slammed the driftwood that shoved Toby ashore and pinned him against the northern bank of the river. He offered up a stronger prayer answered with a rush of water that shifted the log enough for him to wiggle from beneath it, but carried his food tote along as it was washed downriver.

His leg, injured in the crossing, made him to grimace when he attempted to put weight on his foot. He hobbled away from the riverbank to avoid daylight due, possibly in less than an hour. Backing himself on his rear, he moved one-footed up a ridge into the thicket. He assessed his injuries but was unable to determine which hurt more, the separation from his sisters and Onyx or his leg. Without question, Toby hurt inside and out.

He drew the drenched fabric bits from his pocket, peered at them, and thought, *I've been separated from the twins and Onyx. I was taken from Ma and then my Ola was taken from me. Now I'm left with wet bits of remnants.* Squeezing them, he moaned, “Sometimes it seems I will die with only pieces of thready rags from the ones I love.”

Heavy-hearted and hungry, Toby rested against a fallen tree. While calculating how he’d forage for food on a battered leg, he fell into a restless sleep. Conversing voices coming up from the riverbank disrupted the miserable sleep that had overtaken him.

The skiff reached the Indiana shore without incident, but without any sign of Toby or the horse. After a good enough holdup, the conductor peered straight at the girls, warning them, “Been ’bout an hour now. Cain’t wait no mo, misses. Gotta keep movin’, or we all be caught.”

In their most desperate voices, the twins asked, “What about our . . . ”

“Somebody be sent ta fetch him.”

The conductor led the girls and the other freedom seekers on a foot trail to the church site. They hunkered low in the bush and waited for a signal to let them know when it was safe to approach. It was nearly one day and a half later before a lantern flashed a welcoming light.

“Let’s go. Be quick. Keep ya heads down. Stay low ta da ground.”

The twins hurriedly gathered their belongings and squat-stepped behind the conductor. “But what about our brother?” they asked again.

“Shush. Don’t talk. Jes’ keep movin’.

“Can’t stay out here any longer, or we be meetin’ dem catchers and hounds dat always be on da move. Dey don’t stand still cause we do.”

The church, eerily still, was dark and hollow. Each seeker, one behind the other, felt their way, pew to pew. Finally, an opening in the floor permitted them access to a basement. Negroes who lined the walls, sat and laid in a petrified quietness. The girls sniveled and mourned for their brother.

Mammy Rose, with a sympathetic eye, handed them tins of warm broth and ash cakes. “Eat. Ya gonna be all right,” she told them.

Lawrence Piper conducted a visual assessment of the hired slave patrol consisting of six men: Sol, the leader, and his assistants, Abe, Bram, Fonza, Long, and Leo, each with a track hound. Satisfied, he said, “If you catch those gals before they reach the Ohio River crossing at Portland, Kentucky, there’ll be a handsome bonus for you when you bring them back. I understand they might be with a buck on horseback.” He gave each catcher up-front money of fifty dollars. They quickly pocketed it with grateful grins and took leave.

By the time the posse got to Kentucky, they had combed both sides of the Ohio River, St. Louis to Louisville, checking every possible hiding place. Each group of townsfolk repeatedly said they’d not seen any mulatto gals or a buck on horseback that weren’t from around the area.

“Best we be headin’ back wid da bad news,” Sol said.

Fonza grasped Sol’s shirt sleeve. “Wait. Up there.” he said, pointing toward the hills. “I heard some movement. Might seen somethin’, too.”

When it was time to join the Underground Railroad to continue on to Detroit, Mary and Molly took a defiant stance, refusing to leave without Toby. The train departed without them.

"Calm down. If ya stayin', ya gonna have ta help around here," Mammy Rose said and showed them to the kitchen. "Ya be washin' dem clothes piled der." She pointed to a shoulder-high heap of laundry in a corner basket. "When ya ain't doin' da laundry, ya be cookin' dem vittles. Go 'head. Git started wid dem shirts. Don't worry none 'bout ya kin. Dey done sent a party ta find him. Dey be da best trackers. Dey be bringin' him back, if he ain't dead."

Toby didn't know where he was. Yet he scooted, crawled, and limped back in the direction he had hailed from. Day and night came and went. He lost consciousness from time to time, unsure how often. He lugged his body as far east as possible before he crouched among the bushes to rest till it was dark again.

Out of nowhere, a captor from behind, gagged him, while another threw a bag over his head and knotted it at the back of his neck. Toby's stomach churned. His heart raced as he thrashed about like a wild animal about to get its throat cut. He was stretched out on the ground and held down while his arms were rope-tied against his body. His legs were secured at the ankles.

A whisper from behind his ear said, "Be still, boy. Been trekkin' ya awhile. Don't wanna be sharin' ya hide wid dem catchers."

The voice Toby was hearing shifted in another direction when the man at his ear spoke to the others. "Bury dat meat fa dem bloodhounds. Den git dat branch and sweep dem footprints leadin' from dat riverbank ta here."

The men he spoke to did as told and were back just as pounding feet and barking dogs were heard above the whistle of the wind. It was Sol and his fellow trackers who trudged and shouted at one another. "Saw somethin'. Certain it was dem gals." He reminded them that Mr. Piper had told them there might be a buck on horseback with them. But there wasn't evidence of hoof prints or droppings. The hounds barked, growled, and tugged their straps taunt as they wildly clawed and sniffed at the mud for the buried meat bits.

"Seems der been campers here. Couldda been dem other catchers. Hope dey ain't got dem gals and dat buck. I saw trackin' marks earlier. Coulda been dars," Fonza said.

The moon was bright enough for the advancing pattyrollers to see Toby and his captors. Concerned their focus might shift their way, a baritone voice near Toby thundered, "Let's git while we can put distance 'tween dem and us. We don't be needin' der company on our tails. Step easy. Don't utter a sound."

Toby's body was looped by two men who lifted him, and advanced on. He heard one say, "'Cause dat water's done moved dis here buck down da river a good piece, we got a good day mo of footslogging' ahead."

Finally, the truss of the Lord's house emerged in the distance. The freedom seekers sang in low-pitched voices delivered on a gliding breeze to the church:

. . . Hold out yo' light
you heaven boun' soldier
Let yo' light shine around de world

O, dea . . . can't yo hold out yo' light,
O, dea . . . can't yo hold out yo' light,
Let yo' light shine around de world

Hold out yo light . . .

A lantern glowed in the distance, and then a door sprang open. The group gleefully advanced, announcing, "We got him," as they descended the steps to the basement. The toters laid Toby on the floor. They cut the ties and removed the hood. Mammy Rose, who waited next to them, put a tin half-filled with chicken broth in his shaky hands that he couldn't hold onto. She patted Toby's shoulder and placed it on the floor next to him.

"Take, ya time. Ya here now," Mammy told him.

Toby turned his head. He gaped at the men who had carried him through the rough and down the stairs. "Thought you were the trackers. Sure of it. I was scared I was going ta die," he said.

"Glad dey done found ya. You rest, boy. Food be comin' soon as day breaks," Mammy said.

"Where am I?"

"You're here at da church in New Albany, Indiana. Jes cross dem waters from Louisville. Des here be a Underground Railroad station. Ya gonna be gittin' on dat train and movin' on soon as ya better," she said with a toothless smile.

The following morning's clacking noises from eating utensils woke Toby. Tired, achy, and groggy, he took in what his eye couldn't discern the night before: low ceilings, concrete walls, exposed joists, bunched piles of clothing, a tunnel that arced to somewhere. Other Coloureds were sitting and lying about along the walls.

"Sir, would you care for something to eat?" a voice he knew well asked.

Toby raised his head and peered into the face of one of the twins. He saw, but his hazy vision was unable to determine if it were Mary or Molly who dropped to her knees, wept, and hugged him.

"We thought we'd never see you again. The conductor tried to force us to leave with the train. Said we needed to keep moving, but we refused. Yet we couldn't be loafers and had to labor as cooks and laundresses. I didn't recognize you at first. You seem so frail. And ailing, too."

"I feel unwell. I lost Onyx in the rush of the river. He's gone," Toby cried.

"He'll be all right. Horses are great swimmers and he's strong," Molly said and then called to her sister, "Mary, come. See who's here."

"My God! You made it!" she said.

The siblings folded into an embrace, thankful they were one again. They closed their eyes and prayed silently, undisturbed as they contemplated one another. Mary and Molly, each with an arm looped around Toby, dragged him to relocate at a corner of the basement where they could chat privately about what they'd do next and nurse his injured limb.

"Let's have a gander at your leg," Molly said and gently pushed Toby's pant leg up the battered leg. "My goodness, it's inflamed, hot as a pressing iron. It must pain you something awful."

Nursed by his sisters nonstop, in just a matter of time, Toby jaunted about with ease. When it was time to get on board the train, he was ready. The twins' loads were much lighter, and what remained of their money was still secured in their pantaloon pouches. Toby smiled and heaved, thankful he'd given his St. Louis salary to them for safekeeping.

The siblings joined twelve other passengers on the Underground Railroad. The freedom seekers left for Detroit, moving nonstop till they were at the Second Baptist Church on Fort Street. "Get ready. Be prepared to move fast. We be leavin' now," Maxwell, the conductor, told the group.

After several days on the trail, a downpour of rain darkened the sky till it was black. Without the light of day or moonlight, the seekers were able to walk day and night, stopping only for snatches of rest, eat, and think a bit.

One day, the sunlit sky forced the passengers into hiding. With the help of abolitionists who provided food, clothing, and shelter, the seekers were able to continue moving along. When a horse and wagon was available, it was possible for them to advance as much as twenty miles in a day, sometimes more.

Back on foot and trekking for days, Toby and the twins sat apart from the others. He told them, "I wish I could tell you what to expect when we get to the church and then to Canada, but I can't." Toby teased a pouch of biscuits out of his jacket pocket to share with them. "On my way up the stairs of the church in Detroit, Mammy Rose tucked these into my hand and told me, 'Ya take care, boy. Dis here not much. We be thinkin' 'bout ya and dem gals, too.' "

Barking hounds jarred the freedom seekers. "Let's go." Maxwell urged.

Everyone grabbed their belongings and trudged behind him. In a rush, Mary stepped on the hem of her cape. Toby caught her by the arm before she was pulled to the ground, "You hurt?" he asked.

"No. I'm fine."

With each step, Mary hopped a bit higher till she seemed to skip. Finally, they rounded a ridge to thick foliage.

"Daylight's comin'. Gonna have ta stay put and wait for da nighttime sky," said Maxwell.

Toby turned to Mary. "You were hobbling. What seems to be the matter?"

"Something's hurting my foot," she said and removed her shoe, juddering it, something fell out. "It was a mere pebble. But it hurt."

Toby left his sisters to join the men digging a cooking pit. When done, he trailed them into the wild to hunt game. Mary and

Molly worked alongside the women to layer the hole with dry grass and twigs. Next, they created a canopy to camouflage the smoke. Afterward, the ladies scavenged for wild fruits and vegetables.

The men returned to the campsite with rabbits, a good size boar, and a half-dozen birds. With flint and a dry piece of wood, Maxwell ignited the kindling in the pit. After the catchings were prepared and layered over the fire, the women dumped their pickings and findings on top of the meat to help disguise the cooking odors. Once the fixings cooled, everyone enjoyed them.

"Save the bones. Don't toss them away. Gonna use dem after the dig," Maxwell told them.

Feeling relaxed for the first time in days, the freedom seekers lazied around the fire, sang their favorite field songs, and exchanged stories about their hopes and what they wanted their tomorrows to be like.

When it was time, the men dug the pit deeper, near to the depth of a tall standing buck and wide as two. The bottom was filled with spiked branches. The top was camouflaged with long woven grass, and topped with crumbled dirt and weeds. The leftover bones were scattered across it. From a distance, the area appeared restored to its natural state and showed little evidence anyone had been there.

The group lolled about, waiting for nightfall, but before the stars appeared, barking hounds in the distance pierced the quiet.

"Grab ya things. Let's go," Maxwell said.

They did and were on the move in a snap. It wasn't long before yelps and whines from the hounds that had fallen into the pit were heard, along with the loud, vulgar voices of the catchers. The rescued dogs weren't much good for chasing.

The runaways trudged till their feet blistered and bled. Helped once more, the abolitionists moved them along station to station by boats, horses, and wagons.

There were additional weeks on the trail before the Second Baptist Church was seen. To their dismay, there were a good number of men wearing dark cloaks and burlap sacks for headgear. They steered about the churchyard on horseback with torches. The gang demanded that a shackled darkie be tied to a cross and burned to death.

"Gotta stay put. Somethin' ain't right," Maxwell warned his group.

The horsemen created a pit in the middle of the yard. The cross was jabbed into the center of it. A fettered darkie was tied to the rood. Dry bush crammed at the foot of the cross was lit at his feet. The painful cry that emerged, and the smell of burning flesh that blistered and sloughed off the body, taunted the souls that waited to approach the church.

Toby gathered Mary and Molly in his arms. They were the lone ones among the freedom seekers who had never seen or experienced such an atrocity. They shuddered and wept into their skirts to muffle their cries. The others, in silence, quivered as they each folded into a prayer mode.

The cloaked men finally left the yard early the next day, but it was sunset before the church people took down the charred cross and buried the remains of the body. At nightfall, a lantern light appeared. Maxwell signaled to his group with a hand wave. In a low whisper, he said, "We can go now. Remember, walk easy, keep ya heads down, stay low, and stay close. Don't talk 'til ya in da basement."

Moving like cats after their prey, they edged nearer to the church where the hand of a ghost seemed to open the door.

Crouched, they eased inside, trailing one behind the other down a set of stairs to a basement filled with an eerie quiet. At the bottom of the steps, clustered and shaken, the seekers didn't budged till prodded by Pappy, an elderly Negro helper.

"Come, come. We all be hurtin' by what done happened ta our friend. You gottta eat and rest 'cause ya be movin' on soon'. When dat train come, ya gotta be ready to git on board," Pappy said.

Maxwell left his group of seekers in Pappy's care to prepare for his return to gather the next group.

Two days later, before sunrise, Pappy handed a chunk of meat to each freedom seeker. When the same door at the top of the stairs opened, they scuttled out to the southern bank of the Detroit River where a steamboat waited to take them across to the Canadian shore to journey on. Midway, across the waters, in unison and unprompted, their heads bowed. They prayed, some aloud and some quietly. Their words came together as one when they crooned:

Deep river
My home is over Jordan,
Deep river
Lord, I want to cross over into camp ground
I want to cross into camp ground . . .

Sidney, an Ontario, Canada conductor, waited for them at the north shoreline to escort the freedom seekers as far as the London, Ontario station. The passengers wasted little time climbing aboard.

22

Canada

1859

Before the bow of the steamboat was secured on Canadian soil, at Amherstburg, the passengers knocked and bumped one another, anxious to clamber out. They dropped their bundles on land and cupped hands full of the river water that sailed them to freedom's shore. Waving their arms and inhaling the fresh air aromas, they danced a *Buck and Wing*, so jubilant they collapsed. The steamboat conductor grinned and waved a robust so long at the celebrants. With a sense of deepened satisfaction, he turned the boat around and headed back across the Detroit River to learn his next assignment.

Sidney greeted the freedom seekers. "Best ya be gittin' up and gittin' all dem belongs tagather. Tie ya shoes on good and balance ya loads. We gonna be walkin' a good piece among da trees ta keep dem eyes off us. We be on the trail 'til we gits ta da church. Some of ya might be stayin' on here in Amherstburg. Some of ya might be goin' on ta Chatham, the next station, and others on ta London. Dat be da last stop fa me," he said.

Sidney gazed at each of them to be sure they understood

what he was saying before he told them, "Den, at London, I be turnin' back ta git da next group of passengers dat be waitin' fa me at da river.

"We won't be movin' from dis here Amherstburg till tamorrow. A wagon gonna take us overnight ta Chatham. Be daylight when we gits der, likely near up ta noon. We be leavin' dat station in two maybe three days. Best we be gittin' on our way."

Eager to start, the freedom seekers tended to their shoes and stood behind Sidney. He swiftly started up a trail that led into forestation. When the group exited, they weren't far from the First Baptist Church of Amherstburg, where each was greeted with hot meals and fresh clothes. Some who roamed about the city were offered jobs and stayed behind to accept them.

Toby and the sisters ate and rested before they canvassed the town to inquire about their mother and younger brother, whom no one seemed to have seen or heard of them. Disheartened, they returned to the church. The next day, theyv continued on with Sidney to Chatman. While four of the seekers stayed behind, three others joined them in a horse-pulled wagon.

The ride, better than four hours, finally ended in front of Chatman's First Baptist Church. Wary and laden with hunger pains, the seekers trailed Sidney to the church hall. The greeter told him that bounty hunters were in town. He looked at Toby and then at his sisters, "Dey seem to be knowin' 'bout dat boy and dem twin gals ya got der."

Sidney told Toby and the girls, "Ya stay put. I'll search fa ya family members. Don't show ya faces or speak to anyone. Stay here and stay out of sight."

After walking street to street, he returned to the church with the troubling news that there wasn't a twosome in town that matched the description he was given–a mother with long, curly hair, pretty, petite, with a mulatto lad, who might be handsome and tall.

Because there was no indication Clarissa or George Henry were around town, Toby told Sidney, "My sisters and I won't be staying on. I don't have a good feeling about our safety here. We'll leave with you and go as far as you do. And, hopefully escape the hands of any pattyrollers lurking about."

"It seems der be only eight of us gittin' on. Da others decided ta stay, at least fa now. Got no wagon so we gonna be walkin' a good amount."

About halfway to London, Sidney started limping and eventually had to stop and sit. "Dis here foot of mine be smartin'. Won't let me go no father. I be real sorry. But I knows ya be fine from des point ta dar. Jes stay on dis here trail. Ya can't git lost. Might see some camper 'long da way. Dey usually be right friendly. Never had no problem wid dem. Don't worry none 'bout me. Der be others comin' and goin' dat'll stop and pick me up."

The seekers moved on, zigzagging through the harsh thicket for better than two miles. Their hiking led to a widened path bitten down by previous travelers. The group decided to rest there. Gathered around a fire, they planned their days ahead before continuing on.

The next morning, Mary and Molly foraged for walnuts they thought they had seen along the way. A scream from one of the sisters caused a panic among the group. Toby rushed to explore what had happened. When he arrived, Mary was on the forest floor, unconscious. He carried her back to the campsite and placed her near the fire. She woke but was queasy. To not slow the others down, he suggested, "We'll stay behind to determine what happened to my sister and ensure she's able to trek the remaining distance before we go on."

It was three weeks later when Toby and the twins reached the Fugitive Slave Chapel where a slim, tall pleasant woman behind a waist-high table welcomed them.

"Come. Come. You must be tired and hungry. I'm Miss Rona. My helper and I will get you settled in with a bath. And a nap if you like. Afterward, you can come back to the chapel for tea and a hot evening meal. There are eats in your cabins if you feel the need for something now."

Miss Rona handed each freedom seeker a set of sheets and towels. Tish, her peppy assistant, was instructed to lead Toby and the girls to what would be their transitional rooms till they found a place of their own.

Walking and talking, Tish informed the newcomers with quick chattering words, "You'll have adjoining quarters to make it easy for you to visit one another. There's a washroom at the end of the hall. Soap is next to the washbasin in your rooms. Water will be brought up daily."

She unlocked the twins' door and handed the key to them before leading Toby to the adjoining room. To ensure he was aware of her presence, Tish revealed a take-note-of-me smile as she unlocked the entrance door to his room and the one that adjoined the twins' room before she handed the key to him. Over wrought by weariness, Toby hardly noticed her or the flirtatious gesture.

The siblings were delighted to bathe off the trail sweat and dirt, stretch out next to each other on a clean bed, and rest without worry for the first time in months. It was the next day when they woke up. Mary and Molly stayed in the sleeping clothes, left on the bed, from the night before. Toby spent the day milling around town, inquiring about job prospects. Not finding any, he felt discouraged and returned to the church to check for possible postings.

Two years before Toby and the twins arrived in Canada, George Henry, Toby's younger brother, had completed a vocational program for future barbers and had nailed his certificate to the barbershop wall. Jef, the master barber he grew up working for, had aged and saw only enough customers to keep his skills as sharp as his shaving blades. He was proud of his gifted and talented intern whose ethics he admired. The old man decided to sell his shop to George Henry, while he could still mentor the lad.

The new owner, young and energetic, didn't hesitate to recruit barber apprentices from the vocational school. After leaving the shop each evening, he distributed announcements about his ownership and job openings. The number of clientele doubled in a short time. Their savings, plus Clarissa's laundry money, and George Henry's increased income generated enough funds to purchase a house on a busy corner. At the foot of the rear yard, one street dead-ended into another. The two-story structure had a dining room, living room, kitchen, and a staircase that ascended to four bedrooms, plus a bonus room in the attic.

On move-in day, filled with wonderment, Clarissa and George Henry unloaded their meager belongings in the larger-than-most kitchens with a wood-burning stove, icebox, and a good-sized backdoor that opened to a deep rear yard wide enough to accommodate large washtubs, washboard, battling sticks, and laundry lines with wooden props.

"What do you think, Ma?"

"Son, dis here house be makin' me plenty happy. I can do mo laundry and don't have ta be collectin' it. Gonna hire me a gal, maybe two."

George Henry painted *The Perfect Wash* on a shingle, which became the business name. He hung it on a pole, extending from the corner of the house, where the side met the back. Customers who entered the swing gate were able to drop off and retrieve laundry from the back porch.

Clarissa's days began with the first blip of daylight and lasted till darkness soaked it up. Folks around town swore, "No one can press like Miss Clarissa." Whites and Negroes raved about her work and paid handsomely for her services. Some added a monetary gratuity or a live chicken, bags of rice, even a piglet now and then. She became the preferred laundress around London and never had a shortage of to-do wash and pressing.

Back at the room, the twins and Toby weren't faring well. He was gone all day in search of work, and the money was severely depleted. Mary and Molly, disgruntled, meandered the streets only to repeatedly be told there was no need for their kind of work–tutoring nannies–especially two at a time. The twins didn't want to be separate.

Toby returned to the Freedom Chapel where word had gotten out that he was learned. Several townsfolk came around to request assistance with letters and notices to be sent back to their families and legal documents that needed help. Miss Rona, feeling he wouldn't refuse such an opportunity to help them, had a small desk brought into the vestibule where he could sit, greet the newly arrived freedom seekers, and offer to do their penning if he was willing to. Not only did he agree, he quickly plopped on the chair as if it might vanish. At first, work was slow coming but eventually took an upturn. For those who struggled financially, their payments were delayed with a promise to bring them back later. They did without failure. Word of his services continued to spread. His increased pocket change reflected the earnings. His friendship with the locals flourished. The farmers who became aware of his agricultural knowledge also paid for his council.

Dr. Harper, Chancellor at University College, who had learned about the talented scribe, decided to visit him, incognito, with queries about farming, crops, soils, and bookkeeping. Toby was never perturbed by any question, regardless of its difficulty. The Chancellor, so impressed with Toby's depth of knowledge, right then offered the scriber a teaching position. Toby could hardly remain seated as he humbly accepted the offer.

"Come by my office the first chance you get for a tour of the facility and a proper introduction to the agricultural staff," he told him with a handshake and left. Once Toby closed his mouth, he sprang up and spun around, clutching the sides of his head. Miss Rona and Tish raced to his side. They feared something might be wrong, but found that he was drunk on an overdose of elation.

Meanwhile, at the apartment, Molly reminded Mary that they were educated, knew their subjects well, and could speak French without faltering. "Miss Grace, our tutor, always told Miss Virginia such things about us. So, why not start our own school? We can do for children around London what she did for us. At least, till we get proper jobs. There are enough working people in town. It shouldn't be a challenge to gather a few boys and girls for lessons. Toby has contact with an impressive number of local people since his appointment at the college. Plus, he scribes for clients in better than a ten-mile radius. If we create an appealing advertisement, he can distribute it among his colleagues and contacts. We can also advertise in the church bulletin."

When the time came, Miss Rona cleared out a closet at the slave chapel for the twins and their young learners–four girls and three boys, with varying skills, between the ages of five and nine. They occupied it till being shifted to a rear room that had enough space for the students, the furnishing, and a proper window to open and close.

Mary and Molly were paid mere pittances for lessons; but the class number bloomed and made up the difference. Even Dr. Reed, the vocational school's headmaster, who took a fancy to them, eventually inquired about their availability for staff positions.

Never being apart and not wanting to abandon their pupils, the twins accepted the offer with the understanding they'd establish a back-and-forth schedule that permitted them to be at the chapel half the time and the vocational school the other half. Dr. Reed graciously accepted their terms.

One day Toby left work early to let his sisters know that Miss Rona informed him, "The living quarters are nearly full. We'll be needing your rooms as soon as possible. A good number freedom seekers are on their way."

He knew his sisters were at home organizing lessons and school supplies. After Toby delivered the message, he peered earnestly at the twins. "We'll be fine. I spoke with Mr. Jef when he came to University College to give Chancellor Harper a haircut and shave. I inquired about the rooms above his barbershop. 'Got three up there. Take ya pick. I be here a while,' he told me and handed the keys over. I carefully explored each flat."

"When will we need to pack?"

"I suggest now, if possible. Take what you can. I'll come back for the rest. Tish'll help me move things to the flat after she finishes her work at the chapel."

Mary and Molly packed the school supplies in delivery boxes they had set aside, and then gathered their clothing in tote bags. Carrying what they could, they bustled across town, climbed the side stairs of the building, and leaned against the railing. They waited for Toby to open the door to a narrow hallway. Once inside, twins stopped at the first unit on the left. Toby opened the door to a fairly spacious area.

"I chose this room because it's the largest of them. It cost a bit more, but was less than paying for the two smaller rooms. The washroom is at the end of the hall. I don't know who our neighbors are. So, I suggest you go together when you need to use it, at least for now."

Choking and coughing, they cried into their hankies, feeling as if they were spinning inside a dusty upside-down world.

Mary whimpered, "Are you sure we can live here? It's so dank and dirty."

Toby showed them the cleaning supplies he had collected: bucket, lye soap, mop, rags, and a whisk broom. They dolefully eyed Toby as they tearfully said, "We'll try."

"I'm sorry I have to leave you alone with this problem, but I've got to get back to school. My class will start soon."

The only place to sit was on a chaise, so Mary took it upon herself to push the clutter off the seat of it onto the floor. When the two plopped down, the roiled dust provoked sneezes.

"What a mess," they sighed.

Eyes closed and tears falling on the backs of their hands clasped in their laps, the girls mourned for Tipper, who had taught them the details of housework when their missus never demanded such of them. Mary turned to Molly. "Tipper always said, 'Ya don't know where ya be endin' up and what ya be needin' ta know.' She was right, although we were rebellious, she knew how to be stern. If only there was a way we could send for her, but knowing her age and Missus' ways, she would never survive such a grueling journey. I pray Miss Virginia's punitive hand didn't clobber her because we took leave."

Molly dabbed her eyes. "I feel Tipper hugging me. Can hear her voice in my ear say, 'Don't ever be thinkin' ya cain't be doin' 'fore ya be tryin' ta."

Mary laughed as she recalled, "And, taking Massa's money, which gave me an abundance of joy. I love imagining his face when he pulled the drawer to see his notes gone and then the lower drawer to see the fat money bag gone."

"That's enough about him. We've got work to do. We'll take the drapes and rugs outside for a good airing and whisking. Then, we'll start cleaning in the far corner and work our way around," Molly said before answering the door.

It was Tish with a basket. "Thought you might be needin' somethin' ta eat and some clean towels and linen." She smiled, handed the goods over, and scampered away.

It was late evening before Toby returned and knocked on the door. He entered the apartment baffled at how the sisters had converted such a ratchet space into a delight for the eyes. Glad he ventured to the edge of town to pick wildflowers for them, he took in a cough-free breath and fingered the blooms, dividing them.

"I never dreamed this was possible," he said, and gave half of the bunch to Mary, and the other half to Molly. Giggling with glee, the girls placed them in a cup of water. With oversized smiles, they gathered him in their arms, but this time, with tears of joy.

Downtrodden, George Henry sat in a rocker on the rear porch watching his mother wash and hang laundry.

"Son, what gotcha in such a way?"

"Bad news, Ma."

Clarissa let loose of the shirt that she fisted against the washboard to take a seat on the step. "Bad news can gnaw away a good deal of ya innards. Tell me what be troublin' ya, boy."

"Mr. Jef's gone on. The nurse from the infirmary brought the news to the shop. When I finished with the customer I was working on, I left and told the others I wouldn't return till tomorrow. Ma, it hurts so much. What am I gonna do?"

"Ya gonna thank God fa da time he done give ya wid Mr. Jef. Den ya gonna tell him dat ya be keepin' dat shop da way he done taught ya ta.

"Ya been tryin' to git me ta dem church meetin's fa a long time. Ta night we be goin'. Ya tell folks about Mr. Jef and how he take ya in, and hep ya be a good man like ya pa, Jake, want ya ta be. Don't ya be sad, boy. Mr. Jef knowed what he be doin' when he left his footprints fa ya ta follow. Ya rest. Ya pray. Things gonna be all right."

Toby and the twins gathered around the table with barely enough space for their dinner plates and drinking goblets. They discussed finances and the upcoming events around town.

Leaning on his elbow, their brother said, "My work at University College is going well. There seems to be mounting interest in farming around these parts. Next semester, I'll present weekend lectures for those coming in town from neighboring communities. With the new classes, our monthly account at the bank will increase. In two to three years, we can purchase a nice house.

"But tell me, how are the two of you doing?"

The girls laughed as they recalled the events with their young students at the chapel and the older ones at the vocational school who were not able to tell them apart. They compared it to the frustration the Pipers experienced with their likeness as they grew up.

"Only Tipper and Miss Grace could tell us apart," Mary said.

Clarissa pondered the clearness of the sky as she stood on the front porch admiring the blues transforming into a chiffon of sunset-oranges. Dressed in a fresh pressed blue plaid shirt and trousers, George Henry joined his mother.

"Son, let's walk ta da chapel. It seem ta be a night dat God done sent. I can do some thinkin' as I be walkin'. Got a strange feelin' down inside dat I can't git hold ta. It be makin' me uneasy. Pullin' me ta dat chapel in a way dat it ain't never done before."

"Ma, you know if we walk and don't take the carriage I ordered, we'll never gits der in time for da openin' prayer. And probably not get a seat."

"Son, dat be fine wid me, 'cause I don't rightly be knowin' what be waitin' fa me der. I jes be knowin' deep inside, I don't need ta be rushin'. Ain't been ta dat chapel fa a good piece of time. Cain't 'member when I last be der."

George Henry raised his forearm toward Clarissa, who looped hers around it as the hired carriage pulled alongside them. George Henry flagged the driver on his way. He and Ma walked the few miles, not hurrying at first, but soon a spiritual floating on a breeze from the chapel quickened their pace.

As predicted, no seats were available, and the chapel was packed front to back. George Henry scooted along the rear wall, tugging Clarissa behind him. Once their bodies were entirely inside the church, they noted the families and individuals meandering through the crowd, forcing their way to the front of the chapel to tell about their crossings and how they survived the bloody trail from enslavement to freedom.

Mack, a farmer, told how he left Kentucky with his wife and four small children and crossed the Ohio River. His wife and only two of their four totes reached the northern bank. "Our hearts be heavy. But when we got on board da train, we be told ta keep da faith, 'God got dem little ones and dey gonna be all right.' We still hurtin', but we got da faith. Now we's free."

Mae, a chambermaid, relived how she joined a bunch of others on the Underground Railroad. They ran and walked for days and nights with track hounds on their heels before they reached the Detroit River.

Jeremy, was the coach driver for a well-to-do businessman named Jay Brown. He told how on numerous occasions his owner tied him to a pole and whooped him till he called for death. "It be my wife, Ruby. She wouldn't let me meet my maker 'fore da time be due, even though I beg her ta. Den da missus had huh hung 'cause she took care of me too good. Dat's when I run. I's be on dis here Canadian soil 'fore I stopped runnin'," he said.

Sadie, about four feet tall, fought her way through the crowd shouting, "Move over. I's here now, and I wants ta tell my story 'bout how I be beaten like da rest of ya and my babies took from me soon as dey could stand, all six of dem. My man, Ian, read a old newspaper. It say dat da president's gonna free us, so we decided ta go ahead and run right den. When Ian hear dat da train be comin', he tell me, 'We's gonna git on board.' We's real excited. Planned fa our run. We's listenin' ta dem songs comin' up from da fields. When dey say 'git on board' and da night come, we hides out on da edge of da farm. When Massa be lookin' fa us, he find da lil book dat be buried in da bedin'. Be da one missus done give my man. When Massa learn Ian be able ta read, he send dem hounds fa us. We's caught 'fore we run. My man's eyes be put out wid dat hot poker. Den he be beat 'til he couldn't stand. I's locked in a stall. When Massa come ta check on me he push me down, rip my clothes off, and climb on me like I's a animal. He did what he want ta, den he walk out. He keepa comin' back night afta night. I's hurtin' bad. Bleedin' and cryin', too. I don't be knowin' what happen ta Ian, 'til he be dead. So, I runs. I's no swimma and 'bout drownin' mo den once 'fore I gits ta dis here place where I gives birth ta Massa's boy. I's so full of hate fa him, I didn't be wantin' dat baby, but I be lovin' it some now and ask God ta help me wid it.

Clarissa, along with the other parishioners, wept and prayed for those who recounted their passages. It was the voice of a young man and two young ladies that caused her to raise her head. Her knees wobbled and her body weakened, so she tightened her grip on George Henry's arm to steady herself.

"Ma, ya all right?"

Clarissa let go of George Henry to ease forward. The voice of the lad speaking drew her toward the chancel.

"I was put on the auction block when I was a boy and sold away from Ma and my family. While waiting to be claimed as property, I heard a man say, 'Dem pretty little gals was sold to a Missouri businessman.'

"Prior to my escape, I was owned by slavers, one ornery as the next. Knowing my sisters were in Missouri kept me hoping. I ran from my last owner, who caused the death of my wife, who was my life, and his baby that she carried. Before I ran, I burned his farm down to the ground. Then, I went straight to St. Louis to find my siblings."

Scared and fearful of what might be, or might not be, Clarissa forcefully pushed aside parishioners as she jimmied her way to the front. Her heart pounded and thudded inside her chest. The voice that recalled parts of his life's past, also beckoned to her.

"When I found my sisters, I plotted a way to take them from their owner to a passenger ship. They acted high class. I was their slave. We boarded for Kentucky to find Ma and the rest of our family, but they had run. No one knew for sure where to."

Clarissa felt that the handsome gentleman speaking was indeed her boy, Toby, and that the identical young ladies, who stood next to him, were Mary and Molly.

"Dem gals be lookin' alike," she mumbled under her breath as she stepped into the core of what seemed to be an unreal world. With her neck stretched, her eyes consumed more of the young man who stood next to them. Could he possibly be Tall Man, my Toby?

She continued to shove the tight-knit bodies aside without taking her eyes off Toby for a second. He turned his head when he said, "Like some of you, my sisters and I joined the Underground Railroad that was northbound. We stayed with it till we got here. We haven't found my ma or baby brother yet, but we'll never give up our search."

The butterfly-shaped birthmark on the back of the young man's neck fluttered. A resounding yelp that bolted from Clarissa parted the crowd. Heads turned as she frantically shoved her way up the aisle. With outreached arms and a tear-washed face, she cried, "Tall Man, dat you?"

"Ma!"

Sobbing, she pushed harder, straining to reach for her children, who caught hold of her collapsing body as they gathered her into their hugs. Each wept tears of joy.

23

Reunion

Clarissa and her children gathered on the rear porch, a favorite spot to sip apple cider, nibble on crispy, molasses cookies, and enjoy the storytelling of past events. On this bright, sunny, just-right-for-sitting day, Clarissa felt a deeper than usual inner peace. Her vision bounced face to face as she painted mental pictures of the years she had lost with her children as they grew from tumblers to tall-walkers.

To consume the vision of all her children at one glance, Clarissa expanded her gaze and then said, "Ya here. I be seein' ya but not believin'." She reached out to them. With her fingertips, she, ever so softly, stroked each of their cheeks. "Tall Man, I can still see ya scamperin' through dem fields and jumpin' over dem stonewalls wid ya long grasshopper legs. Ya be a handsome one, too. Dem mammies in da quarter be mighty envious of me," she chuckled and smiled. "Mary. Molly. Ya two be da happiest lil youngin's I ever knowed. Ya always be movin' about. Keep me laughin' and a hoppin'. Sometimes I be 'bout oudda breath tryin' ta keep up widcha." Clarissa's voice quietened. She focused on

George Henry. "I keeps tellin' George Henry how he be reminin' me of ya, Tall Man. Oh my, my, how I be missin' ya. Ain't a day go by dat I don't be ponderin' on ya whereabouts. I pestered George Henry wid my story tellin's about da days dat was. He listen. God listen, too. 'Cause he brung George Henry and me ta dis here place. Den, he brung ya, and ya, and ya."

Clarissa gestured to say more, but instead became hushed. With her head bowed, her whole body became still. Only her eyes ogled at her hands that rested on her lap. She heaved as she pulled her head back and shoulders up to scan the perplexed stares of her children. She told them, "We done all come tagether on dis here porch mo den once. I been wantin' to ask 'bout how ya got ta here. Never could git up da gumption ta do so. Negroes done suffered so I's scared ta hear 'bout ya journey. But I be ready now and be needin' ta know."

Toby caressed his ma's hand. Taking his time, he said, "Like a lot of folks, we had troubling times along the way. But I got a message for you. At the Kentucky farm, a young blacksmith named Bo, Little Bo, said to tell you he cried for you a many a night. Said he felt like you were his ma and missed you a powerful lot."

Clarissa, wide eye and opened mouth, gasped and said, "My, my. Dat boy be a son ta me. How I be missin' him, too. Her eyes rolled back in prayer. She swayed side to side before she finally said, "Go head. Tell me mo 'bout ya passage."

"Ma, we knew you wanted to know about our journey, but we were hesitant to burden you with the naked truths. Too many days were hard, ugly, and painful for us as we trudged from St. Louis to Louisville, Kentucky, where we joined other runaways seeking passage on the Underground Railroad. From the banks of the Ohio, River we made our way to Detroit. Church people along the way took us in; gave us food, warm clothes, footwear, and a place to lay our heads. At the Detroit station, once we were well-rested, we were taken across the Detroit River. On the other side, our group began another leg of our adventure: some on foot, some by boat, and some in a horse-drawn wagon.

"One day we came upon a campsite of hunters roasting a deer over a fire. They shared their meat and tents with us. The following day we gathered our things and moved on with the other passengers. As we did, the hinterlands grew more troublesome, causing us to stumble over the thicket as we trekked along. The flesh of our feet and legs were ripped and our clothing clawed. At times, we were battered and bruised which slowed us down, making me fearful of what might haunt us up ahead.

"Another time, hunger stopped the group, Mary, Molly, and I sat against a large stone. We shared our dreams of what we hoped our experiences would be once we embraced a place that we'd call home. That's when Mary and Molly saw walnuts scattered about on the ground.

Knowing what Toby was going to say next, the twins scooted close. Holding hands, they sucked in their lips, squeezed their eyes shut, and hardly took in a proper breath.

"Mary thought they would go well with what we were about to eat and ran to pick up a few. When she reached for them, she was stung by an insect or bitten by a snake.

At the thought of losing her sister, Molly layered her arm across Mary's shoulder as Mary lay her head on Molly.

"At first we didn't think it would be a concern because there was no redness or swelling at the site of the bite. But the next day she was feverish and puffy all over. Her breathing was so shallow she could hardly move. Her hand was near the size of a small melon. The two red puncture marks on her hand gave me cause to think it was a snake bite. Luckily, some hunters came along and left a tent for us. Because that night was cold and the tent was too small for everyone in the group, the other seekers moved on. We remained behind."

Clarissa tapped the scar. Lifting Mary's hand, she kissed it and said, "I be wonderin' what dem tiny marks be, but wasn't sure I wanted ta know." Gandering at her big boy, she asked, "Den, what happened?"

"When Mary thought she could endure tromping for some distance, we started on our way, but her body was aching, and her breathing was laborious. So, we moved slowly and stopped frequently. One day when the weather was dreary with a light snowfall and was unusually dark, God smiled on us. A Canadian fishing boat captain named Moore came ashore to collect seamen for his ship, but they weren't at their assigned post. It seemed we were there instead. The captain waited for some time, but the men never showed, so he agreed to take us on board. 'Take ya as far as I can. Then, I'll come back to get my mates,' he told us. We were so obliged we nearly stepped on our own toes as we stumbled behind the captain to a rowboat butted against the shore. After we clambered in it, he took us out to his waiting ship. About sixty-five kilometers south of London, Captain Moore told us, "This be as far as I can take ya. Gitten late. I can't stay longer. Got ta get back ta find my men."

From there we trotted another three days, following the shoreline. That's when a skiff full of freedom seekers came along."

Clarissa clasped her hand in prayer and pressed them to her chest. Mary and Molly let the tears they had held back roll down their continued to tell, "It was Sidney, the conductor, who helped us along the way before he had a foot problem and had to turn back. Weeks later, leading another group, he made room in the skiff for us and brought us to London. When we arrived on the banks, we took in all the freedom air we could and thanked the Lord for letting us plant our feet, on this soil.

"Ma, the girls and I are thankful to be here with you and George Henry. Many times we felt we wouldn't make it. Although we did, we were sure we'd never see you again."

Quiet and statute-like, Toby peered out at the blue and white marbled sky before he glimpsed at Clarissa. "Ma, we got something to show you." Along with Mary and Molly, the three teased their indigo raiments from their pockets. They patted them out on the floorboards for Clarissa to see. Her face beamed. Unhurriedly, she gathered the wrinkled cuttings against her cheeks. Moaning and sniveling, she rocked them as if they were newborns. She waved the fingers of her left hand, gesturing to George Henry. "Go get it, boy. Be quick footed."

He leaped up, rushed inside, dashed up the rear steps to Clarissa's bedroom, and was back in a flash with an old dusty trunk balanced on his head. George Henry ducked, coming out of the door to place it in front of Clarissa. She lay both hands, palms down on its dusty, splintered lid. It was four-shoulder width and knee high. With smileless lips, pulled tight, she lifted the catch on the chest up and slowly eased up the lid. She scooped out a purple paisley scarf; a pair of over-worn shoes, with nearly no soles; colorful, non-matching, thready socks that were stuffed inside them; and another worn-out, faded muffler.

"Ma, those things are so dirty and worn. Do they mean something?" asked Mary.

"Dey be treasures left on da stoop fa George Henry and me da night we fled. We talks 'bout dem later. Dey each got long-hurtin' stories dat be fa another day."

Underneath closed eyes, Clarissa snugged the treasures close to her hip before she drew out her auction skirt. Consumed with emotion, her fingers trembled as she spread it out on the stoop boards and adjusted the puzzle pieces of remnants into their original places, making the skirt appeared whole again. Filled with a deepened sense of satisfaction, she didn't want her eyes diverted from what she saw.

"Ma." Clarence reluctantly raised her. "What was that puffy fabric I saw beneath your skirt when you took it out?" asked Mary and Molly.

Released from the hold the skirt had on her, Clarissa began to recall, "Dat be da quilt dat my ma, her ma, her ma's ma, and da mas 'fore dem made to tell which way ta go ta find freedom."

Clarissa collected the quilt from the chest and laid it on her lap, with only the homespun-fabric side showing. Her emotions revved again when she meticulously unfolded it, exposing the map side. She soft-touched each appliqué. Her mind flashed back to the many cold, snowy, wet, and miserable days she and George Henry spent wrapped in it as they hid from the pattyrollers and the catch hounds.

Nearly whispering, she said, "Da women in our family made dis here coverlet. Dey pass it down, one ta 'nother. Finally, it gits ta me. See dem birds scattered about? Der be one fa each of dem dats gone on. Some I know, some I don't." Clarissa tapped a bird in the center of the quilt. "Dis one here, it be my ma Alice. She be da one dat birth me. Don't remember her. She be sold away when I's a wee gal." Clarissa paused before she tapped another bird. "Dis one be my great-granma. Ya be named from her, Mary."

Clarissa continued to call the names of the remaining birds. Dis be Granma Molly. Ya be named from her. Then, Clarissa beckoned. "See des two birds flyin' close tagatha. And da dog bone next ta dem?"

"Yes, and they're white as snow. They seem to be fresh and new," said the twins.

"Maybe they've been to *The Perfect Wash*," said George Henry laughed.

"Jes stitched dem two birds and dat bone down on dis here

coverlet. One be Ola, the other Will. Da little bone, it be fa Partner. Gonna put a bucket of oats on der fa Onyx, too."

Toby got up on his knees. He hugged his ma. "What you did fills me with a warm gladness."

Clarissa unhurriedly drew her finger down the quilt to the cabin in the lower right-hand corner. "Dis here be tellin' when ta run and what direction ta be movin' in."

"How so?" asked the twins.

"Dat cabin be built wid dem logs pointin' up ta da Big Dipper and da North Star tellin' which way' ta run. Da firelight in da window, it tell ya ta run when it be dark. Da cross and dat bright light from da lantern, be tellin' ya where ta git help along da way. If ya lean back ya be seein' a ma and ha baby. I puts dem on after I's auctioned away from the three of ya and Jake. It be fa all dem babies separated from der ma. Dey got no eyes ta see da ugly, no ears ta hear painful cries, or lips ta taste da bitter tamarrows."

Clarissa's finger meandered up to the river that crossed the quilt's center, east to west. In a more speedy tempo she said, "George Henry and me, we gits ta da river. We tries ta cross, but I nearly drowns in it. Be George Henry dat pull me out of da frozen water. He thought I be dead. I did, too, cause I's hearin' my man, Jake, callin' ta me from da trees. It wasn't him. It be dem singin' freedom seekers waitin' fa da train. Dey come out der hidin' place up in da hills and takes us on board. Dey share der fire and give us victuals. Den dey bundle us in fire-warmed blankets. I's sure one of dem was Tall Man. He 'bout ya age and size. My heart be broken when it wasn't you.

"When time come ta git on board da train, I 'member how we be singin'. Our eyes be closed and heads be tilted."

Clarissa layer the quilt around her neck, snuggled it against her cheeks, and lowered her eyelids. Crooning, low and slow, she sang:

Steal away
Steal away
Steal away to Jesus!

Steal away
Steal away to home
I ain't got long to stay here

Steal away
Steal away
Steal away to Jesus!

Clarissa rocked a bit and hummed a bit, and then she called out in prayer: *Granma, my gals and Toby be here wid me and my boy, George Henry. We's all tagether. But I don't be knowin' where my man Jake be. I pray, ya watch over him if he be in heaven, like ya done George Henry and me when we be runnin'.* Eyes still closed, Clarissa raised her head heavenward. She moaned, *Lord, be wishin' dat Toby's Ola, his boy Will, da horse Onyx, and der dog, Partner, be here wid us. Tell da angels ifin' dey see em, protec' dem fa us. My boy be lovin' and missin' dem an awful lot.*

After her prayer to the Lord and the angles above, Clarissa sighed and said, "Gonna take dis here skirt and cut it inta strips." Her children gasped wide-eyed. Clarissa smiled. "Not ya pieces. Ya gonna keep dem safe so ya can tell ya babies 'bout how we be parted and den be brung back tagether. And, I be givin' George Henry a wedge of da skirt fa his babies. Gonna sew dem strips tagather, make one long piece, den tack dem 'round dis here quilt. When I be done, da coverlet be havin' a sturdy frame."

Toby, filled with puzzlement, gazed at Clarissa for some moments before he asked, "Why would you do such, Ma? You just put your skirt back to gather to see the whole of it once more.

"Dat frame gonna hold us tagatha. Forever!"

"Let's take the quilt to the next church gathering and the

one under the *Meeting Tree*, and share our trail stories with the others," said George Henry.

Clarissa nodded her head as she tenderly folded and rolled the quilt. Again, only the homespun side showed. She put two fingers to her lips, and then flipped them around. Her children's faces beamed with surprise. Beautiful smiles emerged when they did the same, elated that they remembered the code of love she had taught each of them to use when Massa wasn't looking.

Clarissa extended her arms. Palming the quilt, she said, "Mary. Molly. Dis here be fa ya ta keep. Now, da story be yours ta tell."

The twins reached for the *Freedom Quilt*, but weren't which lap to rest on.

The End

Epilogue

Toby, Mary, and Molly moved out of the flat over the barbershop into the house with Ma and George Henry. Clarissa became a successful laundress with several employees. Toby continued his formal education and expanded his classes at College University. He became Dean of the School of Agriculture. He never stopped scribing for the townspeople, who grew to trust and depend on him for communications with family members left behind. He married Tish, from the Fugitive Slave Chapel. She started a dressmaking shop, finishing uniforms for Mary's and Molly's pupils. The couple, together, had two sons, Jake and Harry, and a daughter they named Caroline. George Henry's barbershop flourished. He added a shoeshine bench with three boot polishers. Hattie, his bride-to-be and a student from the university, who lived a town over, caught his eye. They eventually married and, together, had three daughters–Georgia, Sue, and Lucile–and built a house not far from Clarissa. The twins started the first multi-academic finishing school for girls in London, Ontario.

Discussion Questions

1. What did you learn about antebellum auctions because of Toby's character?

2. Social justice is based on the principles of equality and solidarity and recognizes the value of human rights of every human being. What violations of justice occurred in Bloody Trails: Enslavement & Freedom?

3. Freedom seekers, the Underground Railroad, and abolitionists are significant in Bloody Trails: Enslavement & Freedom. What was it about these concepts that moved the story forward?

4. Joe Jammer purchased Toby and embraced him as a brother. Were the townspeople's reactions toward the two living under the same roof warranted? What elements gave this relationship such a strong foundation?

5. Joe Jammer's wealth and social status were procured because of Zach's knowledge and shared labor, yet Francine despised Zach. How would you describe her relationship with Zach?

6. Joe Jammer traveled to New Orleans to negotiate a hemp deal and get a bride. What events from those visits stand out for you?

7. Clara arrived with Avida Maria, the child from Francine's, maybe, unplanned pregnancy. Do you agree with how Francine handled her pregnancy?

8. Joe Jammer breached his understood oath of brotherhood with Zach. Was his drinking or something else the cause?

9. Will and Partner were significant in the lives of Ola and Zach. Francine lashed out at Will, killing him, and Joe shot Partner, the dog. What were your feelings about these events?

10. Ola birthed Jammer's baby. What came to your mind when Zach and Amos stood by the bed viewing the baby's corpse?

11. Enraged by the deaths of Will, Partner, and then Ola, Zach sought revenge. Were his actions justifiable? What would you have done?

12. Joe Jammer and Francine's lifestyles unexpectedly reverted from wealth to destruction management. Describe their lifestyle after the fire.

13. Raised with privilege, Mary and Molly did not grow up as most children in bondage. How did this influence the dynamics of their lives?

14. Tipper and Miss Grace were significant in the lives of Mary and Molly. What were the pros and cons of their relationships with the twins?

15. Mary and Molly, educated mulattresses and French-speaking, passed for white. What were your thoughts of the incident on the pier with the two strangers and Toby's experience below deck?

16. When Lawrence learned Mary and Molly had run and his money was missing, should he have sent trackers after the twins or let them go?

17. How did Toby's time in St. Louis on Perry Street and his friendship with Ezra impact his life?

18. How would you compare the Ohio River crossing with the Detroit River crossing? What were the gains and losses?

19. The story ends with Toby and his family recalling the past and what brought them together. What were your thoughts about the back porch gathering?

20. Chapter 23, Reunion, is the last chapter in Bloody Trails: Enslavement & Freedom. If "The End" didn't follow the last sentence, what would the next chapter be titled?

Figure 2: The First African Methodist Episcopal (AME) Church (referred to as the Fugitive Slave Chapel) 275 Thames Street, London, Ontario c.1926

Figure 3: The *Meeting Tree*, London Canada, The City of London

Glossary

barter – bargain for a preferred price
bell cord or pull cord – rings a bell in the kitchen or linen room to alert the hands that they are needed (cords run from the main rooms of the house to a roll of wall-mounted bells in the kitchen or pantry area)
bit – part of the horse bridle (line or cable) that goes in the mouth
bloodhound – a Balkay Hound, a breed of dog that extends the hunt range to mountains, swamps, forest, and can outrun freedom seekers, sometimes referred to as Negro hounds, catch hounds, or track hounds used to hunt freedom seekers
butt knot – tip end of whip handle
catch hounds – see bloodhound
cat-o-nine tails – whip made of nine lines with knotted tips and joined with a handle
cauldron – large kettle
chamber pot – portable container with lid kept under beds for urine
chancel – front area inside the church where preachers stand
chemise – woman's or girl's dress-like undergarment
cloudage – cloud cover
coiffure – styled hair, usually elaborate
crinoline cage – hoop skirt
crumpets – small, round, soft, unsweetened griddle cake
cupola (Italian) – small dome atop a larger dome mounted on the roof
duster – light, loose-fitting, long coat
dysentery – infection of the intestines that causes bloody diarrhea
facade (French/Italian) – front of a building
fetter – restrained by chains
fleur-de-lis (French) – a stylized lily or iris commonly used for decoration

frippery – elegant and showy garment
friezes (French) – a sculptured or richly ornamented band of an interior wall
frock – coat
frog – part of the horse's hoof located on the underside of the hoof
fugitive – a person who flees or tries to escape
gruel – porridge; boiled breakfast cereal made from crushed starchy plants
hands – enslaved persons who work in the Big House
hoecake – cornbread batter cooked on the blade of a hoe
homespun – fabric used to make quilts and garments worn by enslaved Africans
horse crop - short horsewhip without lash (flexible part of a whip)
huckaback towel – heavy linen towel
indigo – blue vat dye obtained from plants
linsey-woolsey – a coarse twill or plain-woven fabric with a linen warp (yards extended lengthwise in a loom) and woolen weft (horizontal strands)
malaise – feeling of unwellness
mulattress (French) – first generation female offspring of an African and a white person
mulatto (Spanish/Portuguese) – first generation male offspring of an African and a white person
mutton – sheep
neckerchief – a square cloth worn around the neck
nefarious – extremely wicked or villainous
Negro cloth – cheap, rough, unbleached linen used for making clothes for enslaved Africans
palladium window – large window with a central arch
pattyroller – person sent to catch Negro freedom seekers
platform bed – a bed consisting of a shallow box holding a mattress

piazza (Italian) – large porch on a house
pickaninnies – children of enslaved Africans
pinafore – sleeveless apron-like garment worn over a young girl's dress and typically tied or buttoned in the back
popper – leather or metal end of a whip
portico (Italian) – from the Latin word porticus, structure consisting of a roof supported by columns/pillars
quadroon (Spanish) – a person who is one-quarter African
quill pen – dip pen used for writing; made from a bird's feather
reins – long straps attached to the ends of a horse's bit
shoe button hook – a tool pushed through a buttonhole to hook the button and pull it; catch hold of a button to facilitate the closing of shoes, gloves, or garments
skiff – small boat propelled by oars
slave quarters – buildings constructed for the express purpose of housing enslaved Africans
smite – strike with a firm blow
swing basket – 19th Century basket with a swing handle
tignon (French) – a madras (plaid) handkerchief used especially in Louisiana as a headdress (turban) worn by Creole women
tufting – a bunch or cluster of small, soft and flexible parts
wagon box – body of a wagon
waistcoat – vest
vanity set – a box that can include: mirror, grooming items for hair and nails, glass powder jar with lid, clothes brush, etc
zephyr – gental breeze

Figure 4: Judith C. Owens-Lalude
Photograph by A. O'tayo Lalude

About the Author

Judith C. Owens-Lalude is the great-granddaughter of George Henry "Pap" Johnson born 1850 to his mother, Clarissa, and later enslaved on Ben Miller's 600-acre farm in Spencer County, Kentucky, southeast of Louisville, Kentucky, where Owens-Lalude grew up. After listening to tales told by her family members, she wanted to know more and visited the farm where they had been enslaved. Owens-Lalude strolled the grounds, reflected at the fireplace hearth where a slave cabin once stood, wandered along the streams and creeks, and photographed the outstructures that were once part of her family's daily world. She was inspired to write *The Long Walk: Slavery to Freedom*. Her readers wanted a sequel; thus Owens-Lalude wrote *Bloody Trails: Enslavement & Freedom*. For inspiration, she referenced the lives of Isaac Johnson who wrote *Slavery Days in Old Kentucky*, and Harry Smith, who wrote *Fifty Years in Slavery in the United States*. Both authors were enslaved in Jefferson, Nelson, and Spencer counties Kentucky, where Owens-Lalude's family was held in bondage and later lived as free people.

National Park Service, National Underground Railroad Network to Freedom program has applied rigorous scholarship in identifying and awarding membership to more than 695 sites, programs and facilities in thirty-nine states, plus Washington, D. C. and the U. S. Virgin Islands. Additional members are added twice a year. *The Long Walk: Slavery to Freedom,* by Judith C. Owens-Lalude was accepted into the Network to Freedom as an interpretive program for students and adults.

Made in the USA
Columbia, SC
25 April 2023